ADVANCE PRAISE FOR *THE BILLIONTH MONKEY*

"This book is endlessly creative. If you even *think* you like weird fantasy, you will love *The Billionth Monkey*."

—Steve Englehart, creator of Star-Lord,
Coyote, and the definitive Batman

"This is funny and magic(k)al. Kaczynski has written a crazy quest novel equals parts of Dan Brown and Terry Pratchett. Can Professor Belanger and the quantumly impossible Destiny Jones defeat _____? (Can't write the Dread Name). In some universes this is already a Hollywood blockbuster."

—Don Webb, *Through Dark Angles*

"*The Billionth Monkey* is an adrenaline shot to the heart of twenty-first-century American cultural consciousness, an outrageously intelligent alternate universe where urban legends are real. Kaczynski's playful wit belies a profound wisdom that affects the brain like an overdose of smartness pills. One cannot resist the temptation to evoke Douglas Adams and Robert Anton Wilson when describing the experience. As delightfully funny and entertaining as it is enlightening."

—Lon Milo DuQuette,
Accidental Christ: The Story of Jesus as Told to His Uncle
and *Aleister Crowley: Revolt of the Magicians*

"It's super! …except for the naughty bits."

—Cohor Woolstenhulme, *Arouse!* magazine

"You'd be nuts not to reach into your coin purse and slap a pair of sheckels down in vast deference to this book. *The Billionth Monkey* just may be the most significant English literary work since *Hamlet Special Edition*."

—Simeon Nichols-Woking, *Shakespeare's Globes*
Central University of Newcastle-upon-Tyne

THE BILLIONTH MONKEY

RICHARD KACZYNSKI

BASED ON ACTUAL FICTIONAL EVENTS

www.thebillionthmonkey.com
www.richard-kaczynski.com

Cover design by Aaron Tatum.

"The Fool" from the *Thoth Tarot* by Aleister Crowley and Frieda Harris is copyright Ordo Templi Orientis and used by permission. Other cover image credits include the Deepwater Horizon (courtesy U.S. Coast Guard), skis in the snow (uploaded to Flickr by Nils Rinaldi under Creative Commons), and an albino alligator (uploaded to Wikimedia Commons by Sherriff2966).

Back cover art by Robert Randle.

Arriving UFO
Words and Music by Rick Wakeman, Steve Howe and Jon Anderson
Copyright ©1978 IMAGEM SONGS LTD. and TOPOGRAPHIC MUSIC LTD.
All Rights for IMAGEM SONGS LTD. in the United States and Canada Administered by ALMO MUSIC CORP. All Rights on Behalf of TOPOGRAPHIC MUSIC LTD. administered by WB MUSIC CORP.
All Rights Reserved, Used by Permission.
Reprinted by Permission of Hal Leonard Corporation and Alfred Publishing Co. Inc.

Calling Occupants of Interplanetary Craft
Words and Music copyright ©1976 by Terry Draper and John Woloschuk.
All Rights Reserved, Used by Permission of Magentalane Music Limited.

ISBN 978-1-51413-992-9 (paperback)

1. Urban Fantasy—Fiction. 2. Fortean Fiction—Fiction. 3. Humor—Fiction.

Printed in the United States of America

PROLOGUE
THREE YEARS EARLIER

T HE APPROACHING MOTORBOAT was too far away to hear, even if the drill, pumps, and other machinery aboard the *Deep Water Lemuria* were to fall suddenly silent. It followed the long white trail of gravel that was continuously jettisoned by the drilling operation and carried away by the current. The small craft glinted on the distant waters as it caught and reflected the summer sun: a glint out of place, as obvious as a splinter in a large hand. A glint drawing inexorably nearer.

From the deck of the mobile offshore drilling unit, Steven Ray Skipton solemnly eyed the approaching vessel. His scowl exaggerated the creases in a leathery face that had seen more than its share of subtropical sun. Furrows peeked from beneath the hardhat and hearing protectors that concealed his omnipresent NASCAR cap, while downturned lips set deep lines in his cheeks and pulled tight the ruddy carpet of whiskers that was his chin. Skipton's long career in offshore oil drilling owed plenty to his intense dislike of surprises. Such as this approaching boat.

Why was it out here?

The vessel was no scheduled arrival like the one that delivered workers ready for their two-week shift, or that ferried exhausted crew back to shore for their two-week break. Nor was anyone likely to pleasure-cruise in the Gulf of Mexico fifty miles from shore in waters nearly a mile deep. No, in Skipton's mind it was but one of two unpleasant options: environmentalists come to protest the

Lemuria for the supposed harm it was doing to the environment, or a surprise visit from federal safety inspectors.

Skipton would take the feds any day.

He had no reason to sweat a safety inspection. As operations team leader, his job was to ensure the smooth running of the *Lemuria*, and he did everything by the book. The unimaginable cost of drilling the deepest underwater well ever attempted weighed heavily upon him, as did his responsibility for the safety of every roughneck, roustabout, and deckhand. For the one hundred and fifty men and women onboard, this went well beyond the call of duty. They spent two consecutive weeks out of every four in each other's company, with little else to do but work, sleep, or bond. This made them a second family to each other, and the oil platform their second home. For some, this was their *only* family, their *only* home.

Skipper, as his crew called him, knew every one of them by name. His deckhand Jesus Rivera from Bay City, Texas, had two children with his wife, Maria, and a third due in two months. Bobby Walker worked the midnight shift ever since graduating from Baton Rouge High School; despite four years on the job, the rest of the crew protected him like a baby brother. Mechanical wiz Raymone Washington from Georgetown, Louisiana, had learned his trade serving in Desert Storm, where he often repaired military equipment using pieces scavenged from several damaged units. Their cook, Dag "Fryer Tuck" Tucker, had been sous chef at a boutique hotel in Philadelphia—the other Philadelphia, in Mississippi—until hard economic times shuttered its doors two years ago; since then, his all-important duty has been to prevent revolt by keeping the crew happily well-fed. Given the chance, Skipper would talk all day long about his team and never run out of names or stories to tell.

For the sake of his family, both on land and at sea, Skipper was Mr. Safety and Maintenance. He was known to tell executives "no" in the most colorful language. Nothing—whether it was expediency, orders from corporate HQ, or instructions from the government—would make him cut any corners that might jeopardize the smooth running of his rig. And he wasn't going to let unscheduled visitors change that.

As the boat drew nearer, Skipper made out only three passengers. He dropped his binoculars, pulled the walkie-talkie from his belt, and radioed his deckhand: "Miguel, looks like we got ourselves some company. Prep the air tugger."

"Roger," Miguel acknowledged. "I'll show 'em some genuine southern hospitality."

"We don't know who this is. Do not—I repeat, *do not*—take them for a swim."

"Shit, man, you're more fun at the start of your tour."

"I go home tomorrow. Last thing I need is to step off the boat and have my ass handed to me for dunking some *federales*."

"You get your ass chewed out so much, *mi hermano*, I'm surprised there's anything left to hand you."

"Better me than you."

"*Muchas gracias* for watching out for us. I'd kiss your ass if you had one left."

"Just do this by the book, and you can kiss whatever is left. But no tongue this time."

"*Muy caliente!*"

With no clever retort, Skipper just shook his head and grinned. He saw the crane already beginning to move. As the basket—a disc with a series of cords around its perimeter gathered together and connected to a hook—rose over the deck, both it and the crane looked small against the full size of the dynamically positioned semi-submersible rig that was the *Lemuria*. In addition to machinery and work spaces, its four hundred by two hundred fifty foot deck capped three lower levels of crew quarters, kitchen, gym, and other living areas. The latticework derrick that housed the drill mechanism towered five hundred feet above the center of this steel behemoth, a height equivalent to a forty-story skyscraper. Four unlikely columns at the rig's corners supported its massive structure and raised the rig eighty feet above the water, far out of the reach of potentially damaging waves. That was enough clearance for a sailboat to easily cruise beneath the structure if not for the drill pipe that stretched from its center to the seabed nearly a mile below; the well itself extended even further.

Skipper watched the empty basket swing over the water toward the boat, then plummet suddenly. With a wince, he imagined the resulting splashdown. *Dammit, Miguel!* he thought. But he yielded to a grin anyway. It served them right, although he would never officially admit it. He hated surprises, and the crew knew that. They looked after him just as much as he looked after them.

The air tugger soon reappeared from below, swung back over the deck, and gently deposited its passengers. Marching over to greet them, Skipper finally got a good look at his uninvited guests. In the basket were two smartly dressed young men. Their hair was close-shorn, and they were clean-shaven. Identical opaque sunglasses covered their eyes, and they wore matching black suits, white shirts, and neckties. Their shoes were polished, the water on them already beaded and rolling off.

Definitely the feds, Skipper decided. Only then did he start to worry about why they were here.

One man exited the air tugger with a black leather book bag. The other followed with a large roller bag. Perplexingly, it looked like they intended to stay a while. Both men removed their sunglasses in unison, caught Skipper's gaze, and smiled warmly. The man with the book bag extended his hand as he approached.

Definitely not *the feds*, Skipper revised his theory. But who then?

"Hello," the visitor remarked as he shook Skipper's hand. The hand was soft, its grip enthusiastic. "I'm Cohor Woolstenhulme, and this is my brother Noah." Noah tipped his head in acknowledgement.

"Howdy fellas," Skipper replied guardedly. "What can I do you for?"

"We're here on this fine summer day to ask just a moment of your time to talk about our Lord and Savior."

On cue, Cohor drew a pinch of pamphlets from his book bag and began to distribute their newsletter, *Arouse!*. The contents of these issues prompted a great deal of chatter among the gathering of curious roughnecks.

One roustabout, Hugo Knight, looked at the cover with a scowl and asked, "A ruse?"

"No, man," his friend Davey West informed him. "It's a*rouse*."

"This one has a cover story on 'The Great Harlot,'" chuckled Bill Faust, also known as Faust the Roust. "She can arouse me any time!"

Davey quipped back, "Is it a porno?"

"No, you dumbass," remarked Peter Grant, who spent his off hours reading the Bible in his bunk. "It's not that kind of arouse. It means 'wake the fuck up.'"

"I'd rather have a porno," quipped Jesus Rivera.

"Jesus, Jesus. It's about the goddamn Bible. Show some respect!"

"This one has a story about how some lady bought the Holy Grail at a garage sale in French Lick, Indiana, for fifty cents," Davey reported as he flipped through its pages: glossy, full-sized, and professionally produced.

Peter noted, "Mine says that a vision of Jesus led Seal Team Six to the room where they killed Bin Laden." The story was accompanied by an artist's depiction of heavily armed men in flak jackets and helmets surrounding Jesus, who stood at the bottom of a staircase and pointed upward.

Skipper watched his crew's reaction for a moment then turned back to Noah. "Are you shitting me? You hired a boat to bring you fifty miles offshore to BFE just to ring our doorbell?"

"No, sir. We're not the door-to-door type."

"Then what are you?"

"Technically, we're missionaries."

"Missionaries on an oil rig?" he snorted. "Don't y'all usually go to other countries?"

"We tried that," Cohor explained. "But France turned us away at customs."

"They turned you away?"

"Yes. They said they were all full."

Noah chimed in, "Yes, they said they had all the missionaries they could take. I didn't realize they had a quota."

"Neither did I," Cohor agreed.

"So we went to Belgium."

"A lovely country."

"Yes indeed. At least the airport."

"Oh yes, lovely concessions."

"They gave us three hundred francs and asked us to leave."

"They were so nice. They didn't even ask for a magazine. Fine people, the Belgians."

"So we moved on to Amsterdam."

"I hear you can buy drugs at the coffee shops."

"And prostitutes at the drug store."

"Sounded like a modern Gomorrah, a place that could really use our help."

"But when we arrived, the whole country switched off their lights and pretended they weren't home."

"A pity they wouldn't let the Lord into their hearts."

"Yes, a pity they'll all go to Hell. Those poor, damned Swiss."

"No, I think they're the damned Dutch."

"No, those are the people from Deutschland. Why would the people of the Netherlands be called 'Dutch'?"

"Why would they be called Swiss?"

"Hmm, good point."

"Europe is a very confusing place for Americans."

"Yes. It's *all* very confusing. Which is why we're here."

"But," Skipper reasoned, "this ain't a country."

"We *are* in international waters, though," Cohor replied.

"Shouldn't y'all at least be on…an island?"

"Oh, no. The islands here are overpriced tourist traps. We can't afford to live there."

"You see," Noah elaborated, "we have to pay for our mission out of our own pockets."

"And we're not from a rich family."

Skipper empathized, "That's rough."

"Right," Cohor agreed. "So, if you let us stay in your smallest room…"

Noah chimed in, "We promise we won't eat much."

"…and you won't hear a peep from us in the next two years."

"Listen, fellas," Skipper clarified, "this is a loud, dirty oil platform. It's a workplace, not a fucking youth hostel. You can't stay here."

"What if we gave you a free magazine?" Cohor bargained.

Skipper shook his head.

Noah tried one last pitch: "Can we at least have three hundred francs?"

In the silence of Skipper's firmly shaking head, the excited roustabouts tittered on about *Arouse!* "Look," Hugo Knight remarked, "this one's even got a story about oil wells."

Davey peeked over his shoulder. "Aw, don't tell me you believe that crap! It's just a made-up story."

"No, it's in print. It *must* be true."

"Let me see," Peter said, rubbernecking to look.

Suddenly they heard a hiss so loud that it was audible above the pumps and drills and cranes and other machinery. Cohor and Noah knew from everyone else's horrified expression that this was bad. Very bad. Before any of them could utter the words on their lips— *Oh shit, no!*—the steel floor beneath their feet rumbled ominously. Alarms sounded. The roar of an explosion released pandemonium on the *Deep Water Lemuria*.

The instant he heard the hiss, Skipper's eyes turned toward the drill, just in time to see a giant fireball engulf the forty-story-tall derrick. The explosion threw bodies in all directions, and the deck lurched violently in response. This was unlike any blow-out he had ever heard of: it came on too quickly, too violently. Even as he made this assessment, his blow-out specialist squawked on the radio, "Skip, this came out of fucking *nowhere*. All readings were normal, then she just blew!"

Everything was chaos. The entire platform lost power, and the drill, pumps, and other machinery fell eerily silent. Those familiar sounds yielded to other uncomfortable noises: the roar of the blaze; the crew shouting, "This is the real deal!" and "Go, go, GO!" as they rushed to their designated emergency positions; and the public address system's dire instruction to "Abandon ship!" Alas, shore was fifty miles away, and the nearest hospital even further. With no lights below deck except for the illuminated emergency exit signs, the crew felt their way through dark hallways and scrambled for the stairwells. Each crew member headed to their designated lifeboat as they had done on weekly drills many times before. Some helped the injured, while others succumbed to an every-man-for-himself panic.

The *Lemuria* had four satellite beacon-equipped lifeboats, each with a fifty-person capacity. However, the explosion had blown two boats off the deck, leaving only two for one hundred fifty crew. On each lifeboat, the officer assigned to get a muster called out the names of designated passengers and checked them off on a clipboard as they boarded. The process had to restart several times because screams from those already on the lifeboats to "Put 'er in the water!" and "Let's get out of here before the deck collapses on us all!" drowned out the officer with the clipboard. Accommodating extra evacuees to make up for the two lost lifeboats only slowed things down and made the alarmed cries louder and more urgent.

Meanwhile, the computer-coordinated thrusters that dynamically positioned the deck directly over the well went offline. This allowed the gulf waters to toss the *Lemuria* about at will. The rig soon listed to one side.

As commander, Skipton should immediately have gotten on the radio, barked commands, called in rescue boats and helicopters, and alerted response crews to ready their fire boats and water cannons. But as mud and oil rained all around, his attention focused in the direction of the conflagration. Its flames shot hundreds of feet into the air, a holocaust beyond imagining. It was almost too bright to look at directly, and the heat from the flame was nearly unbearable, even at this distance. A few crew members unfortunate enough to have caught fire leapt off deck into the now-oily water below: if their burns didn't kill them, dropping eighty feet and hitting the water at fifty miles per hour probably would.

But this was not what absorbed Skipper's attention. It was the glowing, smoldering figure striding boldly and purposefully out of the center of the fireball. How anyone could have survived at the heart of the explosion was unthinkable. Never mind how someone with such painful injuries was able to walk at all. If anyone on the *Lemuria* had cause for hysteria, it was this person. Yet he was the only one who was measured, fully composed amidst this maelstrom.

He was walking directly toward them.

Lean yet muscular, the figure drew nearer by regular, confident strides. He appeared to be naked, every inch of his skin either charred or covered with a thick armor of ash. This outer coat was crazed by a web of deep cracks that exposed a red-hot glow beneath the surface. His eyes burned with a bright crimson flame. The air around him rippled from the heat he radiated, creating a blurry, distorted aura as he approached.

He reached the small group and saw them—Cohor, Noah, Davey, Peter, Jesus and the rest—standing slack-jawed with vacant expressions. All except Skipper, who was obviously in charge. The smoldering being focused his attention on him, and spoke in a voice as deep and thunderous as the ominous rumble that preceded the rig's explosion.

"Mortal! Tell me now: What place is this?"

"P-place?" Skipper asked. The question did not compute.

"Yes. What city is this?"

After a pause, the query finally sank in. Skipper shook his head. "This ain't no city."

"What do you mean? Explain yourself!"

"Mister, you're on an oil platform in the middle of the Gulf of Mexico."

For the first time, the smoldering man looked to his left, to his right, overhead, then down and around past Skipper. *"Crap!"* he exclaimed, lingering on the "r" so long that the word had two, almost three, syllables. His voice was now at least an octave higher, squarely in the "annoying teenager" register. He drooped his head down, defeated. "I was so focused on making a bodacious entrance that I didn't even look to see where I was. I am *so* stupid!"

The surreal situation finally transformed Skipper's face into another slack-jawed canvas for astonishment. Meaningless words of comfort just poured out of Skipton's mouth; his brain was no longer in control. "Nah, it's cool. It could have happened to anyone."

The smoldering man looked around again to survey his location. "Thanks. Which way—" He stopped himself, then switched back to his basso profundo. *"Which way is the shore?"*

Skipper—every bit as shell-shocked as the crew around him—simply raised his right hand, turned, and pointed due north, over his left shoulder.

"*Thanks, dude. You are totes wicked dope. Um…I mean…I shall remember your kindness, mortal.*"

At that, he stepped past them, first at his original purposive pace, then accelerating to a fast walk, and finally to a full-out sprint until he dove off the platform and landed with a hiss where the oil sheen spread quickly across the sky-blue water like a dark, threatening cloud. The only trace he left behind was a flaming footprint on a dropped copy of *Arouse!* magazine. Its cover boasted the story within: OIL RIG DRILLS HOLE TO HELL.

CHAPTER

1

*A*CROSS A NONDESCRIPT stretch of Basin Street on the north edge of the French Quarter, a high brick wall, white and cracked, ran the length of an entire city block. Black iron gates at its midpoint provided the only entryway to New Orleans' oldest and best-known cemetery, Saint Louis No. 1. Here, row upon row of tightly packed crypts in various states of disrepair filled the prime real estate. Scattered among a handful of immaculate and pristine monuments, the sun-bleached plaster exteriors of most crypts grayed and crumbled with age or the elements, exposing the dark red brick beneath. Some had shed several of their ruddy blocks, either whole or in pieces, onto the surrounding grounds. Still others were reduced to nothing more than a pile of incoherent bricks and mortar.

A permeating sense of decay befitted this famous "city of the dead." The crypts—with their wrought-iron fences, access doors that doubled as memorial plaques, and assorted pitched, barrel-vaulted, and parapet roofs—indeed resembled the closely-spaced shacks or small homes of a once-thriving ghost town. This city was miniaturized, however, as its homes were not quite tall enough for an adult to stand in, and barely long and wide enough to lie down for a very long sleep.

These sleepers did not want for company. Just as the city's high water table necessitated above-ground interment, its long history and limited real estate required each tomb to house multiple guests, frequently generations of a single family. The hot and humid climate turned these structures into brick ovens that rendered their dead into a pile of bones within two years' time, ready to be moved to the side or rear of the vault to make room for the next guest.

Niels Belanger walked through the cemetery gates early in the morning, before the continuous parade of visitors and guided tours began. Although the flood of Mardi Gras revelers had by now departed, the city—temperate in climate only—would continue to draw flocks of tourists until the return of cool weather in late fall. However, in the early morning most of them were still sleeping off their indiscretions of the night before.

Belanger was a British Yankophile and junior faculty at nearby Tulane University's Department of American Studies, where he specialized in urban folklore and contemporary legends. His affiliation with academia was clear from his straight black and slightly tousled haircut with its hint of Harry Potter, and unabashedly nerdy eyeglasses with thick lenses. He also wore the uniform: loafers, denim slacks, a pale blue Oxford shirt with a business-irregular British bowtie, and a tan corduroy blazer with elbow patches. The ensemble was warmer than he normally wore on campus, but it was perfect for a February stroll through the cemetery.

He came to visit the tomb of St. Louis No. 1's most famous resident, Voodoo Queen Marie Laveau. She and her legend were his current area of study, and he found it helpful on writing days to stop by the cemetery and immerse himself in the milieu from which the urban legends sprang. An abundance of local folklore and legend surrounded Laveau in life and even after, awaiting an exhaustive ethnography. This made primary research much easier than exposing myths from some part of the world that he had never visited. It was immediate and tactile, and connected him to his subject in a more visceral way than any electronic journal article could.

Born in the final years of the eighteenth century, Marie Laveau was a mixed-race widow renowned as much for her beauty as for practicing Voodoo. She was believed to have been the wife of Haitian immigrant carpenter Jacques Paris, who mysteriously vanished a year after their 1819 marriage. Neither wife nor widow, Marie took on a lover and common-law husband in Captain Louis Christophe

Dumesnil de Glapion, who had served as an ordnance officer during the War of 1815. In their fifteen years together, she bore him fifteen children. While precious little was known about her magical career, newspapers reported that she and her followers met in deserted places on St. John's Night to engage in wild naked dances. She also provided gris-gris (protective amulets), advice, and other services for all segments of society, as her powers reputedly swayed lovers' hearts and determined enemies' fates in favor of her clients. As an accomplished herbalist and healer, she ministered to any sick person who called upon her. From the poor to distinguished legislators, lawyers, and other high-society denizens, all of New Orleans sought her counsel. After her dear Louis died in 1855, Marie turned her attention to the work of the church until her death in 1881 at the ripe age of ninety-eight.

In death, her powers only grew stronger. One early and well-known legend had a customer at a nearby pharmacy fail to recognize her, at which the displeased spirit slapped him across the face then flew out the door and away over the city. Her legacy was further preserved by her daughter, Marie Laveau II, who adopted the Voodoo Queen mantle and invited the public to her own elaborate rituals and events. To the present day, visitors and ghost tourists regularly report sightings, healings, and granted wishes.

Laveau's tomb—actually the Glapion family tomb—was left of the entry gate, on the cemetery alley running parallel to the Center Alley. Since the Voodoo religion concerned itself with ancestral spirits, legend had it that, even in death, Laveau still granted wishes to supplicants at her tomb. Thus the doorway to her crypt, dubbed "the wishing vault" by some, was strewn daily with the requisite offerings of her tradition, left by seekers and idle tourists alike: flowers, beads, candles, candy, cigars, cash, and rum. Patterns of red triple Xs densely covered its walls on all sides. Visitors left these marks by scratching on the plaster exterior of her tomb with an eroded chip of brick; ironically, the practice damaged the very structure that visitors had come to honor. Most made these marks in the folk belief that the act would bring them good luck. A handful believed that they represented the crossroads, and hence referred to Papa Legba, the Voodoo *loa* or spirit who is the opener of ways and to whom an offering is made at the beginning of any ceremony, even though Legba's traditional *vévé*, or symbol, actually looks nothing at all like an X.

Already, offerings from the day before—collected and disposed of by the grounds keeper—had been replaced with new tributes that would accumulate over the course of the day. Belanger silently observed as several of these were left by early-morning visitors like himself. One was a young man in sunglasses and a top hat, which formed a stark contrast with the rest of his wardrobe: a vintage t-shirt for the death metal band Behemoth (the name printed in Fraktur above an ominous double-headed eagle), a pair of ripped blue jeans, and sneakers. A moment later, up walked a woman clad entirely in black, from her reversed baseball cap to her plain spaghetti-strap tank top, even down to her skirt and combat boots. Although these two arrived separately and did not behave as though they recognized the other, the similar occult and tribal tattoos on their exposed limbs suggested that they were at least kindred spirits. Each kept a respectful distance as they set down their contributions: he left a fifth of rum, while she brought freshly cut flowers. Both touched the tomb reverentially, and paused for silent meditation.

Belanger was not here to petition the Voodoo Queen, nor to conduct field observation on those who did. However, observing the graveside reverence of these solitary petitioners impressed upon him the genuine and sincere spirit of her legend-makers and perpetuators. It reminded him of the responsibility that he shouldered in trying to summarize the Laveau legend for his fellow academics.

The loud proclamation "Next on our tour we will see the tomb of New Orleans' most famous Voodoo practitioner" announced the arrival of the day's first group. It was Belanger's cue to head into the office.

Turning to walk away from the crowd, he recognized further down the alley the familiar figure of Gabriella in front of one of the tombs. He didn't know her last name, and only knew her first name from her waitress nametag at the Café du Monde, his traditional coffee stop on his way to the office on days when he *wasn't* at the cemetery. On those days, he always sought out and sat in her section.

Bree, as she preferred to be called, had the kind of beauty that caused people to stop and stare. At least that was her effect on Belanger. Her long, straight, and onyx-black hair hung neatly to the middle of her back. Her eyes were large and intense, the effect amplified by the contrast between their icy blue color and her bronze skin. The rest of her features were likewise striking, from her pronounced cheekbones, ever so slightly raised nose, full lips, and graceful jaw that drew into her narrow chin. She was in her early to mid twenties, and her youthful appearance was exaggerated by her girlishly thin figure, slight stature (barely over five feet), and small breasts. Even after months of seeing her perhaps three times a week, he would still stare at her and wonder why she was serving coffee rather than modeling in some exotic location for a magazine cover.

Despite carrying a torch for her, Belanger was so socially awkward that whenever Bree was anywhere near, he felt like a matinee monster that would sooner run from a torch than carry it. He was determined to ask her out, to court her if at all possible. But whenever he looked at her and fell into those enchanting eyes, it took everything he had to muster even small talk. She always smiled at him, though, and mercifully knew to bring his regular order, which spared him from stammering "café au lait." He normally wasn't tongue-tied, but he had never seen such ethereal beauty in the flesh. Perhaps today, here in the cemetery, he would finally manage to ask her on a date. If only he could speak to her reflection in a shield, or have a hidden Cyrano help him with his lines.

Walking nearer to Bree's location, he saw that she wore a black cotton mini dress whose hem terminated in a four-inch cotton fringe that strained to reach her knees. Silver and turquoise jewelry—attesting to both her fashion sense and strong connection to her heritage—covered her fingers. She held something, but he couldn't quite make out what it was. What was she up to? His fascination with her distracted him so much that he gracelessly stumbled right into a cluster of squat, bushy palms. Despite body-slamming the unfortunate hedge, he managed to remain upright.

Belanger hopped a step backward, however, when the plant exclaimed, "Oi!" It was a deep, gravelly voice, strident and irate.

He had never met a talking plant before, and was unsure how to respond. "E-excuse me?"

"Watch it, brah! You're going to give me away."

Belanger pondered this statement for a moment then looked about. Assured that neither of them had attracted attention, he concluded, "I should think that you're giving your*self* away by speaking at all. How could anyone not stop and say, 'Ooh, look, a talking bush!'" His accent was a mix of the West Country and London.

"I'm not a talking bush," the voice protested. The shrub rustled and from behind it rose a man with long brown hair, wild and matted, as were his beard and moustache. His eyes were intense, and his teeth, to the extent they were visible beneath his moustache, were cocked. He wore a black ribbed tank top and a pair of jeans that were weathered and torn in places. Towering over Belanger at six feet three inches, he looked especially unkempt, like an Alan Moore who had completely let himself go. "I'm a hermit."

As Belanger processed that information, he thought out loud, "I thought hermits lived in caves."

"Don't be insulting! That's an offensive stereotype. 'Oh look, honey, that poor hermit must be lost and unable to find his cave.' Give me a break! I suppose you think all Asians are good at math. Or all Irish are drunks. Or all Welsh enjoy bog snorkelling."

"No, of course not." *Bog snorkelling?* He intended to ask, but the offended hermit pressed on.

"So tell me, Mister Cultural Sensitivity, how many caves have you seen in New Orleans?"

Belanger paused to think for a moment. "None that I know of."

"Precisely. The best caves are always taken, so we urban hermits need to be crafty and improvise. This cemetery is, if you will," he concluded with air quotes, "my *cave*. But the prejudices persist, and people still say things like 'I'm sorry, the civic center is for sociable people only.' Or 'Oh, I don't want a hermit living next door. Why doesn't he live in a cavey neighborhood with other hermits?' The reason I don't is because *I'm a hermit!*"

"I apologize. This is the first time I've encountered a homeless person here."

"Homeless?!? Why not just call me a hobo, sidewalk surfer, or aqualung? How very privileged of you to stumble drunkenly into my home after your all-night Bourbon Street bender and call me homeless."

"But I'm not—"

"This," he grabbed the palm shrub from which he arose and gave it a good shake, "is my home. I'm not homeless, I'm a hermit. There *is* a difference, you know. We don't all look alike. We don't all smell like limestone. And we aren't all crazy old wizards living in the desert. Believe it or not, my kind live in *all* communities, not just those subject to speleogenesis. We are productive members of society. We pay our taxes and do the miserable jobs that sociable Americans don't want to do."

"I'm very sorry, I had no idea. That sounds dreadful! What miserable job is it that you do, precisely?"

"Tech support." He nodded to affirm the horrible truth.

Puzzled, Belanger looked around the vicinity. "But I don't see any equipment. Or electricity."

"Ninety-nine percent of all calls are user error. Doesn't take a bunch of people packed in close quarters in a call center, breathing the same air, smelling and hearing each other, being *sociable*, to help the stupid. My job allows me my privacy, plus flextime and great benefits. If I ever need to shamble into the office, I'm near the Central Business District." Suddenly Jerry Lee Lewis' classic rock tune "Herman the Hermit" emanated loudly from his trousers. "Speak of the devil," he remarked. "Excuse me, I need to take this." The hermit pulled back his hair, tapped a button on the Bluetooth device on his left ear, and the ringtone stopped. "Thank you for calling tech support," he began the call with a faux Indian accent. "My name is Bobby, how can I help you? Have you tried cycling the power off and on again? There you go. You're very welcome. Have a good day. Namaste, baby." He reached up to his left ear again to disconnect the call, then turned his attention back to Belanger. "See? Code ID 10-T."

"ID ten tee?"

"Write it out, idiot."

"Hey! I'm not...oh, I get it."

The techno hermit simply shook his head.

Belanger was now a prisoner of his own curiosity. "So why would a hermit pick St. Louis No. 1 of all cemeteries? It's the least secluded cemetery in the city. Don't all the tourists bother you?"

"I'll have you know I'm pretty adept at how not to be seen. On the odd occasion when I am spotted…well, people keep a respectful distance from the scary homeless person who's misplaced his cave. And bonus: all the rum and cigars I want."

Belanger nodded his head.

"F'true, the hermit in Lafayette No. 2, she's lucky if she gets some edible flowers or an occasional rat."

"Really? Is there also a hermit at Metairie?" That was near his home.

"Oh, you'd be referring to 'the King of the Vampires.' He's a complete nutter: read one Lestat book too many. Now he just wanders around all day saying 'SUH-kay.' I don't know how he can wear all that black velvet in the summer."

At that moment, a young man in a business suit interrupted them. Although nicely dressed, his ensemble clearly came off the rack from some suit warehouse. It fit reasonably well, but the entire garment—pants, coat, and vest—was made of the same red, orange, and white plaid fabric. Thus the suit gave the impression of a chameleon hiding in a Scotsman's kilt. The illusion was spoiled only by his white dress shirt and tie with purple and gold diagonal stripes. "Excuse me, might I have a word with you?"

"Count me out," the hermit raised his palms. "Two's a crowd, but three's a social anxiety disorder nightmare. I'll be in my cave." The hermit took a single pronounced step sideways, then folded his arms and watched them with nervous curiosity.

Belanger meanwhile glanced down the path, anxious about missing his opportunity to speak to Bree outside her work hours.

Before he knew it, the man in the suit was grasping Belanger's right hand very tightly and shaking it. "Hello. I'm Cohor Woolstenhulme, and I'm with Godco Insurance."

The professor pulled his right hand free and rubbed it with his left. "Is that the one with the new talking lizard mascot?"

He shrugged. "It's a talking serpent, actually."

"Ouch, how's that working out for you?"

"It tested great among herpetologists, but disappointingly it isn't doing as well with the general public. We needed a new mascot to replace our old one."

"Right, the talking bitten apple. I remember seeing that in the news." Godco's commercials originally featured an actor in a red foam apple suit. A piece was chomped off the upper edge, and their motto was "We take a bite out of insurance prices." They found themselves slapped with a trademark infringement lawsuit from a well-known tech giant who had recently prevailed in a major patent violation case against a competing cell phone company whose product, like theirs, required the use of fingers. Ordered to cease and desist their trademark infringement, Godco hastily produced a new mascot. The consulting company they hired—which turned out to be a one-hermit operation run out of the reptile house at the San Diego Zoo—insisted that a CGI serpent would be "totally awesome and badass." The head of marketing at Godco was sacked shortly after approving this ad campaign.

"Super, so you've heard of Godco, then."

Belanger hesitated. "Are you trying to sell me life insurance?"

"What? No!" His was a drawn-out, emphatic denial. "Trying to sell someone life insurance in a cemetery would be creepy."

Belanger nodded. "I agree."

"No, what I'm offering you today is *after*life insurance."

His nose wrinkled with perplexity. "Afterlife insurance? I've never heard of such a thing." This was turning out to be a very strange day, even for New Orleans.

"It's the newest trend in monetizing return on policyholder surplus. Unlike all other life insurance policies, we pay out directly *to you*."

"To me?"

"Yes, to you."

"After I'm dead?"

"Exactly. It's super."

"How can that possibly work?"

"I'm glad you asked!" Cohor pulled a business card from his vest pocket and pressed it into Belanger's hand. "Simply keep your agent's card on you at all times. Especially after you're dead. On Judgment Day, once you've crawled out of your grave, just reach into your wallet, pull out my card, and call me to claim your death benefits."

"Seriously?"

"'Dead serious,' eh?" he chuckled. "That's our new motto. When the Rapture comes, you don't want to be the only person in your cemetery who hasn't made provisions for himself. Your thrift-shop clothes may look nice today, but how do you think they'll look at the End Times, especially after you've broken out of your grave and clawed through six feet of dirt?"

"These aren't thrift shop—"

"After all that time in a New Orleans oven vault, you're going to smell worse than Bourbon Street the Wednesday after Mardi Gras. Who wants to stand before God almighty during their Assumption, being judged while wearing clothes that are out of fashion and stinking to high heaven—and I don't mean that in a good way! Sure, we like to think we'll be judged by our acts and the contents of our soul, but The Lord is only human. You should dress your best for the most important interview of your life. Our policy makes this possible."

"I don't think so." Belanger again cast his glance sideways to confirm that Bree was still there, kneeling now but still manipulating the objects in her hands.

"Don't say no until you've seen how low our rates are, using our handy new app." Cohor produced a smartphone and tapped on its screen. "First, let's see what discounts you qualify for." Cohor looked up from the device. "Have you ever killed anyone?"

"What?!?" That got his attention.

"Have you ever deep-sixed, 187ed, dusted, fragged, iced, kevorked, offed, or popped a cap in anyone's ass?" Belanger stared at him aghast, and after a pause the agent raised a finger and clarified, "Manslaughter and negligent homicide count."

"No," he shook his head emphatically, "of course not!"

"Oh, too bad." Disappointed, Cohor returned to his screen. "Did you disrespect your parents?"

"I *loved* my parents."

Cohor shook his head ruefully. "We're going to have to try harder then. Do you now, or have you ever, worshipped false gods or graven images?"

That coaxed a wistful smile from Belanger. "When I was a boy, I had a Spider-Man poster in my bedroom. I loved Spider-Man."

Cohor grinned widely and elbowed him in an overly familiar manner. "Oh, you little sinner, you! I'll count that as a yes." He tapped the touch screen, scrolled down, then looked up again. "Do you work on Sunday?"

"I often grade papers on weekends, though I have a great TA now. That gives me more time to write on weekends."

He tapped the phone. "Does *not* keep holy the Sabbath day. Super. How about adultery?"

"Excuse me?" Belanger scowled, shifted his weight to his backmost leg, and placed his arms akimbo.

"Ever have a bit of how's-your-father with Mrs. Girl Next Door? You know, get some stankie on the hang down? Take old one-eye to the optometrist?"

"That's rather personal!"

Cohor leaned in and stage-whispered, "Don't worry, your answers are confidential. Just between you and me. And God, of course. It's nothing to be ashamed of. Plenty of men have had a little too much nog at the office Christmas party, or slipped the leash at a convention and tried some of the local cuisine." With a devilish grin, he winked and elbowed Belanger's arm again, "If you know what I mean."

"No!"

"Are you saying you don't know what I mean, or—"

"No. I have *not* had an affair with a married woman."

Cohor's lips curled downward with disappointment. "If you were French rather than British, I bet you'd have answered differently. All right, have you ever checked out your neighbor and *wanted* to storm her cotton gin? Coveting your neighbor's wife is a popular discount: you don't need to have actually *done* anything to qualify."

"Absolutely not. I'll have you know my neighbor is a perfectly respectable lady."

"All the better, I'd say." He chuckled knowingly, as if they shared some inside joke.

Belanger was not amused. "No."

"Sodomy?" He winked and leaned in again. "Either gender counts."

"No!"

"No in through the out door. That's barely *Two Shades of Grey*. How about bestiality? Ever take Fido for a ride? Shagged a sheep? Porked a pig? Pounded the duck?"

"Of course not!"

"All right then, I'll just put you down for masturbation." He tapped the screen some more.

As Cohor did so, Belanger glanced down the path again. Bree was slowly beginning to collect her things. "I'm really not interested."

"Super. All right, I can see that you're a busy man, so I'll cut to the big discount: have you ever sinned against the Holy Ghost?"

Belanger halted mid turn-away. "What's that?"

"Nobody really knows. But it's the one unpardonable sin. Between you and me, I'd answer 'yes.' We can't verify it, and added to your admitted idolatry, Sabbath desecration, and wanking, you qualify for a *substantial* multiple-category discount."

"You offer a discount for committing sins?"

"Absolutely! Unlike our competitors—for example, Imprudential—we are the *only* insurers that reward our customers for engaging in risky behaviors and lifestyles. The way we see it, the more things you do to endanger your immortal soul, the better the risk you are. After all, if you aren't called out of the ground at the Resurrection of the Dead, we don't pay out."

"That's the most ridiculous idea I've ever heard."

"Ah, but is it more ridiculous than bog snorkelling?"

"As I've told you, I'm not interested. I don't believe in Heaven. For that matter, I'm not sure that I even believe in God."

"Oh, then you'll want to hear about our 'Godless heathen' discount!"

"Good day." With that, Belanger turned sharply and walked down the alley toward Bree.

The hermit, who had been eavesdropping the entire time, raised a finger and quietly confessed, "I killed both my parents on a Sunday."

The crestfallen agent's expression lit up again. "Oh, that's a triple. Super! Hello, my name is Cohor Woolstenhulme, and I'm with Godco Insurance."

After several brisk steps toward Bree, Belanger stopped abruptly, dropped his shoulders, and heaved a long, slow sigh. The tour group had crossed his path from the adjoining alley and come to a full stop right in front of him to admire the crypt there. He neither noticed nor cared what the crypt looked like. He was too perturbed by the sea of cameras, plastic Mardi Gras beads, and New Orleans Saints jerseys that stood between him and Bree. He was equally disinterested in the tour guide's words, which may as well have been the *wah-wah-wah* tromboning of Charlie Brown cartoon adults.

He ducked into a space between two crypts as an improvised detour around the crowd. Stepping carefully around brick fragments and brush, he wound around the back of a tomb toward the path perpendicular to the one he had just left. As Belanger pushed his way through some tall weeds to emerge into the road, he caught the briefest flash of Bree just before colliding with her. He instinctively reached out and caught her forearms, preventing her from falling backwards. Unfortunately, her cards dropped out of her hands and onto the ground.

"Bree!" he exclaimed. "I didn't see you there."

Having seen Belanger's conversation with two other fellows, she had taken a similar shortcut on the other side of the tour group to say hello to one of her favorite customers. "Small worlds collide, eh? Funny bumping into you here." She stooped down and began to collect her belongings off the ground.

As he helped her, he remarked, "Believe it or not, I'm here doing fieldwork. You?"

"Today is the name day of *mi abuela*. I like to visit her here, and take some time to meditate on life."

He looked down at the handful of cards that he had gathered off the ground. Their graphic backs featured a stylized cross unlike any he had seen before. Each of its three-lobed arms was a different color: yellow on top, green on the bottom, and red and yellow on the left and right sides. At the center bloomed a rose, its three concentric rows of petals arranged and painted to look like an artist's color wheel. Three green triangles radiated from behind each pair of arms. The whole image sat on an earth-toned background of tessellated diamonds that radiated from a central point invisible behind the rosy cross. "And to read cards?" he asked.

"They help me to focus my thoughts." Bree stood up again. "I suppose you might say my tata was a *bruja*. She always had folk remedies whenever one of us kids got sick. And whenever we had to make a major decision, she helped us to consult *El Tarot*."

"Right. A colleague of mine organizes a Tarot panel at the annual meetings of the Popular Culture Association." That was the extent of his knowledge of the subject: he was more likely to attend a paper session on folklore or comic books. At an awkward impasse, he decided to pivot to his original motive. "Listen, I was wondering if I could ask you—"

"To read your cards?" she guessed eagerly. She put her hand upon his, which held the few cards he had gathered from the ground. "Sure. It looks like you've already selected your hand."

He looked down, then back at her. "What? No. I wasn't thinking of a question."

"Even better. You hold the answer to an unasked question."

Belanger smirked and muttered softly, "My only unasked question is whether my clothes look like they came from a secondhand shop."

"Yes/no questions don't work well," she answered, utterly serious. She took the small stack of cards from his hands and, without flipping them over, counted through them. "Seven cards, that makes for a pretty good spread. Let's see what you have."

The first card depicted a figure dressed in green with yellow boots, spread-eagled across the card as if he were about to burst through the borders of the artwork. A pair of horns protruded from his yellow head, and a tiger grasped and bit his left leg. Various objects swirled around this person: a dove, a butterfly, a caduceus, even a crocodile. These creatures traced a swirling vortex around the green man, creating the impression that the viewer might fall into the card. It was *The Fool*. Its number was zero.

"This is your significator," she announced.

"Significator?"

She nodded her head. "It represents you."

"*Pffft*," he replied. "*The Fool?* Thanks a lot."

"It's not like that," she reassured him. "The Tarot recounts the journey of the Fool. *El Loco* represents someone at the beginning of their journey, the journey of life. He is innocent, carefree, spontaneous, maybe a little naïve. But he also represents air, the intellect. So he isn't stupid. He's just idealistic, has his head in the clouds. Since *The Fool* can also be put at the end of the Tarot, this tells us that he may *appear* foolish, but he is really blissed out with the wisdom gained on his journey."

"Kind of like the Beatles' 'Fool on the Hill.'" Bree smiled back blankly, and Belanger mentally kicked himself: The Beatles were probably what her tata listened to. *Way to charm the ladies.* "Well," the drowning man flailed, "I *am* on my way to the Popular Culture Association's annual convention."

"There you go." The next card she turned over resembled a cubist nightmare of Tolkien's Barad-dûr: A large, fiery, unblinking eye in the dark, radiating chaos and menace, hovered atop a tower which collapsed in unnatural shapes and sent black crystalline figures of people plummeting toward what looked like a fire-breathing lamprey. Numbered XVI, it was *The Tower*.

"That looks pretty unpleasant," Belanger mused.

"This card says that something is going to turn your world upside down. It will change the status quo, shatter your assumptions, challenge your prejudices. You will have to rethink the situation you are in. But it will be liberating."

"Oh, kind of like Thomas Kuhn's idea of the paradigm shift."

She paused for a moment. "I'm not familiar with that."

"In his celebrated 1962 book, *The Structure of Scientific Revolutions*, Kuhn described instances when new data in the natural sciences required re-evaluation of existing paradigms. A shift in the scientific worldview was necessary to incorporate this new information while still continuing to account for the established body of data. The concept was embraced by social scientists who found much fruit in the metaphor." He stopped mid-exposition, reminding himself that this encounter was not a graduate-level seminar.

Her expression was even more blank than it was in response to his Beatles reference. Bree finally just smiled and nodded politely.

Really smooth, Don Juan.

The next card showed a ten-spoked wheel floating on a purple background. Lightning bolts flashed behind it, starry shapes hovered all around, and swirls extended tentacle-like beyond the borders of the card. A sphinx surmounted the wheel, while an ape ascended the left side and an alligator man with a sword hung off the right. Card number X was *Fortune*.

"Oh, this is very good," Bree remarked. "It's the wheel of fortune. You will reach a turning point for the better. You may come into wealth, take a relationship to the next level, or maybe even meet your destiny."

Belanger liked the sound of taking a relationship to the next level. That presumed, of course, that he had a relationship to level up. He wondered if this prognostication included *starting* a relationship, perhaps with a beautiful cartomancer. Wisely, he avoided dating himself by mentioning Vanna White.

Flipping over the next card revealed a Mercurial nude with chartreuse skin, orbited by a variety of similarly yellow objects that he was juggling: a winged egg, loving cup, engraved disk, Egyptian staff, stiletto, torch, stylus, and papyrus. From below, a baboon climbed the geometric latticework of lines emanating from behind the central figure. This card was *The Magus*, and its number was one.

"A magician changes the world through sheer willpower, bending the universe into line with his intentions. He is an enlightened being and teaches the truth. But," she tapped the lower right corner of the card, "he is shadowed by the Ape of Thoth, who repeats the magician's words to others. These words come off sounding incredible or nonsensical, which is why the magician is called the Lord of Illusion. This is his curse, his cross to bear. You have the opportunity here to take charge of your life and make some changes for the better."

Belanger nodded, not so much in agreement but to acknowledge her impressive command of fortune-telling jargon. She obviously believed this stuff, even if he considered it to be nonsensical. Much like his references to the Beatles and Kuhn.

The next card depicted a three-eyed goat with extremely long, twisted horns and a Fu Manchu moustache. Although standing, the goat seemed to float in space while some kind of shaft rose into the skies behind it. A caduceus stood guard in front. Below the goat's hooves rested two balls, each filled with four bluish-white figurines. This was card number XV, *The Devil*.

"This card," Bree explained, "is a warning about materialism. Success can make someone a prisoner to their bank balance. In his *Robin Wood Tarot* book, Michael Short says this card is the monkey trap: a box with a small hole and a banana inside. The hole is just big enough for the monkey to reach in, but too small to pull his hand out while holding the banana. If the monkey refuses to let go, he's trapped by his own greed. So, while you may enjoy good fortune," she held up the previous card, then switched to the current one, "be careful not to get too sucked in. Too much desire is a trap."

The next card showed a golden coin, its outer rim engraved with the Greek letters "ΤΟ ΜΕΓΑ ΘΗΡΙΟΝ," the inside inscribed with a seven-pointed star. It rested on an opalescent bed of blue-green-brown ovals that may have been shells or wings, he wasn't really sure. The card was numbered one, and its title was the *Ace of Disks*.

Belanger quipped, "Is that like that Ace of Base?"

She shook her head, his reference once again lost on Bree.

Bugger, I thought for sure that was a good one.

"That isn't one of the suits," she continued undeterred. "So far everything has been a trump, one of the twenty-two cards of the Major Arcana which represent major events. The *Ace of Disks* is a pip, one of the fifty-six Minor Arcana cards. They reflect influences on those events, like people and circumstances. The *Ace of Disks* is the root of the powers of earth, or the physical world. Disks are coins, symbolizing money and all the things that it can buy. They also represent metaphorical riches. Tied in with the other cards, this confirms that you will be fulfilled, either inwardly or outwardly."

As she turned over the last card, she stopped halfway and remarked, "Oh, how cliché." It depicted the figure of a very animated black skeleton, gamboling away from the viewer with a scythe in hand. On its bony head was a black pharaonic crown, and with its scythe it stirred egg-like bubbles of new life from the decaying sediment of spirits of the departed. Other imagery around the edges of the card included a scorpion, a serpent, an eagle, and a fish. The card was numbered XIII, and its name was *Death*.

"What?" Belanger asked, unsure why she made that remark.

She flipped the card the rest of the way over and laid it face-up on top of the previous five. "If this was a crappy movie, I'd say, 'Oh, it's the butterfly card,' and then you'd die horribly."

Belanger scowled. "*That* sounds rather dodgy!"

"But it *is* the butterfly card," she stressed, gesturing at him with her free hand for emphasis. "It represents transformation, sublimation, change. Death is only one form of that. It's similar to *The Tower*, but the change is natural. Think less cataclysm, more cocoon. This card represents Scorpio in the zodiac, and if you know any Scorpios you know how reserved, hard to read, and even secretive they can be. Any change with them is under the hood, not to the paint job."

"So a horrible yet subtle demise."

She chuckled. "What I see is that you're about to set out on a journey. The first card is you. The next and last cards, *The Tower* and *Death*, are bookends. They are both ruled by Mars, so these events will create boo-coo change in you and how you see the world. But, like *The Magus*, you have the opportunity to influence how things turn out. Then we have all those materialistic cards in the middle—*Fortune*, *The Devil*, and the *Ace of Disks*. These suggest that you'll come out ahead. Just don't get trapped by the illusion."

"That seems kind of vague, doesn't it?"

"It's pretty coherent for a handful of cards that you randomly knocked into the road. You'd get a lot more information from a formal session. We can schedule that, if you're interested. It's how I make extra cash."

"That would be brilliant," Belanger lied. He really didn't have much use for pseudoscience. Folk ways were something to be studied, not practiced. But he was perfectly willing to compromise his principles and have a Tarot reading if it meant spending more time with Bree.

"Let me give you my phone number. That way you can call me to schedule an appointment for a full reading."

"Absolutely!" He pulled out his phone and tapped at it. "What's your number?" Then he scowled at the screen. "Wait, gave me a second." He tapped some more. "Hang on. This rubbish phone isn't working."

A voice from several tombs away called out, "Have you tried cycling the power off and on again?" It was the hermit.

Belanger pressed a few other buttons and nodded. Then he called out, "Yes, that fixed it!"

"You're welcome," he shouted back. "Namaste, baby."

CHAPTER

2

THE ANNUAL MEETINGS of the Popular Culture Association were like the San Diego Comic-Con without celebrities and cosplay. For each dry, academic presentation such as "Séances and Suffrage: The Victorian New Age and Equal Rites," there were dozens of equally dry papers on every imaginable aspect of modern pop culture. Droves of fanboys and fangirls, bolstered by their advanced degrees, gathered in New York's Javits Convention Center to present papers on their particular passion: How journalism's coverage of electronic dance music has moved from scorn to championship. The influence of *The Hunger Games* on post-apocalyptic young adult fiction. The craft of synthesizing multiple literary sources into a screenplay for the *Hobbit* trilogy. How "geek chic" gained mainstream acceptance through *Big Bang Theory*. Rebooting franchises and culture, from Marvel's *Spider-Man* to J.J. Abrams' *Star Wars*. And, de rigueur, several panels—collections of papers—dealt with all things related to that perennial favorite of academics, Joss Whedon: from *Buffy the Vampire Slayer* and *Serenity* to *The Cabin in the Woods* and *The Avengers*. In all, the conference consisted of four days' worth of fifteen concurrent tracks of papers, panels, and symposia; an exhibit hall refilled hourly with poster sessions; nightly receptions and banquets with distinguished academics; and a vending hall full of book publishers, scholarly journals, and other related professional resources.

Niels Belanger stood in the cavernous atrium of the Javits Center between sessions, trying to locate the meeting room for the next presentation that he wanted to attend: "The So-Called Burning Man of *Deepwater Lemuria*: A Case of Partial Human Combustion?"

A loud, familiar call—"Hey, Monkey Boy!"—jarred him from his conference center orienteering. In a facility this large packed with this many academics, certainly a handful answered to that epithet. It was like crying "Honey!" in a crowded shopping mall. But Belanger knew the voice all too well. It belonged to his department chair, Octiana Martens. And that made him cringe all the more.

Belanger had acquired the nickname "Monkey Boy" toward the end of his graduate studies at Tulane. He had devoted three semesters to working on his dissertation about the urban legend that live monkey brains are a culinary delicacy in parts of the Far East. According to popular myth, this meal requires a special table with a hole in the center: a live monkey is strapped beneath the table with the top of his head protruding through the hole, which facilitates removal of the skull cap and consumption of the exposed gray matter with a spoon. It was xenophobic nonsense, he argued convincingly in his dissertation. Alas, a month before he was scheduled to defend his dissertation, Jones and Ford at Marshall College published their study, "In the Maharaja's Kitchen: Debunking the Trope of Eating Monkey Brains," in *Contemporary Legend*, the leading journal in the field. Hailed as definitive, the paper effectively flung poo all over Belanger's dissertation and ensured that his own research on the subject would never be published. He passed his defense—it was after all no fault of his own that some colleagues had beat him to publication—and it was no small consolation to be accepted as junior faculty on the strength of his research. But his department chair never let him forget that setback by nicknaming him "Monkey Boy." In Belanger's mind, it was more than just good-natured ribbing or collegiate hazing. He suspected his boss of insinuating that he was always two steps behind, that he was good enough to teach but would never shake up the field with original research. And that perception, he was convinced, guaranteed that he would never make tenure.

Before he turned in the direction of his master's voice, Belanger replaced his wince with a feigned expression of pleasant surprise.

Doctor Octiana Martens was a beautiful woman with straight black hair, flawless chocolate skin, and perfect makeup. Her gray herringbone jacket, matching skirt, and black silk blouse projected her confident, authoritative, and exacting nature. Black heels added to her already tall stature, and her matching cultured pearl earrings and necklace completed the look. She may have dressed like a CEO, politician, or news anchor, but Belanger imagined her as a wicked witch. He prayed for a tornado carrying a farmhouse.

"Sorry about the nickname, Niels," she began. "Seemed like the best way to get your attention in a crowded room."

You could have used my name, he thought to himself. *'Niels' isn't exactly common.* But he merely nodded in acknowledgment. As he did so, he glanced at the name tag dangling from his lanyard to confirm that it did not, in fact, read "Monkey Boy, Assistant Professor."

"I'm glad that I bumped into you. I need you to proctor my midterm exam this Wednesday for Introduction to American Studies."

"Sure. Not a problem." The request wasn't at all unusual. Faculty, particularly department chairs, often had meetings, travel, and other schedule conflicts, and an exam—where the only responsibility was to pass out and collect the tests—was an easy session for a substitute. Especially one hoping to make tenure. Belanger was happy to do what amounted to a professional courtesy.

She then looked directly in his eyes. "I also need you to take over the rest of the course for me."

His eyes and brows widened briefly with surprise. "Of course. Is everything all right?"

"Couldn't be better. But I am retired effective immediately. I tendered my letter of resignation to personnel and the president before heading to this conference. And I told my class at their review session."

This was most surprising of all. "Retiring? That's unexpected."

"I hadn't planned on it either. But I recently received an email saying that a distant relative in Nigeria had left me a fortune."

This gave Belanger a good belly laugh. "Let me guess, you had to wire them $500 to cover legal expenses."

"Yes. How did you know?" This time it was the newly former chair's turn to be surprised.

"Octiana, you know that's a scam, right?"

"No," she protested, shaking her head.

"Yes, it is. Lisa Atkins was scheduled to give a paper on it over in 1B. You probably should have gone."

"Oh, Lisa wound up never presenting."

"Why not?"

"She spent the entire morning demonstrating that you *can* dry a cat in the microwave."

"What? That's monstrous and irresponsible! You *can't*—"

The sound of a bell from the food court caused him to turn his head. There—in the area where attendees found ketchup for their fries, cream for their coffee, and a microwave oven to warm up their pastries—stood Lisa Atkins like a circus performer ringed by onlookers. With the push of a button, the just-finished microwave opened its door and out poked the dry head of a kitten, who announced its presence with an adorable little meow. Atkins gestured like a magician's assistant toward the emergent kitten with both hands, and the onlookers expressed their enjoyment with oohs and aahs and offers of polite golf applause.

Once he returned his gaze to his boss, Belanger's dumbfounded expression again became serious and focused. "The Nigerian email scam is the most notorious advance fee fraud in the world. They convince victims to wire money to them because such transactions can't be canceled or traced, and then they are never heard from again."

"But I have the money."

Belanger continued his mini lecture as if he didn't hear, or process, that information. "The dead giveaway in this scam is the awful spelling and grammar in the email. No professional bank or lawyer would send such a message."

"Niels," she emphasized, "I *have* the money."

"What?" At this point his dear departed mother, had she been there, would have warned him to stop looking like a complete prat or his face would freeze that way.

"Fifty million dollars was transferred into my bank account last week. For God's sake, I'm not stupid. I wouldn't have quit unless I actually had the money in hand. But I do, and I am *so* out of here. The last you'll ever see of me is my bootylicious backside walking out of this conference hall."

Belanger was stunned. "Huh. It's such a famous scam, I'd never think it could happen for real."

"That's right: *you'd* never think that. But I *do* have relatives in Nigeria. So this isn't all that implausible. I swear, Niels, you need to get your head out of the ivory tower, forget all those contemporary legends, and see the world the way it really is."

That was the smack-down he was anticipating: her parting shot, one for the road. "Yeah, I'll work on that."

"You do that, Monkey Boy. Who knows? With me out of the picture, you might make tenure yet." She smirked, turned away, and headed toward the exit.

Watching his frenemy leave, Belanger begrudgingly noticed that she did indeed have an awfully nice booty. For a witch. An evil, ball-busting, mind-reading witch. Looking out of the glass façade of the Javits Center, he was disappointed to see bright blue skies. No chance of tornadoes today.

CHAPTER

3

*L*ISA ATKINS HAD THE BEST VISIT to New York City. Her demonstrations at the Popular Culture Association meetings astounded endless throngs of onlookers. She took a "me day" to see the Statue of Liberty, Strawberry Fields, and Times Square. And she visited her old college roommate who now lived in Brooklyn. After these accolades and reminiscences, she was ready for a leisurely drive back to academic life in Brattleboro, Vermont. All that remained was to grab some road snacks and take one last bathroom break before setting out.

She steered old faithful—her red 1995 Honda Civic, a posh ride by liberal arts junior faculty standards—into the parking lot of a Williamsburg gas station and convenience store. She left her car and trotted through the crisp late-February air toward the entrance, passing a pair of colorfully dressed women in their early twenties. They looked conspicuously nonchalant loitering by the NYC Bike Share station.

One of them intently puffed an American Spirit cigarette, her expression masked by an oversized pair of Ray-Ban sunglasses. From the brightly colored floral headscarf that completely contained her hair, one might assume that she was a cancer survivor rather than an extremely unorthodox Orthodox Jew. She wore her latest thrift-store swag, a vintage flannel gingham dress in red, navy, and white, buttoned all the way to the top and collared with an ironically oversized floppy purple bowtie. The abject failure of this, her favorite accessory, to coordinate with her outfit telegraphed her contempt for the opinions of others. An alligator courier bag hung from her right hip, its strap crossing her body to her left shoulder. Unpaired and mismatched bracelets—some chunky and plastic, others hand-made of craft beads strung on hemp—adorned her wrists. Black leggings and a big pair of cowboy boots finished her unlikely unsemble.

The other dressed completely differently, but in an equally random-yet-intentional fashion. Her hair was relaxed and dyed into a dishwater version of Beyoncé…although she did her hair this way first. Her shaggy and unstyled look was uncovered except for the wreath of dried rosettes that crowned her head. Red wide-rimmed eyeglasses, without lenses, popped against her hazel eyes and toffee complexion. She sported what, at first glance, looked like the iconic "I ♥ NY" t-shirt, except the heart was replaced by the red scrawled letters RO. Over this she wore an old leather biker jacket, unzipped, that she had scored at a tag sale on her way home one day from her stepfather's summer home in the Hamptons. A pair of distressed high-waist jeans from American Apparel and old red and white checked gym shoes upgraded with lime laces completed her look. Whatever this outfit may have lacked in color she redressed with several bright beaded necklaces, a pair of purple knit fingerless gloves, and a different color of neon nail polish on each finger. Instead of a purse, she carried a metal lunch box from *Josie and the Pussycats*, an early 1970s Hanna-Barbera cartoon so far before her time that she could only have known about it from YouTube, if at all. Although her nose pressed intently into a worn paperback copy of Jack Kerouac's *On the Road*, her eyes peered over the top edge and watched Lisa Atkins enter the market.

As the door closed, so did the Kerouac. "Let's do this," she declared.

Both women walked briskly to the driver-side door of the Honda Civic. The first planted her cigarette between her lips. She reached into her messenger bag, between her iPad and the latest copy of *Nylon* magazine, and withdrew a slim jim. She quickly slid it between the window and weather stripping of the door, peered inside, then—without doing anything else—immediately pulled the lock pick back out again.

"Are we in?" her friend asked.

"Is that what you said to your boyfriend last night?" the other replied, returning the slim jim to her bag and rolling her eyes. You couldn't actually see her eyes roll behind those enormous sunglasses so much as you heard them roll in her sarcastic tone.

"No, Ione, it's what I said to *your* boyfriend last night."

"Girl, you need to moss." Ione pulled up the handle and the door cracked open. "Can you believe this stupid bitch left her car unlocked?"

"What a derp," the other scowled with contempt. "And did you notice the Vermont plates? I'll bet she left the door to her house unlocked, too. And her neighbors brought in the mail for her."

Ione shook her head. "My God, nobody respects people's property anymore." She pulled the car door fully open, reached in, and hit the unlock button. At first sight of the interior, she wrinkled her nose. "Ew, leather seats. Doesn't she know that meat is murder?"

"Chuh, just like that burger you ate for lunch."

"*That*, Piper, was a bacon double cheeseburger. And I ate it to show my indifference to keeping kosher. Now who's going to drive this piece of shit?"

"Are you kidding? I wouldn't be caught dead behind the wheel of a Honda Civic! I mean, this car is as old as I am."

"Then why are we stealing it?"

"Duh, because we're stealing it *ironically*."

"Fine, get in. We better make tracks before she returns."

Piper boarded the car on the passenger side and watched as Ione, behind the steering wheel, reached into her courier bag and pulled out a #2 Phillips screwdriver.

"Do you know how to hotwire one of these?"

"Trust me, I was hotwiring cars long before people like you decided it was cool."

"Hey there, just because I'm black doesn't mean I know how to steal cars."

"I'm totally with you there. During that summer in high school I spent hitchhiking across Europe, some Asian guy taught me how to do this in exchange for tutoring him in math. You just never know."

With screwdriver in hand, she removed the steering column's plastic cover. Then she reached into the exposed wiring and extracted the bundle for the battery, ignition, and starter. Once she pulled the ignition and starter wires free, she stripped off an inch of colored insulation with a small pocket knife to expose the bare wire. Her fingers twisted together the two red ignition wires, and the lights on the dashboard came to life. Finally, she sparked the bare starter wire against the connected ignition wires and revved the engine. "Mission accomplished."

As Ione shifted the car into reverse and backed out of the parking spot, the car stereo made some clicking noises and began to play music. Neither of them knew the artist, but they recognized it from when they first met in middle school. They both had shunned the song because the artist was too popular. It had been a bonding moment. "Hey, check it out!" Piper noted as they sped away from the convenience store. "This lady still listens to cassettes."

Ione nodded authoritatively. "The format *does* sound better than MP3. It's the next best thing to vinyl. As Robyn Patton writes on *Pitchfork,* 'always analog.'"

"Yeah," Piper remarked skeptically and tapped at the face of the player in the dashboard, "but she still has the factory sound system. If it was me, I'd totally trick this out with a set of Focal speakers."

"I'll bet she listens to Katy Perry and Beyoncé." Ione shuddered. "Or even Nickelback."

Piper rifled through the small collection of plastic cases stuffed into the gaping glove compartment. "Does she have anything decent or underground like DJ Rashad or Fuck Buttons? I'd even settle for Radiohead."

As she drove, Ione reached into the storage bin in the door and pulled out a cassette. "Hah!" she remarked with genuine surprise. "She has *The Best of Radiohead.*"

"She does?" This provoked a momentary flash of cognitive dissonance in Piper's consciousness. "Oh my God, that band *sucks*! I was talking about their early work, before they sold out and went commercial. Ick, now I have to get the bad taste of pedestrianism out of my mouth." She flipped open the lid of her lunchbox, pulled out a can, and cracked a Pabst Blue Ribbon beer. After a long, grateful swig, she sighed. "That's better."

Ione was quite perturbed. "What are you *doing*?"

"Hey, beer is the new Bordeaux."

"But we can't have open alcohol in the car!"

"Now *you're* the one who needs to moss. We're already stealing a car, who cares about open alcohol?"

"True. Plus here I am operating machinery on Shabbos. What would my bubbie say?"

Piper shook her head. "Don't look at me. I'm not your Shabbos goy."

"You've got *that* right. You're too much of an enabler." Ione pressed the eject button on the stereo and threw the cassette out the window. Then she popped in Radiohead just to tweak her enabler. When the song "Creep" began playing, it elicited a smile which indicated that, since it was the band's first single, this was acceptable. She reached over and took the can from Piper's hand. Raising it toward the roof of the car, Ione let out an unreserved whoop before taking a big swig of her own. Then together the friends sang along about their angelic skin.

After a few more blocks, they drove into a secluded parking lot. It was just off Kent Avenue, in the shadow of the Williamsburg Bridge. Ione pulled into a vacant area along the East River, practically under the bridge.

Piper asked, "Are we stopping here?"

"I'm not setting foot in Manhattan if I can help it." Ione reached into her bag for her iPad, turned it on, and launched her camera app. "Now lean in." Both women slanted toward the center of the car and looked disdainful. Then Ione held up the tablet and snapped their picture. "This is so going on Tumblr."

Piper was aghast. "Oh my God, you're not actually posting a selfie, are you? I can't be seen in a picture next to someone making a duckface!"

"Chill," Ione reassured her. "I have a killer app that makes photos look like they were shot with a Holga. You probably never heard of it." With just a few taps on the intuitive interface, the picture was online. "Done."

"So what now?" Piper asked.

Ione gestured with her head toward the back seat. "Let's check out what swag we scored. As old as this car is, the contents of her suitcase are bound to be way more retro than that thrift store we shoplifted."

Piper turned around and peered into the back seat. "Hey, look, she has a cat carrier."

"I hope it's a rescue."

"Let's see." She reached for the door of the carrier. Once she squeezed the squeaky release mechanism, the door swung open. Piper peered over the seat and looked into the opening. "Hey there, sweetie" was the first thing she had said that day without derision.

Within was Lisa Atkins' kitten. However, repeated bombardment with microwaves all week had transformed her, like a feline Bruce Banner, into her feral alter ego. Many times her barely-two-pound size, her fur now dark black, her eyes fierce and her claws sharp, she had become one of the legendary Anomalous Big Cats. The carrier quivered in the back seat, and a moment later the cat launched itself at Piper's face.

Hissing and yowling erupted from both woman and beast. Hands and paws flailed the air. And flesh tore from the onslaught of razor claws and needle teeth. Piper's vegan, French-pressed blood spattered on the windshield so artistically that most people wouldn't understand it.

Overwhelmed with the swift ferocity of the attack, Ione—sitting sideways in the car—reached behind herself and pulled on the handle. The car door swung open from her weight against it, and she fell flat on her back in the parking lot. She hastily rolled onto her hands and knees, pushing herself upright while scrambling away from the disturbing sound of her friend's gurgling and the obscene, purring satisfaction of the predator.

"Fuck me. Fuck me!" Ione stammered while she retreated from the horrific scene. Running along the East River—just like Thom Yorke was telling her to—she struggled to slow her hyperventilation, to take a deep breath, and to regain her senses. She finally stopped and hid deep in the shadows of the Williamsburg Bridge.

A stirring in the shadows, swift and silent, startled her. Before she was able to process that information, she found herself next to a twelve-foot-long alligator: a freakish albino with glowing pink eyes and a sickening white bumpy hide. Even in the shadows, the bright skin broadcast its details: five webbed toes on each leg; rows of osteoderms along its back and tail; and teeth of varying length exposed by a truly ironic and threatening grin.

The warm- and cold-blooded animals regarded one another for a moment. Both stood transfixed with their mouths agape, albeit for decidedly different reasons. One was in shock while the other was in preparation. Ione dropped her right hand to her side and brought her courier bag into view. She considered its alligator skin, then looked back to the creature in front of her. "Ohhhhh," she gasped, "this isn't someone you knew, is it?"

No answer was necessary. The beast lunged toward Ione's legs, knocking her to the ground. Once she was down, the alligator clamped its jaw around her midsection and quickly dragged her into the East River. Her arms and legs flailed the air until she and the alligator vanished under the water, replaced by a pool of blood that spread along the surface.

Meanwhile, Radiohead's "Creep" continued to blast out of the open door of the Honda Civic. Its plaintive final chorus asked what they were doing there, and cautioned that they didn't belong there. The warning fell on deaf ears.

CHAPTER

4

NEWCOMB QUAD on the southwestern edge of Tulane University is a verdant stretch of campus bounded by McWilliams Hall, the Woldenberg Art Center, the Newcomb Art Gallery, the Dixon Hall and Performing Arts Center, and Newcomb Hall. The latter, set back fifty yards off Broadway and surrounded by oak trees, is a century-old Colonial named after Josephine Louise LeMonnier Newcomb, who donated $3.5 million to Tulane in 1886 as a memorial to her daughter, Harriet Sophie. Wide and rectangular, Newcomb Hall is a four-story building of red brick with white window moldings and stone accents. Cement stairs rise from the Broadway-facing side of the building to meet its wooden double doors, which sit beneath a pedimented façade of four Ionic columns so majestic and oversized that they nearly overshadow the entryway. The back of the building, facing the quad, features a curved portico with a balustrade on top and a tall curved palladium window that spans the two stories above.

The Department of American Studies occupied the top floor of this building, where Niels Belanger peered over the shoulder of his teaching assistant and gesticulated at the computer screen. "A student can't claim a religious exemption from the midterm just because someone said 'the devil's in the details'!" the exasperated professor insisted. So began Belanger's return to Tulane and his less-than-welcome job of filling Octiana Martens's shoes. He had by now convinced himself that his former boss was punishing him by making him responsibile for her undergraduate class rather than one of her graduate seminars, which went to more senior faculty.

Belanger's teaching assistant, Rusty Piquot, dutifully clacked away at his keyboard. With neat and shortly coiffed hair, the TA was of average appearance but made up for it in earnest dedication. His blue jeans and combed ringspun red cotton t-shirt were typical grad student apparel. He sat at a modular desk cubicle, with a sliding keyboard drawer beneath his monitor and a hutch against the wall above it. Pens and various stacks of papers covered his desktop. As he typed, he assured Belanger, "I'll let her know. Bad student, no opiate of the masses."

"It isn't a Biblical quote anyway. Some people have traced it to Gustave Flaubert, asserting that one of his catchphrases was *Le bon Dieu est dans le detail*—or roughly 'God is in the details.' Which would be ironic considering that Flaubert's *Temptation of St. Anthony* and *Salammbô* are classics of the Decadent movement and notorious for their treatment of sex and sadism. But even if we admit Flaubert's original phrase, no one is sure how it became 'the *devil's* in the details.' The phrase doesn't even appear in print until 1975." With that off-the-cuff exposition, Belanger demonstrated the encyclopedic grasp of popular culture that prompted Tulane University to take the unusual step of recruiting one of its own graduates as a promising new faculty member.

"So does that mean she can't bring an exorcist to class either?"

"Did she really request that?" Belanger glowered at Piquot's computer screen. Then he backed up and regarded the graduate student's wily grin. "Rusty, have I thanked you lately for offering to help me with this new course load? I know you have your hands full TAing my other classes, not to mention your own coursework, but I just don't have the time to deal with this nonsense. People can believe whatever they want, of course, but I think Aristotle had it right with the golden mean: all things in moderation."

Rusty sat back in his chair, caught the professor's gaze, and raised an eyebrow. It was his "academic debate" posture, which Belanger knew all too well from previous friendly and spirited discussions with his grad student. "Mathematically speaking, in the long run varying your excesses produces the same mean as all things in moderation," offered Rusty.

"Oh," said Belanger, adopting a mock father-figure tone, "is that what they teach in philosophy class these days?"

Rusty shook his head. "No, I got that from my roommate. 'Vary your excesses' is the motto or something of his fraternity." Indeed, it was the motto of House Beta Poppa Kappa, whose founder, Albus Weinstein, coined the group's Theory of Relativism.

"I don't buy it. Someone still needs to clean the chunder out of the sofa."

The student nodded and stroked his chin thoughtfully. "So what you're saying is that the thesis full of feces has a précis that is pure."

Belanger chuckled despite himself. And that is why Rusty Piquot—whip-smart, perpetually enthusiastic, and fearlessly funny— was the best TA ever. "Were your parents even alive when that sketch was popular?"

"No, and neither were yours. But I consider myself a renaissance man."

"Better than rain man, I suppose." Belanger glanced at the clock on the wall and remarked, "Well, Mr. da Vinci, it looks like it's time for me to do my penance for Dr. Martens."

He collected his briefcase and stepped out of the office to administer the midterm exam in his first meeting with his new class. A hallway paved in light beige linoleum and lined by deep burgundy walls, white Doric columns, and ornate entablatures ran the length of Newcomb Hall and bisected the floor into two rows of facing offices. Belanger proceeded midway down its length to the stairwell, where flyers for upcoming student events, services, and brown-bag seminars lined the walls: "Wax Cylinder Recordings of Early Mime Performances." "Dothraki Tutor Available." "Professional to Format Your Theeses or Discertation." He descended three flights to the level where his classroom was conveniently located.

The lecture hall was laid out like a small auditorium. While it seated perhaps seventy-five, it was comfortably spacious for this class of thirty students, with room for one or two empty seats between each other. Two sets of doors flanked the rear of the room, but Belanger entered from another door located at the front, where he found the customary whiteboard, lectern, and table. He placed his briefcase on the latter, popped its latches, lifted the lid, and removed a stack of papers. As he considered the students before him, they became aware of his gaze upon them and grew gradually silent. Belanger took a black erasable marker and wrote on the whiteboard his contact information: name, email address, office number, and telephone extension. Then he turned to address the room.

"Hello, I'm your new step-teacher. I realize that a midterm exam doesn't start our relationship off on the best foot, but I hope that, with time, you'll come to think of me not only as Dr. Belanger, but as *your* Dr. Belanger. For today, the exam is multiple choice and you have the entire class period if you need it. Answer each question as best you can, and if you have any questions come up to the front and ask me quietly."

Belanger distributed the exams row by row using the time-honored "take one and pass it down" method. Then, sitting behind the table at the front of the room, he scanned the classroom and visually confirmed that everyone was diligently at work. He next pulled a yellow steno pad from his briefcase. Although he appreciated the benefits of smartphones and tablet computing, he preferred the old-school feel of pen and paper. As he scratched away, he paused frequently to hold the pen to his lower lip—sometimes tapping it there—and pondered his next words.

His frequent pensive gazes soon caught one student behaving suspiciously. Seated about two-thirds of the way toward the rear of the room, a young blond man alternately leaned casually left, right, or forward, and craned his head in an obvious attempt to peer at his neighbors' answers. He was good, Belanger noted: this student was handsome enough to grace the cover of *GQ* magazine or endless romance novels, and whenever one of his female neighbors caught him peering, he flashed such a disarming smile and wink that she immediately looked away with a blush.

His highlighted hair was trimmed short around the back and sides, but blended into a longer, jagged-cut on top whose shaggy and spiky look added height to his round face. He wore a hint of stubble, just enough to add rough masculinity to his good looks but not enough to appear unkempt. Indeed, he must have spent a great deal of time in front of the mirror applying product. His eyebrows were dark and his eyes deep-set, giving him an intense look from which gazed his gorgeous electric blues. His nose was perfect and his lips petulant; his chin was long and pointed. He was broad-chested, with muscular arms protruding from his shirt sleeves. His every move projected a combination of confidence in himself and disdain for others.

Belanger rose and slowly walked up the center aisle of the auditorium, glancing left and right in a nonchalant effort to thwart this student's dishonesty and force him, through proximity, to keep his eyes on his own paper. Once satisfied, the professor returned to the front of the room, took up his pad of paper, and considered the words written there: THESIS, FECES, PIECES, GEESES. No. He shook his head and crossed out the last word. Then he jotted down another, MEECES, which he likewise crossed out.

Before long, Belanger again detected the wandering eyes of his student, and so again took his discouraging walk up the center aisle of the classroom. Then for good measure he strolled around the rear of the auditorium, where he paused for a moment before slowly pacing down the middle back to his table. Returning to his note pad, Belanger jotted a few more words: NIECES, RHESUS, TEASES, BREEZES, CHEESES, JESUS. Soon, however, he was forced to take a third and then a fourth walk around the classroom. By that time, the students who were seated near this problem student had all placed their completed exams at the end of Belanger's table and left the auditorium.

With no one to copy from, the student fidgeted with displeasure. He straightened his legs into the vacated space before him. He locked his fingers behind his head, elbows stuck out to either side, and stared at the ceiling. He blew air over his upper lip with a heavy sigh. He even stared occasionally at his paper but never successfully brought himself to actually touch his pen to it. Finally, he folded the stapled pages over so that the first page was again on top. He rose to his feet and brought the exam to the front of the room where the other students' exams had been deposited.

"You're done?" Belanger asked, somewhat rhetorically.

"Yeah," the student replied sullenly. "I've done the best I can."

Belanger leaned forward, caught the student's gaze, and commented quietly so as not to distract any of the other students, "You know, if you spent as much time studying as you did peering at your neighbors' answers, you might find the exam isn't so hard." It would have been routine for Belanger to simply confiscate the exam and charge the student with academic dishonesty, but he thought it was enough on this first day of class to thwart the cheater and let him know that his professor knew exactly what he was up to.

Instead of taking the bone offered, the student's face creased up with fierce indignation. "Are you accusing me of cheating?"

Belanger smiled knowingly at his defiant student, who gasped, rolled his eyes, and shook his head.

"I don't believe this. Do you have any idea who I am?"

Belanger cocked his head and held out his open hands as he stated the obvious. "No. This is my first day in this class. I don't know any of you."

"Good," the student remarked, then hastily shoved his test into the middle of the stack of completed exams and ran out the door behind his professor.

Belanger sat in stunned silence for a moment before an ironic smile crossed his lips. He wasn't sure what was funnier: that he, a contemporary-legend expert, completely fell for this legendary scenario, or that a student actually had the audacity to try such a well-worn trope. The student in the traditional version of the tale wasn't cheating but attempted to turn in his exam long after the teacher announced that the allotted time was up. This student's brazen denial was close enough, though. Touché.

A good shake cleared Belanger's head of the incident. Then he took up his pad and wrote again. FLEECES, GREASES, PLEASES. Not too long after this, the last of his students turned in their exams.

He walked back up the stairway to his department and found Rusty at the cubicle exactly where he had left him. Belanger dropped the stack of exams on the desk and proclaimed, "The essay that is messay has the penmanship that's poor."

Rusty giggled and exclaimed, "Not bad, Doctor B!"

"You might want to hold off on awarding me that Pulitzer. It took me the entire period to come up with that, and it isn't even an essay exam."

"Not to worry. Today's Wednesday—I'll email you a spreadsheet with the grades by Friday night."

"Wonderful. You can give yourself until Monday morning if you need it."

"I'll return the exams to you on Monday, but I want to have them graded before the weekend. I have big plans with Cindy. It's the one-year anniversary of our first date, so we're going to dinner then catching Blue Man Group at the Jackson Theatre."

Belanger smiled warmly for Rusty. It was a bigger weekend than he had planned. "Say no more. I'm chuffed for you—have a good time."

"Thank you, student loans! See you Monday."

As he headed out of the room, Belanger paused in the doorway and turned his gaze back. "And Rusty?"

"Yes, Doctor B?"

"Remember to vary your excesses."

CHAPTER

5

ONDAY MORNING BEGAN like any other. Belanger dropped his briefcase in his office. He turned on his computer, grabbed his Café du Monde mug, and walked down to the shared open office area which also housed the clerical support staff. There he filled his mug from a waiting coffee maker and checked his mailbox. *Hmmm*, he thought at the absence of last week's graded exams. Strolling down the hall to Rusty's office, he saw the door locked and the lights out. *So much for "vary your excesses,"* he chuckled to himself. *Point and match to Doctor B.*

Upon returning to his office, Belanger found his computer now booted and his coffee cool enough to drink. The office was standard junior faculty fare: not too big, with neutral beige walls. His desk—cluttered with books, various stacks of papers, a pen cup, his computer and printer—nestled against the wall opposite the door, leaving the center of the room clear. Over his desk, two wall-mounted adjustable shelves held assorted textbooks and academic works in his specialization, plus several years' worth of the journal *Contemporary Legend*, which he had received ever since he first became a graduate student member of the International Society for Contemporary Legend Research. Kitty-corner from his desk stood a bookshelf stocked with more titles, many of which were remnants of his graduate studies or inherited from other faculty who had retired or otherwise pared their collections. The bookcase flanked a filing cabinet filled with old exams, syllabi, journal offprints, photocopies, drafts of research articles, and copies of grant applications. On the opposite wall hung his Ph.D. diploma from Tulane, a calendar from the teachers' credit union, and two photographs. One was a portrait of his parents, Diane and Roger Belanger, while the other was an autographed photo of actor Roddy McDowall signed "To Diane." Beneath these sat a simple dark purple office chair for students or other visitors.

As Belanger sipped his coffee and skimmed the subject lines of his unread emails, a knock on his open door interrupted him.

Turning toward the doorway, Belanger encountered the familiar face of Wednesday's anonymous cheater. A purple fleur de lis baseball cap peeked out beneath the hood of his student's black Tulane hoodie. The combination all but obscured his golden locks. The effect was to emphasize his wide blue eyes, which peered into the professor's office both earnestly yet vacantly. He wore baggy blue jeans and tennis shoes with untied laces. One hand was stuffed into his pocket, the other held a to-go cup of coffee from Café du Monde. As his eyes quickly scanned the office, they widened as they came to rest on the coffee mug in Belanger's hand. "Hey, you like Café du Monde too!" he exclaimed.

"Yes," Belanger conceded. "It's part of life in the Big Easy." He was being ironic: locals never referred to their town as the Big Easy.

"Man, I love their fucking beignets."

Belanger nodded and said "Mmm-hmm," more in acknowledgement than in agreement.

"Fuckin' beignets!" The student left no doubt about his enthusiasm for sugary fried breakfast pastries. "Right on."

Belanger's enthusiasm was unequal to the conversation, and he wearied of it quickly. "So, what can I do for you, Mister…"

"Oh! Young. My name's Nicholas Young, sir." He pulled his hand out of his pocket, extended it toward the professor, and gave a cursory shake. Belanger's hand came back slightly greasier than it began. Evidently his student had gotten some of those lauded pastries along with his coffee.

He looked Nicholas Young squarely in the eye and winked. "Ah, now I know your name."

The student smiled and pointed at Belanger. "You got me. Good one, Doctor B!"

"You realize, now that I know your name, I could throw out your exam. Although"—he referred to his spreadsheet of midterm grades—"in your case that would almost be an improvement."

"Well, you see, that's why I'm here this morning." Nicholas clearly felt awkward.

This should be good, the professor mused silently to himself, and wondered what yarn the student would produce this time. "Yes?"

"Um, well, my roommate killed himself this weekend."

Belanger's jaw dropped at the revelation. This was no dog-ate-my-homework excuse. "Dear Lord," he responded with sincere empathy. "I'm so sorry. What happened?"

"I got in Sunday evening from a frat party and found that he had hung himself. Majorly not mind safe."

"So you were also the one who found him. Oh, that's dreadful! It must have been quite a shock for you."

"It was totes Donny Downer, that's for sure. I couldn't sleep last night, so I needed the caffeine this morning…" His mind wandered fancifully to his paper cup, which he examined and rotated in his hand. "Even though it's part chicory." Nicholas chuckled and held out his cup for Belanger to click with his mug. When that didn't happen, the student took a sip as if he had completely forgotten about it.

"Were the two of you close?"

"No, man," Nicholas shook his head emphatically. "We both liked girls."

"I was wondering if you had known each other for a while."

"Oh," he greeted the dawn of understanding. He nodded while answering, "No, no. We got paired up by student housing. But I saw the guy every day. It was like he was my roommate or something."

Belanger gave him the benefit of the doubt that grief was talking. "You're not going to be able to concentrate after all this. Consider yourself excused from today's class. In fact, you can skip Wednesday too if you need to. Just let me know."

"Thanks." Nicholas nodded and smiled. "But I think it would be best if I just got my A and took the rest of the semester off."

"Pardon?" The remark left Belanger confused. "If you need to, I'd be happy to give you an incomplete and you can finish the course next semester."

"No, I think I'll just take my automatic A." If Nicholas seemed scattered before, he seemed focused now.

"Automatic A?"

"Yes. My roommate committed suicide."

In that moment the light bulb went on for Belanger. Many students share the misconception that various universities—typically extremely competitive ones—give an automatic A for the semester if one's roommate commits suicide. This belief was, of course, completely wrong. "I'm very sorry about what has happened, but you're mistaken," Belanger gently counseled Nicholas. "We don't give students an automatic A for this."

Nicholas looked shocked, even incredulous. "But," he complained, "Dr. Martens gave me an automatic A last fall after my roommate committed suicide!"

Belanger was doubly taken aback: first, because his predecessor had given an automatic A at all, against university policy; and second, because Mr. Young had a previous roommate who had recently committed suicide. "Oh God, you had another roommate kill himself?" That was some extraordinary misfortune for this young man.

"Two, actually. The first one was the worst: during the night he threw himself out the fucking window and landed—smack!—in the courtyard ten stories down. The sidewalk where he hit never looked the same. It was like the impact forced his blood and guts into the pores of the concrete." His face had grown intense, his eyes wild. Then, just as suddenly, he snapped out of it. "It's kind of fucked up to think about. After the last two, they stuck me into graduate housing hoping I'd wind up with someone more stable."

"How terrible!"

"Yeah, but it was still gnarly squared to come home last night and find Rusty's body."

The coffee mug slipped out of Belanger's suddenly slack fingers and dropped with a clatter onto the desk. Coffee splashed everywhere, but he didn't even notice. A horrible picture took shape in his mind's eye, the pieces made from the exams not being in his mailbox, Rusty's absence from his office this morning, and Rusty's roommate being a frat boy. The blood suddenly rushing through Belanger's veins sounded like a howling wind and drowned out everything else that Nicholas Young was saying.

"He knotted one end of a rope to the doorknob of the crapper, threw it over the top of door, and tied the other end into a noose. There was like no slack at all. He had to schlep over his crappy Ikea dorm chair and stand on it just to get the noose around his neck. Then he just stepped off and choked out."

As Belanger struggled to regain his composure, his eyes pleaded, "Rusty?"

"Yeah," Nicholas nodded. "That's my roommate's name. Rusty Piquot, or some shit like that. I guess he was French."

The dread confirmation that his TA had taken his own life just the night before churned Belanger's stomach. He broke into a sweat. The room began spinning.

"Anyway," Nicholas concluded, "if you just give me my automatic A, I won't bother you anymore."

Belanger lost his temper. The best TA ever had just taken his own life, and all this pathetic, dim-witted excuse for a student cared about was how to turn the tragedy to his advantage. It was callous beyond Belanger's comprehension…and tolerance. "Get out!" he barked. He rose suddenly to his feet and thrust his index finger toward the door. Had they been in the UK, Belanger would have rapped young Master Nicholas over the knuckles with a ruler. "I've already told you, we do *not* give automatic A's at this institution. *No* university does." As the words poured out aggressively, Belanger intruded into the comfort zone of the student, who instinctively backed up. "You'll get whatever grade in this class that you earn. And not a point more!"

Once Belanger backed Nicholas into the hallway, he slammed his office door shut to establish his privacy. Seeking respite behind his desk, he crumbled into his chair, his head dropping into his hands.

CHAPTER

6

I T IS FINAL EXAM WEEK for the fall semester, mid-December, just before students and faculty alike disappear until classes resume mid-January.

The faculty and staff of the Department of American Studies are grouped around several tables at Le Bon Temps Wine Bar for our informal holiday soirée. I am seated across from Octiana Martens, who is being uncharacteristically pleasant. My trusty research assistant, Rusty, is seated kitty-corner to my right.

Trusty Rusty. Of all the happy people in this bar, even more so than Dr. Martens, he is by far the happiest. But is it just the alcohol? Is it just a lie? No, he seems genuinely contented.

He lifts his glass, swirls the wine around, and gives it a deep sniff. In a deeply affected British accent, he declares dramatically, "This private-label wine is a varietal blend of grapes grown in the New Orleans bayou. It is notable for its alluring bouquet of plum, oak, spices, and crawfish, finishing with grave dirt and alligators. You might say it is my Number One." He concludes his celebrity voice impersonation with a sip.

"Oh my God!" Octiana is laughing. "That sounds *exactly* like Patrick Stewart!"

He takes up the second glass in his wine flight. "This one," he says in a scratchy, gravely bass voice, "reeks of the filth of the underworld. It's the smell of shattered childhood. But it's also the satisfying scent of vengeance. It's the smell of fear: the fear that I strike into the hearts of villains throughout Gotham."

I am nodding and laughing too. "Very good, Batman!"

Octiana finally catches her breath and asks, "I know, can you do Arnold Schwarzenegger?"

Rusty is shaking his head. "*Ah-nold* doesn't drink wine. Being from Austria, he likes German lager. After one look at the menu, he'd just say '*Ahmber Bock*.'"

She's laughing again.

"You know his favorite band?" Rusty is grinning, hamming it up. "It's *Neeckleboch*."

Now she is slapping the table and whooping.

"Dr. Martens," Rusty continues, "you'd better keep it down. The guy at the next table in the Bubba Gump hat is saying, '*Life is like a box of whatever she's having*.'"

I am laughing too, but mostly I'm smiling at my delightful company: the best TA ever. "You know, Rusty," I tell him, "if you can't secure employment after uni, you always have a promising future as an entertainer! Or as a publican."

He is sitting back, his hands behind his head, and smiling. Such a wise smile for someone so young. He is grinning with his entire being. "You said it! The world is my oyster bar. Life is good."

Life is good. Those words prompted Belanger's recollection of that evening from just two months ago, and he brought those words back with him to the present. He refused to accept that the happy young man in that wine bar had just taken his own life. It made no sense.

The night found Niels Belanger wide awake in bed staring at the ceiling, haunted by memories of the hardest day he'd had since his mother died. After the awful news of the morning, police investigators and campus psychologists had contacted him in hopes that the professor's final interactions with Rusty would provide some insight into his motives and actions. But the clues simply weren't there. Rusty had graded the exams and emailed the scores as promised. He had a date that weekend. And his last words were "See you Monday." He showed no symptoms of depression, no telltale cries for help such as giving away possessions or displays of anger. Belanger left these interviews for class and, despite being upset and distracted, he managed to get through his lecture. A sad early dinner followed. Then he came home, sat in his armchair, and ran the events of the day in his head, over and over, as he stared blankly into space.

He also struggled to make sense of his bewildering conversation with Nicholas Young. The student's emotional response did not match what one would have expected of someone who had come across the corpse of his roommate mere hours before. At first Belanger attributed it to shock, but very soon Mister Young's cold and calculated position seemed darker: He had come to Belanger's office not to apologize for cheating, nor to be excused from a few class sessions. No, he was there to claim what he mistakenly believed he deserved, an automatic A for the semester. But even this deplorable stance did not nag at Belanger nearly as much as the revelation that Nicholas's two previous roommates had also committed suicide, and that Octiana Martens had given him an A for last semester. That made as much sense as her Nigerian inheritance. Something simply did not compute. Even in bed that night, all he could do was stare at the ceiling and think and think.

Finally Belanger shot upright in bed, his eyes wide with insight. Then he reached for the telephone on his nightstand.

On Tuesday morning, Niels Belanger did not go to his office. Instead he stopped by the Office of the Registrar. Located in Gibson Hall, it was on the west end of campus just off St. Charles Avenue. Named for Confederate General and first Tulane Board of Administrators President Randall Lee Gibson, it was the first building to be built on the present campus in 1894. Its sprawling white stone-over-brick structure was in the Richardson Romanesque style, with numerous gables, characteristic semi-circular arches over all windows and doorways, and arcaded corbel tables running horizontally along its edifice to break up the stories.

To the receptionist at the Office of the Registrar—an imposing and matronly African American woman whom no one would dare disrespect—he explained, "Hello, I'm Doctor Belanger from the Department of American Studies. I rang early this morning and left a message asking to see the academic file on one of my students."

The receptionist disappeared into a back room and soon returned with a manila folder. "I'll need you to fill out this form with your campus contact information," she instructed. "After that you can take the file *temporarily*."

Belanger nodded.

She peered at him over her horn-rimmed glasses and emphasized, "We need this back, so don't make me come hunt you down."

"No ma'am. I'm certain that wouldn't end well for me. Rest assured that I'll return this file promptly."

"All right then," she smiled.

"Cheers."

From there, he continued to his campus office. At his desk, Belanger produced the manila folder and examined it. The first thing that struck him was how much thicker it was than a typical student's file. Within, however, he found no SAT scores, high school transcripts, nor letters of recommendation. Because Nicholas was a transfer student, those documents resided with his freshman institution. That was one of Louisiana's private schools, the Sacred Heart Institute of Theology, which he had entered at age eighteen, presumably straight out of high school. His was a typical freshman curriculum: English composition, basic math, American history, and introduction to film. He received mostly C's and D's. He left after only one semester with a grade point average of 1.93. Belanger laid the transcript on his desk.

The following winter, Nicholas Young was a transfer student at Juan de Fuca University in nearby Houston, Texas. His transcript read like a repeat of the last one. He took a predictable set of courses—art history, introduction to psychology, English literature, peace and conflict studies. He earned straight C's. He again stayed for only one semester, and left with a grade point average of 2.0. Belanger placed this transcript beside the other.

In his second year of college, Nicholas spent the fall semester at the less prestigious and even more distant Friends University of Central Kentucky, where he finished the term with a dismal 1.87 grade point average. In the winter, he studied abroad at the Central University of Newcastle-upon-Tyne, located in Northumberland in northeast England. The story was similar: his course load was typical, including some "blow off" classes, yet he left after one semester of abysmal grades. As with the others, Belanger arranged these transcripts on his desk, as if setting out the pieces of a puzzle.

That summer found Nicholas as a transfer student at Tulane, the first of three semesters here. In sharp contrast to his previous two years' worth of grades, he carried a 4.0 grade point average—straight A's—in both the summer and fall semesters. Belanger nodded, impressed with the student's turnaround. The next pages in the folder contained letters from Nicholas's professors. The first few showed that, in the summer semester, all his professors gave him A's because his roommate had committed suicide. The next few said the same thing, but for the fall semester. Thus, on closer inspection, this remarkable turnaround in academic performance was due to an unfortunate pair of self-destructing roommates. Given Rusty's death, Nicholas naturally expected the same for this winter semester.

The last document in Nicholas Young's student folder was a letter from campus psychological services. What Belanger read there raised his eyebrows:

My concerns about this student have escalated ever since I began counseling him about a creative writing project wherein he described beating his professor and classmates to death with a copy of Strunk and White's *Elements of Style*. As it is such a slim book, the incident in his paper was extremely drawn-out and brutal. Over the course of our meetings, this student has displayed a constellation of behaviors that, in my professional estimation, place him at high risk of danger to himself or others. These behaviors include noncompliance with University policies, disruption of the classroom environment, disrespectful and derogatory verbalizations, difficulty managing his frustration level, fascination with violent video games and movies, and veiled threats of violence. Most recently—and most concerning—he began to spread a campus rumor that a psychic in Jackson Square has predicted a Halloween mass murder in Tulane's honors residence, Butler Hall. Consistent with APA's *Ethical Principles of Psychologists and Code of Conduct* and Tulane University's standing policies, my duty to warn requires that I breach confidentiality and report this to campus police.

Although the student's behavior was reported as a potential danger, no police action was taken because Nicholas had made no specific threat. In the end no Halloween massacre occurred. However, Belanger mused, Nicholas Young's presence *was* a danger to three of his roommates.

The professor stared at the documents that now littered his desk and tried to piece them together. Three roommate suicides in three consecutive semesters was outrageously unlikely, even in the estimation of a liberal arts professor who was never good at maths. Despite that sticking point, Belanger's curiosity repeatedly returned to the counselor's letter. A campus scare over psychic predictions of a mass murder was a popular trope in contemporary myths. Halloween was an especially common date for the foretold homicides, and the source of the prediction varied from local radio programs to a major network broadcast like *The Oprah Winfrey Show* or *Late Night with Jimmy Fallon*. But no such prediction had ever been documented; it was nothing more than an urban legend. Like the belief in an automatic A. Or the anonymous test-taker.

Gradually the pieces began to fit. Returning his attention to the transcripts before him, Belanger looked more closely at the names of Nicholas Young's former colleges: Sacred Heart Institute of Theology. Juan de Fuca University. Friends University of Central Kentucky. Central University of Newcastle-upon-Tyne. These, too, were the stuff of urban legend: colleges that discovered too late that their acronyms on spirit shop apparel formed inappropriate words. The exception was Juan de Fuca U, where the pun was more straightforward. None of these storied institutions actually existed. With the exception of Tulane, all of Nicholas Young's transcripts for the past three years were forgeries.

Shite, Belanger realized. *His entire file is a parade of contemporary legends.* But if the transcripts were bogus, why did he give himself such lousy grades? And how did these forgeries fool the seasoned eye of the registrar?

Those posers notwithstanding, Belanger now had a hypothesis, a profile and a modus operandi. Nicholas Young was evidently obsessed with acting out contemporary legends. He started out innocently enough with forged college transcripts and by spreading the Halloween murder prediction rumor, but his obsession drove him to serially kill his roommates and make them look like suicides in an effort to get those mythical straight A's.

For the second time in twelve hours, Belanger reached for the phone to make an urgent call. This time, however, it wasn't to the registrar. It was to the police.

CHAPTER
7

"**H**ELLO?" BELANGER SPOKE into the telephone after the receptionist transferred his call. "I'd like to report a murder."

After a pause, he responded to the question from the other end of the line. "No, sir, I haven't killed anyone. This concerns a case you're currently investigating as a suicide."

He listened some more, nodding, and then responded, "Yes, I understand that suicide doesn't count as murder."

"I agree, you very well can't arrest the perpetrator of a suicide. But I think you will find that this particular case ought to be treated as a homicide."

After a longer pause during which Belanger shifted in his chair and slumped sheepishly, he continued, "No, sir, I'm not trying to tell you how to do your job."

"No, I don't want to run this investigation."

"No, I don't want you to come and teach my class either. I just want to share some information that might be helpful. You see, the deceased was my TA—"

"Teaching assistant."

"No, that isn't the piece of information that I thought would be helpful."

"You see, I spoke with Rusty on Wednesday—"

"Yes, Rusty Piquot, that's him. He was perfectly happy, and very excited about his big date this past weekend."

"No, sir, I did not also have a big date this weekend."

He mumbled self-consciously into the telephone. After a pause, he repeated, "I said 'I read a stack of journal articles.' After that, I got take-away from the local curry shop and listed to some old radio dramas on NPR."

"Radio dramas? They're like podcasts for old people."

"I can assure you I am *not* jealous of Rusty's weekend plans."

By this point, Belanger had picked up a pen and absently, even impatiently, tapped it on his desktop. "No, I don't think my personal feelings are clouding my judgment. The thing is, he wasn't showing any suicidal behavior. I don't believe he would have—"

Belanger's head cocked and his expression fell. "He left a note? I see. Might his roommate have forged it?"

"No, I don't claim to be a graphologist. But I have reason to suspect that the roommate was the perpetrator." By this point he had set down the pen in his hand and, with his elbow on the desktop, supported his forehead.

"*Two dozen* witnesses placed Nicholas at a party that night? As you say, that's 'a shitload of people.'"

"I see. He danced on the dining room table in his underpants and tube socks."

"With an inflatable love doll?"

"While lip-syncing to Ke$ha's 'Die Young.' I never suspected he had that much talent."

"Yes, it *is* a clever choice of a song given his last name."

"Then he vomited in the punch bowl? Yes, I can see how that would attract 'boo-coo attention.'"

Belanger sat up and leaned over his desk, his body language suggesting he was ready to push his point. "All right, but don't you think it odd that he's had a roommate commit suicide three semesters in a row?"

"Yes, I've seen the cost of tuition."

"Yes. I also have student loan debt."

"I am indeed lucky that after graduating I found a job with Tulane." He sank again into his desk chair.

"No, I don't expect I could have found work outside of academia."

"Yes, I suppose it is depressing to be a student."

"But three suicides? That's highly unlikely." He waved his free hand in the air for emphasis, for the benefit of no one in particular. He then turned his open hand palm-up. "What about his roommate last fall?"

Disbelief quickly spread across Belanger's face. "Seriously? He locked himself in the bathroom and attempted to commit suicide by firing a hunting rifle at his reflection?"

He shook his head. "No, of course it didn't work."

"Oh dear, I'm sorry to hear that the cartridge killed a parrot in the next dorm room. The owner must have been very upset."

"He was also struck and killed by the bullet? Huh, what are the odds of that!"

"Odds. Not aughts."

"A thirty aught six?"

"So, realizing what he'd done, the student ran outside in a panic and threw himself in front of a slow-moving food cart. How very tragic."

"Yes, I imagine a lot of students went without a burrito that day."

"Okay, then," Belanger renewed his argument. "What about the previous semester? I understand this one happened during the night, so Mr. Young must have been present at the time of death."

Belanger's face communicated his clear disappointment at the detective's reply. "He was in Cancun for summer vacation?"

"And he was shown on *Tosh.0*?"

Belanger closed his eyes and shook his head. "Indeed. If I stole a police cruiser and had my friend drive around town with me on the hood, naked and spread-eagled like a ten-point buck, I would expect to attract some attention."

"Yes, especially with the flashers and siren going."

"No, I don't think 'I was too pissed to drive it myself' would have been much of an alibi."

"There's also a YouTube video of his arrest?"

"Yes, sir, I'll Google 'Police Car Naked Planking.'"

"Thank you, I'm relieved to know that the naughty bits are blurred out."

"Yes, it sounds like Mr. Young is in the clear."

"No sir, I do not know who killed the Kennedys."

"Thank you for your time."

"Yes, sir, I'm sorry to have wasted it."

And he hung up the phone.

With a sigh, Belanger reclined limply in his chair. Octiana Martens' words haunted him: *I swear, Niels, you need to get your head out of the ivory tower, forget all those contemporary legends, and see the world the way it really is.* Did his profession taint his view of the world and make him see monsters under his bed? Was grief—or intense dislike of his new student—causing him to lose perspective? Or his grip on reality? The facts certainly cleared Nicholas of any wrongdoing. At least of murder. Still, something about this just didn't add up, didn't ring true. It nagged him like an unscratched itch.

There was only one way to settle this once and for all.

CHAPTER

8

NICHOLAS YOUNG DID NOT HEAR the knock on his door. He pranced around the confines of his student apartment and muttered incoherent syllables, completely preoccupied by whatever music, inaudible to the outside world, that his MP3 player was pumping through his earbuds. Decked in gym shoes and hoodie, Nicholas was prepared to go out for the evening. The second knock, as inaudible as the first, happened as he grabbed his cell phone and glanced at the screen to check for any text messages or social media updates. Meanwhile, he bobbed his head up and down and sang off-key what sounded like "Baby, baby, nom nom nom." He likewise danced keys into his pants pocket.

As he approached the exit and pulled open the door—shaking his arms and torso while belting out the words to "Gangnam Style"—he was startled to find Belanger standing there, about to knock for a third time. The sight of his professor brought the production number to an abrupt halt. Wide-eyed, Nicholas yanked the earbuds from his ears by the point where the wires branched just over his heart and stammered, "Doctor B! What are you doing here?"

"I wanted to apologize for my outburst yesterday," Belanger explained. "I was also hoping you might help me with something."

"Sure thing, doc." His words said yes, but his mannerisms, expression, and tone of voice all oozed trepidation and nervousness.

"You see, I didn't know that you were roommates with my TA."

"Shit, man, Rusty was your TA? I had no clue!"

"Indeed, until you said Rusty's name, I had no clue that he had committed suicide. I was very distressed and shocked by the news, and regret that I became so emotional."

"No worries, dude. Monday was a complete blower."

"It certainly was."

"You said you needed my help with something?"

"Yes, please. Rusty graded my midterms over the weekend. Although he emailed me the scores, I still need the exams."

"Right, for the class review."

"Exactly. I gave them to him in an inter-departmental envelope. I'd be able to spot it right away if I took just a quick look around." Belanger peered over Nicholas Young's shoulder into the apartment behind him.

"Oh, sure. Come on in." Nicholas stepped aside, flicked on the light switch, and gestured for his visitor to enter. Behind the inviting words and gestures, Belanger sensed tremendous discomfort. It was more than just having his professor enter his lair. There was a feral territoriality about him.

The graduate housing apartment was rectangular, with the door at one end and a window on the opposite side. Inside to the left Belanger spotted a kitchenette, which consisted of a mini fridge, microwave, toaster oven, sink, and trash can. Dirty dishes filled the sink, and trash overflowed the can. On the opposite side of the room was the door to the toilet and shower, where a pile of white towels gathered. Just past these features was the living area, demarcated by two futons sitting at right angles to each other. They were oriented toward the flat-screen television in the far corner. Beneath the television rested a set of speakers, a video game console and controllers, and several cases containing video games. In the space immediately in front of the two futons sat a storage bin that served as a makeshift table. Through the clear plastic sides Belanger identified clothes—whether clean or dirty, he did not know—while the top of the container held empty beer bottles, energy drink cans, pizza boxes, and assorted fast-food containers. On the wall opposite the television, on the left side of the living area, hung a Nerf dart board. Posters lined the other blank areas of the wall. Some were for the metal bands Behemoth, Avenged Sevenfold, Devil's Blood, and Sabbath Assembly. Others were for comic books, including *Guardians of the Galaxy*, *Batman*, and *The Avengers*.

Beyond the living area, through a doorway in the center of the room, was the sleeping area. To either side of its entryway was a lofted bed beneath which sat a small dresser and desk. A bookcase comprised the foot of each bed. It was obvious which bed belonged to Rusty and which to Nicholas. The desk of the latter held a laptop, a stack of notes, and a pair of plastic action figures. One depicted Kratos, the gray-skinned Greek warrior on steroids who served as anti-hero in the *God of War* video game series. The other was of Dante, the cool and stylish white-haired mercenary in the red duster from the *Devil May Cry* video game franchise. The shelves at the foot of Nicholas Young's bed contained several textbooks—excluding, Belanger noted, the one for his American Studies class—and one shelf was devoted to an impressive array of hot sauce bottles with brand names including 100% Pain, Nuclear Hell, Zombie Sauce, Devil's Bitch, Black Mamba, Bernie in Hell, Fire & Brimstone, and Beyond Insanity, all decorated with eye-catching images of skulls and crossbones, flames, devils, grim reapers, and offensively stereotypical Mexicans. Many of the bottles were either empty or partially consumed. Below this was a shelf stocked with a small collection of classic cookbooks, including Irma Rombauer's *Joy of Cooking*, *Larousse Gastronomique*, and *The Professional Chef* by the Culinary Institute of America. Belanger recalled from his student's transcripts that Nicholas, since transferring to Tulane, had taken a culinary course each semester.

By contrast, Rusty's bed was stripped and his desk's contents collected in a cardboard box. This allowed Belanger to peer inside and immediately spot the envelope containing the graded exams. "Here it is," the professor announced as he pulled his excuse out of the box.

"Ivory fabulous," Nicholas replied. As Belanger entered the living room from the bedroom, the student asked, "Is there anything else?" It was a polite way of saying "get lost." But, in contrast to his two previous interactions with Nicholas, Belanger felt he was in control of this one. He wasn't about to yield the situation until he got what he *really* came for.

"Actually, I'd love a glass of water."

"Shizzle." The remark was slang for either "sure" or "shit," and in this case probably meant both. He turned and grabbed a glass from the kitchenette.

Belanger smirked and sat on one of the futons in the living area. "Rusty seemed fine when I saw him at the department last week. Did he give you any indication that he was depressed or upset?"

"Beats me. Between classes, parties, and hookups, we really didn't talk much." He emerged from the kitchen and handed the glass of water to his professor.

Belanger took a sip then continued. "It must still be very hard going through this *again*. Remind me, how many roommates does this make?" He raised an eyebrow as he fixed Nicholas Young's gaze, making clear that he already knew the answer.

"Th-three."

"All since you've come to Tulane?"

Nicholas merely nodded his head and took a step backward.

"And this never happened at your previous schools?"

"No, sir."

"That's very strange. Do you think it's something about Tulane?"

Nicholas felt the noose start to tighten and stepped back more, as if to put some distance between himself and a hunter. "Uh, I suppose you'd have to ask them."

"Fair enough. Too bad I can't." His eyes again drilled into the student's. "By the by, I was looking at your transcripts recently. You know, to sort how this 'automatic A' thing works. I see you've been to quite a few colleges before settling here."

"That's right." By this point, Nicholas had backed himself against the kitchenette. "Um, I guess it took me a while to find a place where I felt at home."

"The curious thing is," Belanger continued as if Nicholas Young's response didn't matter, "I've never heard of any of these schools. None of them have a webpage either. Don't you think that's odd?"

Sweat ran down his brow. His upper lip perspired. His hands behind him, Nicholas braced himself against the wall that divided the kitchenette from the entryway. "I think some of them changed names." He seemed to be searching for an answer. He glanced sideways in the sink in case he needed a weapon. There were only dirty forks. One didn't eat Chinese carry-out with a knife.

"So tell me this: Where did you attend high school?" Belanger sipped the water slowly, indicating that he was ready to wait as long as it took to get an answer. He was poised to spring the trap, to close in for the kill.

Nicholas Young's expression turned blank, with just a dash of surprise. "Wut."

Feeling himself quite the schoolmaster now, Belanger pressed harder. "Come now, Mr. Young. It was only three years ago. Surely you haven't attended enough frat parties to erase that memory."

Much to Belanger's surprise, Nicholas's demeanor suddenly transformed. His back stiffened. He stared darkly back at his professor. He scowled. "You haven't got a fucking clue," he realized angrily. "This whole thing is just a fishing trip. You don't have the slightest idea what you're dealing with, do you?"

What could he say? The student called his bluff, and now he was on uncertain territory. "To be perfectly honest: no, I don't."

Nicholas Young's eyes shifted left, then right. "Good."

Belanger heard the sudden click of the light switch, and the apartment plunged into total darkness. Realizing he was in an unfamiliar place, Belanger remained perfectly still on the futon. If he tried to move quickly, he might trip over the plastic tub in front of him. Or on any of the piles of fast-food containers and other debris scattered around the room. Instead, he listened closely for any clue to what was about to happen next. Uncertain of what Nicholas was capable, the professor hoped that the shuffling sounds he heard continued to move away from, rather than toward, him.

The answer came when a shaft of bright light from the hallway pierced the darkness. The entry door opened wide, and Belanger watched as the student's silhouette stepped into the hall and pulled the door shut. This placed Belanger back in total darkness. He listened to footsteps hurriedly tap down the hallway, then he shook his head and thought to himself, *I cannot believe I fell for that trick twice in one week.*

After allowing time for his vision to adjust, Belanger stood and looked around the room. He spied a faint sliver of light under the door to the main hallway. Moving slowly with arms extended, he carefully made his way around the futon—inadvertently kicking a few fast-food bags along the way—until he found the edge of the kitchenette counter, which he then followed toward the entryway. Open-palmed, he brushed along the wall until he reached the door and, thereby, the knob. Properly oriented, he next felt around for the peephole, through which he peered. No one was in the hallway. He opened the door to let in just enough light for him to spot the switch next to the exit and flick on the room lights. Then he closed the door, set the deadbolt, and slid the security chain in place.

He leaned back against the door, relaxing and sighing for a moment. He had no idea what had set Nicholas off like that. But his was definitely not the behavior of an innocent man. Belanger savored the fact that he emerged unharmed from this confrontation, which he realized in retrospect was extremely foolish.

So what now? He would be safe in the open, he reasoned. And Nicholas would be long gone by now. But where would the student go?

Belanger thought he might find a clue in the small apartment. The living room and kitchen were disaster areas, and nothing looked important amidst the laundry, food containers, and plates. Stepping over to the television and speakers, he looked to see if any important papers were there. All he saw were a few scattered video game boxes: *Dante's Inferno*, *Guitar Hero III*, *Silent Hill*, and *Diablo*. Belanger entered the bedroom and examined the desk underneath Nicholas Young's unmade loft bed. Pinned to the wall next to his laptop was his grinning Mexican mug shot, one hand holding his case number and the other giving a thumbs up. The bare-bones printer to which the laptop was connected had a piece of paper in the output tray. Belanger pulled it out and saw a flight reservation from New Orleans International to Rapid City Regional in South Dakota. *Not your usual spring-break destination*, he mused. The cluttered desk otherwise held no obvious secrets: some Amazon packing slips, a few Doctor Strange comics, his fall report card showing straight A's, and other scattered papers and writing implements. On the upper right corner of the computer screen hung a yellow sticky note on which was drawn an elongated trapezoid, wider at the bottom and narrower at the top, above the letters DT. Belanger reached out, snatched it, and pondered: Delirium tremens? Dream Theater? David Tennant? Dumb Teacher?

His eureka moment failed to materialize, so he stuffed the note into his coat pocket. Casting his gaze back at the entryway, Belanger decided it was best to leave and put this strange day behind him.

CHAPTER

9

NICHOLAS YOUNG SAT at the makeshift desk of a small motel room and sipped his to-go container of coffee. Powdered sugar from the beignets that he had eaten out of a grease-soaked white bag now formed a circle on the worn and stained carpet beneath him. His tablet computer stood upright in the center of the desk thanks to the optional cover that doubled as a stand. The tablet ran a teleconferencing app which divided the screen into nine equal sections for video feeds and document sharing. Most of these displayed an unsavory cast of characters who together made up a sort of malevolent Brady Bunch.

In Marcia Brady's position in the upper left-hand corner was a fierce-looking Hispanic man. His white shirt, open to the sternum, revealed a braided gold necklace nested in his hirsute chest. Over this shirt was a black denim blazer. His face's resting position appeared to be a scowl, and his heavy eyes, stringy chest-length hair, and black bandito moustache only cemented his resemblance to the prototypical Mexploitation villain. If he were in Colorado, the police would want to pull him over and ask to see his papers, but they would be too afraid to actually do so.

A muscular, stubble-haired man appeared in Jan Brady's spot below. His eyes were squinty, and his large broad nose—which looked as if it had been broken a few times—made his eyes look even smaller. He had a broad chin, and fiercely clenched a pipe between his teeth. His wide head would have looked like it was grafted directly to his t-shirted shoulders if not for the Blackletter tattoo spelling "Grandma" on his short thick neck. Not that anyone would ever consider giving him a hard time about that.

The participant in Cindy Brady's bottom-left position was anything but the baby of the bunch. Whereas the others were clearly in their prime, this one was in his early fifties and had just as clearly seen a lot of mileage over rough roads. His complexion was ruddy, and his hair black. A scar ran from the side of his forehead, down across his right eye, and to the corner of his mouth, giving the latter the illusion of curling downward more than it really was. He wore a turquoise bolo tie over a long-sleeved henley liberally dotted with blobs and splatters of paint.

Ironically, Nicholas—barely twenty-one and thus by far the youngest of the conference participants—appeared in the top center, in the matriarch's position. Two spots below him, in the father's spot, was an elderly and gaunt figure in a purple robe, its hood hanging down over his eyebrows.

Over on the right side, the top cell was occupied by a figure in a retro aviator cap made of soft brown leather. Large goggles covered not just the eyes, but the area from brows to cheekbones. Only the brightly red-lipsticked mouth and red hair cascading from under the cap past her shoulders suggested that this person was a woman. Otherwise, the room was so dimly lit that any other details were lost in the low contrast. Had it actually been Greg Brady in drag, no one would have known.

After a computerized voice announced "Someone has entered the conference," a head appeared in the spot below. It wore a hockey goalie mask covering the entire face except for two eye holes and a rectangular mouth hole beneath the nose that gave the mask a strange Hitler-moustache look. Nicholas Young looked down and to his left toward the newest member of the family, sighed, and asked, "Really? Is a mask necessary?" After a shake of the head, the new Peter Brady removed the mask to reveal the most incongruous of all the callers. He was clean-shaven, his hair impeccably neat and closely trimmed. He wore a pressed shirt, striped tie, and suit jacket. He might have been a CEO, if not for the unnaturally wide smile on his lips. If the others seemed like a scowly bunch, his unflinchingly cheery—even psychotic—expression was the most unsettling of them all. "Hmmm," Nicholas mused, "maybe the mask wasn't such a bad idea after all."

The point was moot, however, as the computer system again announced "Someone has entered the conference." In the lower right-hand corner appeared, rather than a face, a penis. Nicholas circled his brow with his thumb and forefinger as if he suddenly had a splitting headache, and shook his head. Dropping his hand, he asked, "Number Eight, who are you?"

With a thick British accent came the reply, "Sir Terrence Snogworthy, sir."

"Of course you are. Is that thing a deadly weapon?"

"No, although I was arrested one night when I was caught having sex with a pumpkin in Old Man Mason's patch."

"Let me guess: It hadn't started out as a pumpkin."

"That's what I told the officer, at least."

"Have you ever killed anyone?"

"I once accidentally burst into my own surprise party naked. Nearly gave both my mum and my wife a heart attack. Does that count?"

Nicholas simply shook his head, tapped the "x" on his video feed to close it, and said "Buh-bye."

"I think that's everyone," the robed man informed them.

"Then behold!" Nicholas called out in an imitation of a 1950s science fiction announcer, his voice deep in both pitch and vibrato. As he did, he extended his arms toward his tablet's camera. "I come to you across time and space!"

The fellow with the long scar made a face and shrugged, "It's only the Internet."

From above, that participant removed the pipe from its teeth, looked down with a scowl, and said, "Shh!"

Nicholas simply continued with a giggle, "I've always wanted to say that. So yo, where y'at?" No one answered, so he assumed a more formal tone. "Thank you for answering my summons. Especially on such short notice. Something has come up and I have a mission for you. We're all very busy, so I'll make this brief." He tapped on his tablet and in the center of the screen appeared a picture of Niels Belanger, below which was a link to his faculty page at Tulane. "This is my prof—" Nicholas caught himself and rephrased that. "My *enemy*."

The woman in the aviator hat leaned closer to the screen for a better look, leaned back again, then looked to the side, where Nicholas's video feed was located. "He doesn't look very formidable to me."

The smiling man looked up at the speaker above him and suggested, "Do you think he meant to say 'enema'?"

From across the screen, the bandito looked to them and offered, "Or maybe '*blasfema*.'"

"He is dangerous," Nicholas insisted. "He hasn't exactly figured out what is going on. But he suspects *something*. I can't allow anything, no matter how unlikely, to interfere with my plans."

"And dat's where we comes in," said the squinty man before putting the pipe back in his mouth.

"I want you to take care of this problem." Nicholas spoke these words clearly and slowly so there was no doubt of his intention. "Locate my enemy and remove him from the equation. Eliminate him." As he elaborated, however, his delivery became more rushed, passionate, frantic. "Let his name be so despised that even his descendants unto the aeons wander the streets, afflicted and destitute. Take out your sword and smite my enemy! Let his annihilation be forevermore through the ages a warning that all those who oppose me shall surely be slain as are cattle to the slaughter. Make no covenant, show no mercy: *Utterly. Destroy. Him!*"

The Hispanic gentleman in the upper left shrugged his shoulders and with a no-big-deal expression said, "Pffft. *No hay problema*."

"The motion is seconded," spoke the old man in the lower center. "All those in favor say 'aye.'"

A chorus of affirmations followed: *Sure. Okay. Sounds good.*

"All opposed?"

Silence followed.

"Then the ayes have it, and the motion carries. Let the record show that the motion to destroy Niels Belanger has passed unopposed." It was strangely comforting to see that even a conclave of hit men followed Robert's Rules of Order.

Nicholas, however, continued his abjuration despite the preceding vote. "I invoke, conjure, and command you: By the Fearful Day of Judgment! By the Moving Sea of Glass! By the Four Beasts before the Throne! Do my bidding. And speak your agreement in a clear and easy voice that I may understand your words. Be obedient in every way to my desires. If thou dost not, I will curse thee, and will cause thee to be stripped of thy powers, and consigned to the Waters of Everlasting Flame, Fire, and Brimstone. Come, then, and obey me utterly!"

"Dude," the smiling man said, his eyes and brows furrowed in an expression of gleeful concern, "we said we'd do it."

"*Mi amigo*," the Mexican said to him as an aside, "it is the only way he knows."

"Is there an objection to consideration of the question?" the elderly Parliamentarian spoke up.

"It's not so much a question, is it?" replied the smiling man. "This motion is merely a continuation of the previous motion, which has already been unanimously passed."

"So you move to close debate on the previous question?"

Nicholas's voice, now booming with intensity, cut them off. "Inimical and disobedient servants! If you do not obey I shall brand thee accursèd: accursèd by Heaven, accursèd by Hell, and accursèd by the Sun and Moon and Planets! By the power invested in me—"

"Yes!" the smiling man interrupted, "I move to close debate! We already said we'd do it!"

"Seconded," said the figure with the braided back hair. "Let's get on with it."

His expression falling, Nicholas looked down and pouted. "Oh, you're no fun anymore."

"I have a parliamentary inquiry," piped up the aviator as she raised her gloved index finger.

"Yes?" the hooded man invited.

"Would it be appropriate to move that we take the proposed curse off the table?"

The old man nodded. "Yes, I think it would be."

Almost instantly, the squinty-faced man jumped in. "Seconded."

"All in favor?" asked the parliamentarian. Everyone raised their hand. "Let the record show that the subsequent motion, to curse the committee by heaven, hell, sun, moon, and planets, has been rescinded. However, the first motion, to smite the chairman's enemy, remains in force."

Nicholas smiled and nodded in acknowledgement. "Thanks for diligently agreeing to my demands, and for being so ready and willing to come at my call. I hereby license thee to depart unto thy proper place: Let there be peace between us, and be ready to come at my call. Go now to your places, without causing harm or danger unto any man or beast."

The fellow in Marcia Brady's spot gave a pained look. "Aww, not even to *beasts*?"

"Well...all right," Nicholas conceded with a smile. "Raise some hell. You know I can never say no to you guys."

"All right!" the aviator said, clapping her hands. "I move to adjourn."

"Seconded," agreed the man in the suit and tie.

"All in favor?" asked the robed one. Everyone raised their hands. "Meeting adjourned."

The squinty man cocked his head and asked, "Did we ever approve da minutes from our last meeting?"

"Shut up," said scarface, who then disappeared as he logged off.

"Someone has left the conference," the software announced.

Jackson Square is the French Quarter's prime location for artists, actors, musicians, and other entertainers to stake out a space and collect money from tourists in the shadow of St. Louis Cathedral and the square's namesake statue of Andrew Jackson. Here, soloists and ensembles perform music for tips. Actors painted silver from head to toe stand frozen and statuesque, moving only when a contribution is placed in their jars. Tarot readers spread cards out on folding tables under the cover of market umbrellas. Some artists paint unearthly landscapes using nothing but cans of spray paint, while others paint wildly colorful and impressionistic oils of local architecture. In front of it all, horses and carriages queue up along Decatur Street ready to take couples on romantic sightseeing tours.

One of the artists near Decatur stood in front of a semi-painted canvas, held out his thumb, and peered intently past it across the street. There stood the famed Café du Monde, which teems with customers twenty-four hours a day. The canvas depicted the small store at the end of a row of shops, whose iconic white and green striped awning covered dozens of round black metal tables and matching chairs. People filled all the spots, while others stood waiting for a seat to open. Birds hopped around, hoping for a piece of beignet to accidentally fall to the ground or to be intentionally offered by a generous customer.

After a few brush strokes, the artist set down his brush and extended his thumb again. He stared intently, fixedly. Then he reached inside his paint-speckled smock and pulled out a pistol with an optical sight attached to the barrel. He straightened his arm to point where his thumb had previously been fixed. Squinting through the sight with an eye whose lids were bisected by a scar that ran from his brow to his mouth, he fixed café customer Niels Belanger right in the crosshairs and squeezed the trigger.

CHAPTER

10

O N THE SECOND MORNING after his encounter at Nicholas Young's apartment, Niels Belanger woke up ahead of his alarm clock and decided to treat himself to coffee and beignets on his way to the university. He settled into a cafe chair under the green and white awning and unfolded the latest *Times Picayune*. Before he could read any further than the headline, DEEPWATER LEMURIA TRIAL FINALLY UNDERWAY, Bree appeared with a "Hey, baby," her usual greeting for customers. He requested his usual—a café au lait and an order of beignets—then sat back and moonily watched her walk off. After she was out of sight, he continued to look at nothing in particular.

As he considered the customers interacting with staff, Belanger's imagination begat a monologue. Police officers are known to be prone to "mean world syndrome," but are wait persons subject to a similar occupational hazard? he wondered. After all, it seems like they always come to check up on you just as you've taken a bite of your meal. "Is everything okay, Mr. Wickersham?" "Fine, fine," he'd reply with a mouthful of kidney pie. "Is the Double Gloucester to your liking, Mrs. Waistcoat?" She'd answer by bobbing her head up and down, wide-eyed; perhaps she'd throw in a thumbs-up. Seeing scenes like these day in and day out, wait staff in restaurants the world over must see their fellow human beings as slobbering gits who speak with their mouths full, or as nonverbal primitives who communicate solely through head and hand gestures.

The sight of Bree at his table with a serving tray brought him back to reality. Prepared with payment, he handed her a ten-dollar bill, smiled, and said, "Keep the change." She took the cash with her free hand and slipped it into the front pocket of her apron. Then she lowered the tray and handed Belanger his café au lait. It was nice and hot, releasing steam into the cool morning air. As Belanger took the cup by the handle, she reached for his order of three beignets.

Surprisingly, the cup shattered in Belanger's hand. Hot coffee spilled everywhere, soaking his pants. Left holding half a ceramic ring that used to be a mug, he sat there thinking, *Well, this is certainly not the lagniappe that I expected!* It all happened so quickly that he didn't connect this event to the whizzing sound that immediately preceded it, nor to the pop an instant earlier.

Before he registered anything at all, the plate of beignets in Bree's hand also exploded, showering Belanger—and the vicinity—in broken china, donut bits, and a cloud of powdered sugar. This time he noticed the pop and whizzing. He also noticed pandemonium break out as everyone in the café realized that an active shooter was in their vicinity. Half the people dove under their tables—which, Belanger concluded, simply made them sitting ducks in an open-air food court. The other half took the more sensible action and scattered in all directions.

Belanger leapt to his feet in order to follow the example of the sensible members of the gene pool. Bree, meanwhile, stood frozen on the spot with shock. He grabbed her hand and, with a tug, said, "Come on!" She dropped the tray and ran with him.

The two pops had come from Jackson Square, so Belanger led them in the opposite direction. They exited at the back of the café near the carry-out window, ducking through an opening in the iron railing. This tactically put distance—and the storefront—between them and the shooter. It also took them in the direction of his car, which was parked in the public lot behind the café.

Their route to the car park took them down the Dutch Alley, a slate pedestrian plaza behind the French Market shops. Today it was a gauntlet. A series of tall, sea-green palladium windows backed the stores on their left. On their right rose a high cinderblock retaining wall dotted with palms, ferns, and ivy. The throng of pedestrians here was more confused than usual in the face of people racing frantically in their direction.

More shots rang out. Bullets sailed through storefronts on Decatur Street and shattered the palladium windows on their way out on the alley side, mere moments after Belanger and Bree passed them. People screamed. The professor squeezed Bree's hand and pulled harder, ran faster.

Ahead of them was a break between the French Market shops: an arcade allowing passage from the alley to the storefronts. Here, a low fountain protruded from the wall on the right. A bronze statue of a woman in a modest two-piece bathing suit perched, semi-recumbent, on the edge of the fountain facing outward. On the wall behind it, sea-green shutters framed a mural that depicted the Dutch Alley of a bygone era. As Belanger and Bree passed this landmark, they heard another pop followed by the sound of a bullet ricocheting off the statue.

At last they reached a break in the wall. Five broad steps rose on their right between a pair of rectangular concrete lampposts stenciled EB 57 in black on yellow. The French Market parking lot awaited. As they entered, Belanger pointed across the stairway to the Dumaine Street stop for the Riverfront Streetcar. His green Chevy Volt was parked beside the shelter.

Arrived at his vehicle, they tugged frantically on the door handles, which turned out to be locked…just as he had left them. Bree glanced around nervously while Belanger reached into his pants pockets and came out empty-handed. Then he reached into his blazer, with equal results. Finally he tapped his thighs, sides, and chest to detect where he had stuffed his car keys. By now Bree looked on with strained and anxious impatience, arms akimbo. The keys turned out to be in his breast pocket. As he fumbled to pull them out, they slipped through his shaking fingers and clattered to the ground. Sighing at his clumsiness, he dropped to his knees and patted the ground just underneath the car until his palm came to rest around the keys. He closed his fingers tightly, stood again, and repeatedly pressed his key fob until the car lights blinked on and off and the doors unlocked. "Get in!" he shouted. Alas, when they opened the doors, his car alarm sounded. This required him to fumble with the fob some more. *Bloody hell,* he thought, *if I weren't a complete tosser I'd have taken out my keys on the way to the car!*

Once they got in and Belanger started the engine, another pop signaled the shattering of his rear window. Pellets of safety glass rained inside the vehicle. Panic spread across his face, replacing the lesser panic that was already there.

"Duck!" he told his passenger. He likewise slid low into his seat and put the car in reverse. It jerked out of its parking spot, then jostled the passengers when Belanger stomped on the brakes every bit as emphatically as he had punched the accelerator. Another pop from behind shattered his front windshield. He cringed for a moment at experiencing—yet again—the destructive force of a firearm trained in his direction. A scraping noise from the rear of the car, too close for comfort, startled him out of his brief reverie. He shifted into drive and punched the accelerator. The car leapt forward, roaring through the lot along the Mississippi River.

The lot itself continued for the length of three blocks—two-tenths of a mile—before exiting past an attended booth. As they zoomed across that distance toward the barrier gate, Belanger cried out in frustration. "Shit!"

"What's wrong?" Bree asked.

"I told you to keep the change."

"*¿Adió?* You're angry that you tipped me?"

"No! Now I don't have any change to pay for parking."

She sighed. "Don't even *think* about stopping!" She placed her hand on his right knee and squeezed for emphasis.

His eyes widened at the unexpected thrill of her touch. Almost involuntarily, his leg stiffened and the car accelerated. They zoomed past the Governor Nichols Street Wharf and the Ursulines streetcar stop, bearing down on the attendants' booth. Guards scattered out of the way as his car crashed through the wooden arm. A splintered section decorated with a sticker reading "Thank You For Parking At French Market District" slid up the edge of his broken windshield and over the roof. Such blatant, disobedient vandalism filled Belanger with guilty satisfaction: it always bugged him that they capitalized "For" and "At."

As they passed the booth, Bree turned and shouted belatedly through the broken rear window, "¡*Abran cancha!*"

The long exit ramp finally deposited them onto North Peters Street, heading away from the Vieux Carré and toward the Faubourg Maringy. From here they had no particular destination other than away. Belanger instinctively headed toward the Ponchartrain Expressway and sped away from the Quarter. As he drove, both he and Bree bandied about the burning question "What was *that* all about?" They agreed that they should go to a safe spot and call the police. After about fifteen minutes of wind blowing through the broken glass, they exited the highway and pulled into the driveway of Belanger's home in Metairie. No shooter could have followed them this far. To be extra safe, they agreed to call the police from inside.

Belanger got out of his car and began to walk around to help his passenger with her door. As he circled the rear of the vehicle, however, he saw something that made him come to an abrupt stop. Deep scratch marks marred his trunk. And dangling from the bumper was a hook.

CHAPTER

11

BELANGER HURRIED BACK into the driver's seat, closed the door, and hit the lock button. With quivering hands to his face—fingers under his glasses—he rubbed his eyes and released a long sigh. This was all happening so quickly. He was uncertain what to do, what to say. Should he tell Bree what he saw?

She touched his shoulder, a gesture combining gratitude and calming. "Thank you for getting me out of harm's way."

Belanger didn't move, didn't respond. Inwardly, his head was reeling.

"Do you think any people back there were killed?" she continued.

He rested his hands on the steering wheel and shook his head. "I hope not."

"We should call the police. 911. Or CNN."

"We can't stay here," he finally declared.

"What? Why not?"

"I've been thinking. It was my coffee that got shot. It was my car that got shot, too. What if the gunman was after me?"

Bree's compassionate concern changed into a scowl. "*¿Qué demonios?* What have you done?"

"Me? I didn't do anything!"

"Someone doesn't get publicly executed for missing a credit card payment. Are you a drug dealer?"

"No!"

"How about a stock broker? Did you screw a bunch of rich people in a Ponzi scheme?"

"No, I'm a professor."

"Are you a hard grader?" She paused and squinted for a moment to think, then her eyes popped open wide with realization. "Oh shit! I'm sitting next to a target!"

This thought brought out the stereotypical British unflappability that was his birthright. "You may be."

"What does that make me? Your human shield?" So much for getting her out of harm's way.

Belanger started the car. "Listen, if someone is after me then we're in danger here."

Bree flashed an index finger at him. "No, hombre, *you're* in danger. I have nothing to do with this—other than the fact that you dragged me into it!" She was furious and seriously freaking out. *"¡Por los clavos de Cristo!"*

Spanish wasn't Belanger's strong suit. "Is that bad?"

"It means you're an asshat."

"Listen, let me drop you off somewhere. Anywhere you'd like. After that, I need to go to the authorities."

"No way, *chico*. Remember I saw your Tarot cards." She got out of the car quickly and slammed the door. Belanger rolled down the window to plead with her. Before he could say a word, she continued, "You seem like a nice guy and everything, but I'm not going to play Bonnie to your Clyde. I'm out of here. Keep your head low. And watch out for falling towers." With that, she stomped briskly down the sidewalk toward Metairie Road.

Belanger watched, gutted and helpless, as the probability cloud representing his chances of dating Bree collapsed to zero. Fine, he didn't want to schedule a stupid "full reading" of his Tarot cards anyway. The cherry on this shit sundae was the fact that someone had just tried to kill him. He started the car and backed out of the driveway.

Unbeknownst to him, a squinty-faced man with a pipe scowled from the bushes in front of Belanger's house, grimly watching his opportunity slip away.

Having driven a safe distance from home, Belanger pulled into the car park of an electronics store. He needed a place where he could think without the distraction of driving, and in the store he could pretend to stare at computers or home theaters while processing his thoughts. The location was also secure: far from both home and the Quarter, it was full of security cameras and guards. It was the perfect place to crawl inside his head without needing to watch his back.

He walked through the sliding glass doors, past the anti-theft security checkpoint and the store greeter. After surveying the aisle signs, he made a beeline for the recordable CDs, DVDs, and other media. Nobody used that stuff anymore, so he would be relatively undisturbed there. To complete the illusion, he picked up a 50-pack spindle of shiny silver discs and pretended to be extremely interested in the label.

Replaying the incident in his memory, Belanger reaffirmed that every gunshot indeed seemed to be trained in his direction. Two decimated his breakfast. Others shattered shop windows as he ran past. The last two took out his front and rear windshields. For the motive, he drew a straight line between the hook dangling from his bumper and his recent encounter with his urban-legend-obsessed student. More than ever, Belanger was convinced that Nicholas Young was a disturbed serial killer whose modus operandi paid homage to famous contemporary myths. This time he was recreating the legendary lover's-lane paramours who narrowly escape a hook-handed killer and speed away, only to later discover a hook attached to their car. Belanger had obviously exposed his unhinged student, who in retaliation planted a hook on his professor's car and staged this failed murder attempt.

Unfortunately, the police didn't see the obvious pattern in three suicides connected to his erstwhile student. Belanger doubted they would find any evidence to connect the hook to Nicholas either. Nor would they realize that he would kill again if he wasn't stopped.

If Belanger was a target, then his home, his office, and his class-room were the most predictable places for a maniacal killer to find him. He would need to avoid those places. That meant canceling class for today.

Taking out his cell phone in order to to notify the department, he saw that he had voice mail. He tapped the corresponding icon and listened: *Hello, Dr. Belanger? This is Miss Nancy from the registrar's office. I'm hoping you can return that file that you signed out on your student Nicholas Young. Yesterday he dropped all of his classes and asked us to forward his transcripts to the Wyoming University for Social Sciences. Thanks!*

Belanger didn't need to ponder the message for long before noticing that the acronym for Young's new college, like those of all the other institutions he attended, would make a lousy t-shirt. Just like the urban legend about that collegiate sports team from Furman University, the Christian Knights. But why Wyoming? Large yet sparsely populated, it would make a great place to hide and lay low. But Nicholas was too brazen to lay low. There had to be another attraction, another explanation. Belanger brainstormed what he knew about the state: The Great Plains. Rocky Mountains. Black Hills. Continental Divide. Grand Teton National Park. Yellowstone National Park.

His eyes lit up with the invisible light bulb over his head. He reached into the breast pocket of his coat and pulled out the sticky note that he had snatched from Nicholas Young's computer screen. He again examined the elongated trapezoid with the base wider than its top, with the letters DT beneath it. The answer came to him:

Devils Tower.

It was designated the United States' first national monument in 1906. The sheer walls of this laccolith, eroded over millennia to its present shape, rise to a height of nearly thirteen hundred feet. Devils Tower is sacred to several Native American Plains tribes, who know it in their native tongue as "Bear Lodge" or "Brown Buffalo Horn." Legend told that the Great Spirit, in answer to two girls' prayers to save them from a marauding bear, caused the ground beneath them to rise too steeply for the bear to climb and high enough to absorb the girls into the heavens to become the Pleiades: probably not quite the rescue they had in mind. The silhouette of Devils Tower imprinted on the popular psyche after it appeared in Spielberg's 1977 cinematic classic *Close Encounters of the Third Kind* as a mashed-potato sculpture.

Niels Belanger didn't know all this off the top of his head, however. He had dashed over to the computer aisle where he used a floor model to look it up on Google.

The computer aisle happened to be adjacent to the home entertainment displays. These caught his attention when a wall of televisions, tuned to the local news program, all flashed the logo "Breaking News." A pretty female newscaster, wearing too much makeup for anything other than television, appeared at a desk and stared intently at her teleprompter. A banner headline across the screen's lower third proclaimed "GUNMAN IN FRENCH QUARTER. Area locked down with two dead, one injured."

"We have breaking news about a deadly shooting that just took place in the French Quarter near Jackson Square," she announced. The visuals switched to a live shot down Decatur Street which showed that the ordinarily bustling road had been cleared of pedestrians and replaced with barricades, police officers, and the flashing lights of cruisers parked across the road. "Earlier this morning at approximately 9:19, an unidentified gunman opened fire near Decatur Street and St. Philip, striking two tourists. One was pronounced dead at the scene, while the other is currently listed in serious condition and in surgery at Tulane Medical Center. The victims' names have not yet been released, pending notification of family. The gunman has not been identified, and police have the area cordoned off as they search the crime scene and look at surveillance camera footage to help identify the perpetrator.

"It is unclear whether a third death reported at the scene is related to the shooting." The shot returned to the news host, with the left side of the screen showing an old file photo of a young Native American man in military uniform, his black hair cropped in standard military style and a battle scar running from his eyebrow to his lip. The caption at the bottom of the screen now read LOCAL ARTIST DRAGGED TO DEATH. "Around 9:25 a.m., French Quarter painter

Michael Powell was dragged to death in the French Market parking lot near Ursulines Street after his prosthetic arm apparently became entangled with an automobile. The as-yet-unidentified driver fled the scene of the accident. Because of confusion surrounding the nearby shooting incident, police have only sketchy details but are reportedly looking for a green Chevy Volt. A special hotline has been set up for anyone who may have further information." The hotline number appeared across the lower third of the screen. "Powell was a fixture in the New Orleans art scene, having taken up his brush while recuperating from the loss of his left arm during the Gulf War. Human statue Angelo Michaels has already set himself up in Powell's spot in Jackson Square as a tribute to the artist. However, he offered no comment as our reporters had no change for his tip jar."

By the time this report ended, Belanger had turned away and leaned into an aisle shelf, gasping for air as his outstretched arm supported his bent body. He felt terrible for the innocent people caught in the crossfire. Although he wasn't the gunman, he *was* evidently the target and thus felt partially responsible for the collateral damage. Even more devastating was news of the artist's death. Until Belanger heard that newscast, he had assumed that Nicholas planted a hook on his car as a nod to urban legend. But evidently it wasn't a gimmick done for show. There really was a man with a prosthetic arm. And Belanger had dragged him to death with his green Chevy Volt. The thought that he had killed someone made him feel sick to his stomach.

What was Powell doing in the parking lot? Was he also fleeing from the gunman? And why did he gouge Belanger's trunk? Did he bang on the car hoping to catch a ride in the escape vehicle? So many questions.

As he struggled to fight the feeling of nausea deep in his gut, Belanger tuned out the ongoing news broadcast. "Scholars at Oxford University have authenticated a previously unknown work by William Shakespeare which had been posted to the WikiBard website earlier this week. Sophisticated pattern recognition and vocabulary matching software have confirmed that the work is by the greatest poet and playwright of the English language. Dame Frances Beye-Cohn,

Professor Emeritus of Shakespeare Studies at Oxford, declared that 'The telltale use of archaic phrases like *come in person hither, nay,* and *thou art* are pure Shakespeare.' The discovery of an entirely new work has aficionados of the Bard worldwide in a tempest.

"The new play was written toward the end of Shakespeare's life, and is a prequel to his most critically acclaimed work, *Hamlet*. It tells the life story of the prince of Denmark's father from childhood to how he became a ghost. We learn that King Hamlet was originally named Menelaus after the king of Sparta, but as a child was an indentured servant who gained his freedom by winning a chariot race. After entering a religious order, the youth changed his name to the familiar 'Hamlet.' Critics are sharply divided over this new work, titled *The Phantom Menelaus*. Traditionalists complain about its stilted language and offensive stereotypes. Shakespearean actor Ian McDiarmid was quoted as saying, 'One may write this shite, but one cannot say it.' Meanwhile, its defenders—mostly younger scholars— say this is much ado about nothing. They argue that the work is every bit as good as the original *Hamlet*, and which one you prefer may depend on which play you've seen first."

By this time, Belanger had mentally clawed his way to some clarity. If he had dragged a man to death, then yes, he needed to turn himself in to the police. But this casualty was the result of a botched attempt on Belanger's life by a serial killer. That killer was still at large and on his way to Devils Tower, where the body count would only continue to grow. Since the police were so slow to put the pieces together, Belanger had no choice but to take matters into his own hands. It would mean missing Rusty's funeral; Belanger's British sense of decorum would ensure donkey's years of guilt over that faux pas. But while Nicholas Young might be a killer, he was also a coward who ran away from both his previous confrontations with his professor. Making him run away a third time might just save a life.

Belanger marched back to his car, restarted the engine, and got onto the westbound Ponchartrain Expressway in the direction of Louis Armstrong New Orleans International Airport.

CHAPTER

12

ELCOME TO RAPID CITY REGIONAL AIRPORT, where the local time is 8:27 p.m. Please keep your bags with you at all times. For security reasons, baggage left unattended will be removed and possibly destroyed.

As this announcement sounded through the terminal, arriving and departing passengers bustled through the small airport. In the baggage claim area, a buzzer announced the imminent deployment of luggage from the most recently landed flight. Nicholas Young waited impatiently for his belongings while engaged in a heated conversation. His cell phone was wedged under the right ear flap of his New Orleans Saints knit wool beanie. With a pom on top and tasseled cords dangling off the ends of its fleur de lis-embroidered ear flaps, this headgear plus his fluffy down jacket showed that Nicholas was prepared for February in the Northern Plains states.

"He dragged the chief to death with his car?!? Whoa, dude, that's *so* fucking hardcore! I didn't think the old man had it in him. He's so candy-ass." As he spoke, Nicholas became aware of the concerned glances from his fellow travelers. Some obviously tried *too* hard not to look at him, as if coping with their discomfort by looking away from a person in a wheelchair. One mother covered her young son's ears and began to inch away. Nicholas covered the receiver with his left hand and sheepishly remarked, "Ummmmm, my...*father*. He—" Then, his cover story manufactured, he nodded and quickly finished his sentence, "finally decided to try *Grand Theft Auto*."

Nicholas took his left hand away from the phone and returned to the conversation. "WHAT THE FUCK DOES THAT MEAN!?! 'He had someone with him'? Why the hell was someone else in that cocksucker's car?" Realizing that he was once again attracting unwanted attention, Nicholas cobbled together a calm and collected cover sentence. "I mean, GTA is a single-player game."

His eyes bulged with a mix of fury and panic as he listened. "I don't give a shit. You have your marching orders: Frag him. And frag anyone else…that…he's playing with. I don't care if there are witnesses, but I don't want anyone left alive who may know…his… high score. Don't take any chances. Kill anyone that he's with. And save often."

Nicholas stuffed the phone into his down jacket and gave a long frustrated sigh. He held both in front of his chest as if shaking an invisible basketball. His distraught state was obvious to even the most casual observer. The people around him tried *really* hard to avoid eye contact and pretend that they didn't notice. He looked broadly to his right and to his left, raised his arms, then flung them downward in a grand gesture. "All right, all right!" Nicholas declared in a loud voice to everyone who was treating him like an obnoxious drunk or dirty panhandler. "Fuck it! Okay, I wasn't talking about a video game!" With that, he grabbed his roller bag off the conveyor belt and stormed out the door.

He stomped onto the waiting hotel shuttle bus—a small model, with a single pair of passenger doors at the front and seating for twelve, most of which were already taken. Nicholas dropped his bag on the luggage rack and fell into a vacant spot on the blue vinyl bench seats. He closed his eyes and leaned his head against the window behind him. A flood of mixed feelings washed over him like a gut-wrenching paella of emotions. What started out as a very simple plan had suddenly become very complicated because of Belanger. And Nicholas didn't like it. While he felt confident that his team would handle his vexing professor, the fact remained that the first assassin had failed spectacularly. And he didn't like that, either. Perhaps Belanger was a more formidable opponent than he appeared to be. Or perhaps Belanger wasn't a cause but merely a symptom that his plan was unraveling. What if things fell apart even more? Might he get caught? He wondered if he should just pull the plug on the whole thing. Lay low for a while.

"Having a bad day, dear?" a thin, creaky voice inquired.

Nicholas raised his head, turned in her direction, and opened one eye.

A sweet old lady was sitting next to him. A halo of white hair surrounded her gaunt smiling face, and large bifocals circled her eyes, large, dark, and warm. Her cheeks and lips seemed sunken around her mouth, and her wrinkled skin hung loosely around her neck. She was bundled up in a double-breasted hunter-green winter coat with faux-fur cuffs and lapels. In her lap rested her small black clutch purse, a pair of chestnut lambskin gloves, and a wool cap that she undoubtedly knitted herself.

"The worst," he confessed.

"It's late and you've had a long day. Here," she extended a trembling arm and handed him a free drink coupon for their hotel. "When you get to your room, order yourself a nice hot cocoa." She patted his knee twice to emphasize her advice. "That's what I would tell my grandson. He's a nice boy, but people misjudge him because of his hair, jewelry, and clothes. You remind me of him. Just sit down with your cocoa, relax, and watch a nice movie." She leaned in and continued *sotto voce*, "Maybe even a porno. The titles don't show up on your bill, you know."

Okay, that may have been a little bit creepy. But the grandma magic worked on him the same as it works on everyone. He smiled, pocketed the coupon, and nodded his head. "Yeah, thanks. Maybe I'll do that."

Nicholas reached into his down coat to retrieve his smartphone. He powered it up, donned his earbuds, and tapped the movies-on-demand icon. As he scrolled through screen after screen of offerings, he pondered how many of these films he hadn't seen before. How many of them would he *never* get around to seeing? For that matter, how many of them would *anybody* ever get around to seeing? It was a sobering thought. It gave him perspective and eased his troubled mind.

Finally he tapped on a movie and sat back. A soothed smile crossed his lips, and his relaxed shoulders dropped away from his head. By the time the shuttle bus pulled under the hotel porte-cochère, he recognized the hypnotic and asymmetrically tinkling strains of Michael Oldfield's "Tubular Bells." He was immersed in the familiar opening sequences of *The Exorcist*. There was nothing like a classic feel-good movie to transport someone to their happy place.

CHAPTER

13

"Yes, that gentleman was here just last night," the bartender told Belanger. He was bald and clean-shaven except for bushy silver eyebrows and sideburns that stood out against his nutmeg skin. Although he wasn't scowling, his downturned lips imparted a severe appearance—an effect accentuated by dark, penetrating eyes, a wide nose, and a broad chin which looked like it was pushed forward in a pout. His disposition, however, was calm, polite, and articulate. The man took his job seriously. He dressed well above the pay grade for this small-town hotel, in a neatly pressed and starched white dress shirt with cuff links, a black bow tie, black vest, and black slacks with a sharp crease down the front of each leg. Belanger imagined that, behind the bar, the bartender also wore spotlessly shined black leather shoes. Perhaps he was a substitute, or a new hire, from a more upscale establishment. In any event, he was in his late sixties and had been at this type of job for a while. He handled his barware and bottles with the skill and confidence of a seasoned professional. "I remember him because most people visiting these parts in February come for the skiing. But he said he just wanted to see the park while he still could. Sounds like school is going to keep him pretty busy."

This was much easier than Belanger had expected. When he hastily set out for Devils Tower, he had no plan for finding Nicholas. But shortly after his afternoon arrival, the professor discovered there was only one hotel in nearby Hulett, the town closest to Devils Tower

National Monument. That simplified his search considerably. Given that Nicholas and his fraternity brothers lived by the motto "Vary your excesses," the hotel bar was the obvious place to begin.

The watering hole was everything one would expect. A shiny hardwood laminate floor supported a pine bar with a marble top, and a row of stools lined up against the brass foot rail. Behind the bar hung a picture-window-sized mirror, with shelves to either side well-stocked with various liquors. A cushioned bench across from the bar ran the length of the wall, with tables and chairs, similar in style to the stools, opposite the bench. Long wires suspended dozens of low-wattage lights from the ceiling for a look that was both artsy and industrial.

Hotel guests in their polar fleece, knit caps, hoodies, and nylon cargo pants dotted the room. Many were just off the slopes, as evidenced by the pile of fashionable goggles, helmets, and ski jackets on the tables or vacant chairs. Their conversation teemed with incomprehensible terms like shredding, ollies, monkey trails, and calfdick. And they were simultaneously on Tinder, making the whole place seem like the Winter Olympic Village.

When Belanger first walked in, he took a vacant spot at the bar. To his right a small group watched hockey on the bar's plasma television. On his left, the only patron not dressed in sportswear was checking her smartphone then began to doodle once he bellied up to the bar. From there, the rest unfolded effortlessly.

The bartender continued, "But mostly I remember him because the little fuck skipped out without paying his bill. He'd best see the park before *I* get my hands on him!" The profanity was a surprising break with decorum for the otherwise refined bartender. With a shrug, he set before Belanger a pilsner glass of the house microbrew, expertly topped off without excess foam. Given that it was the middle of the afternoon, Belanger thought a pilsner was more appropriate than a Pimm's Cup.

As the bartender turned away with a "Pardon me, sir," Belanger took a sip and winced. "That's terrible," he remarked. It was unclear whether his reference was to the beer or to Nicholas stiffing the bartender. "Makes you just want to throw up your hands."

From his left, Belanger heard a woman ask, "What does that even mean?"

He looked in her direction and, for a moment, time stopped. If he, a British-born academic from New Orleans, was an obvious misfit for the Wyoming ski season, she, a china-pale beauty in black leather club wear, was equally out of place. Long black hair framed her face and dangled down to her breasts. Her high forehead left ample room for her thin but arched eyebrows, which pointed down to her long lashes and bright eyes. Her face was narrow, with rounded cheeks that gave the impression of a come-hither smile even when the rest of her face was doing otherwise. Her jaw tapered into a small but smooth chin, her mouth small but her lips full. Her nose was small and unremarkable, but its shape, along with her arched eyebrows, drew the gaze down her face from her eyes to her lips, creating a sort of luscious cycle from which he was hard pressed to look away. She was remarkably pale, but this only served to make her lips redder, her eyes bluer, and her eyebrows and lashes darker. Her looks were so arresting that Belanger barely noticed her piercings: a diamond stud on the left side of her nose, a small silver ring through the outside edge of her right eyebrow, and multiple piercings ringing her ears.

Her neck was long, thin, and graceful. A black lace collar with black Austrian crystal drops adorned her shoulders. She wore a black leather jacket over a sheer black blouse and exquisitely embroidered black bra. Despite the bulk of her coat, her arms were obviously as pencil-thin as the rest of her. Her nails were painted black, and she wore sterling silver rings on each finger. Black fishnets extended from her leather miniskirt and ended in knee-high boots with thick heels. She was a goth, but toned down for the venue.

"Sorry?"

"The phrase 'throw up your hands.' Does that come from biting your nails? If so, people really need to eat better."

He chuckled. "I never thought of it that way. I don't think that's what it means."

"I hope not. The English language is lousy with non sequituri, if you know what I mean. Like doing things 'behind closed doors.'"

He was intrigued, particularly by her correct conjugation of the Latin *sequor*. He leaned back and encouraged her, "Go on."

She held her outstretched hands about six inches apart. "There's only this much room behind an *open* door. You can't do very much back there."

"I certainly can't argue with that."

"And speaking of 'behind,' isn't the phrase 'behind one's back' a double negative?"

"I'd say it's redundant at the very least."

"Sounds like you're looking for a deadbeat friend. Are you some kind of a debt collector?"

"Something like that." He didn't really want to get into it, preferring to keep a low profile instead.

"Oh, I know!" she pointed an index finger at him. "You work for the mob, and you're going to break his legs."

"No, now you're getting colder. I know him from school."

"Are you an exchange student?"

With his best mockney accent, Belanger smiled and replied, "Crickey, my bad teeth and tea-drinking give me away every time as a grockle from Blighty."

"Hah! No, the giveaway was how you hold your pinky out while drinking beer."

He didn't do that, but he appreciated the jest. "I've lived on this side of the pond for six years, but I still can't get used to drinking cold beer."

"Yeah, we have refrigerators here."

"So do we, but we don't use them for brewing. And just look at this poor excuse for a glass: it isn't even a real pint! I can't fathom how you lot managed to beat us in the war."

"So where are you from?"

"Dawlish, originally."

"Sorry, I must have slept through that geography lesson."

"It's a small town in Devon, in the west of England. Devon's history goes back before the Roman invasion. But in my opinion my hometown's main claim to fame is the legend of the Devil's hoofmarks."

With no idea what he was talking about, she fidgeted uncomfortably. This was starting to look like a replay of his failed small talk with Bree at Saint Louis No. 1. "Yeah," she finally replied, "I slept through religious studies, too. Sounds interesting, though."

That was all it took for his mental floodgates to open. Along with his mouth. "Oh, it really is! You see, one winter morning in 1855, the good people of Devon awoke to find a series of mysterious hoofmarks in the fresh snow. Strangely, the marks were all single file, as if something had been hopping about one-legged. They approached small holes in hedges and drain pipes, and picked up again at the other end. They came up to tall brick walls or haystacks and continued uninterrupted on the other side. And they detoured up to homes and continued on the rooftops. These hoof-prints described a hundred-mile-long path through the town and countryside, winding its way up to every home in the village. They had no explanation for what had visited their quiet town that night or what business it had at every single door."

"Sounds creepy cool. So what was it?"

"To this day, nobody knows for sure."

"Oh, that is totally GAF."

"Excuse me? Gaffe?" Suddenly Belanger understood what Bree must have felt like in the face of his references to the Beatles and Ace of Base.

"Yeah, goth as fuck. What was it like growing up there?"

"I'll tell you this much: Even though the Devil's hoofmarks happened more than one hundred fifty years ago, it really messed me up. Winter terrified me as a boy. On white Christmas Eves I used to keep a nervous vigil at my bedroom window, terrified of what might come down the chimney. It wasn't until I got older that I learned that other children eagerly welcomed snow as the bringer of school closures and holiday presents. After my parents sent me to the Torquay School, all my housemates would get excited about the Christmas charity show that they wrote and produced that year for the Gateway Club; but all I thought about on those snowy nights was how the devil would surely find Blake House, with its bevy of posh, defenseless children, to be a veritable candy store of tasty souls." He couldn't say why he was so chatty with this stranger. Perhaps it was because he felt unusually comfortable with her and her demeanor. Or maybe the alcohol content of American beer was higher than he was used to.

"So naturally you came to Wyoming in the winter."

"To be fair, I'm a little bit older now. Plus I live in New Orleans."

"Ah, not many footprints in the snow down there."

"Surprisingly not. But that isn't why I chose it."

"No?"

He shook his head. "When I got older, my family moved to London. It's the gateway to Europe. Paris is just a quick ride through the Chunnel, and the rest of the continent is a short hop on an aeroplane. Berlin and Rome are simply where my family went on holiday. Now it's where the cool expats hang out. Prague is where our version of hipsters go. It's all like the Jersey Shore or Disneyland for Americans. But to me, New Orleans is the most magical and exotic place I can think of. It has Mardi Gras, jazz, voodoo, Creole, plantations, muffulettas, and above-ground cemeteries. Bourbon Street, Little Maringy, and the Garden District. *Angel Heart*, *Interview with a Vampire*, and *A Confederacy of Dunces*.

"After I first moved there, I struck up a conversation with an employee at Faulkner House Books, in William Faulkner's former residence. She had been a grad student in English. One summer, she took a trip to New Orleans and never left. As a new student myself, I asked her why she never returned to uni. Do you know what she told me? 'I live in New Orleans, and I work in William fucking Faulkner's house. What more is there? I'm living the dream.'"

The pale beauty shook her head. "Sorry, my friend, but if you're talking about living the dream then it's New York City. Between Broadway, Madison Square Garden, and Carnegie Hall, everything goes there first. It has world-class museums and World Series champs. People fly there from London and Rio just to go shopping. I'll take your muffulettas and raise you one city that never sleeps."

"We had Katrina."

She met his challenge with a raised eyebrow. "We had Sandy. But, hey, I'm not challenging you to a 'yo hometown' fight. After all, you do have Trent Reznor."

"Ah, so you hail from New York." He took a sip of his drink and tried to shift the conversation to a different topic. "You don't exactly look like a snow bunny."

"Are you comparing me to a sex toy?"

"What? No!" After his initial embarrassment passed, a puzzled look dawned over his face. "Is that really a sex toy?"

"Look it up, doc. Someday you'll make a girl very happy."

"What I mean is that you don't look like someone who...likes the great outdoors."

"Crickey, my deathly pallor gives it away every time."

Belanger chuckled. "Touché. So what's your story?"

"Well, my father was a mortician and when I was a girl, my mother and older sister were murdered by a serial killer. So I grew up obsessed with death."

The smile fell from his face, which turned ashen, nearly as pale as hers. "Dear God, I'm so sorry."

She burst out laughing. "I'm just teasing your dog. Life isn't a comic book: I don't have an origin story that makes sense of everything. I'm just who I am."

"It beats being someone else."

"My dad's a computer programmer and my mom's a painter, so I didn't get the conformity gene. In the cliquey world of public school, it turns out that's a really bad way to make friends. Bitches don't like it when you don't fit into neat, preconceived boxes, and when that happens they show you why they're called bitches."

"Forgive me for saying so, but you're gorgeous."

"You don't need to apologize for complimenting me. But what does that have to do with anything?"

That didn't come across the way he intended. "Your looks must've gotten you some slack."

"Then you don't know girls. Look at it this way: I'll bet you were beat up at school for being a nerd."

"Hey!" he objected, but ultimately relented. "Okay, you got me."

"Trust me, girls are a zillion times worse. If you don't conform, they will mercilessly ostracize you. It doesn't matter how pretty you are. As if I cared what the homecoming queen thinks. My solution to being hated for not giving a shit was to care even less. Fuck them. As long as I can remember, everything that people thought was important just seemed really contrived, artificial, and boring. I'm a city girl: my world is gritty, urgent, and a little dangerous."

"That still doesn't explain what a goth bird from Gotham City is doing in Wyoming."

"Eesh, I'd rather not say." This time it was her turn to avoid discussing why she was here.

"Oh, come on. I just admitted to getting beat up for being a nerd."

She wrinkled her face. "Pfft, it's not like I needed confirmation."

"So what was it? The skiing? A job? A boy?"

She took a drink before continuing. Hers was a Death in the Afternoon. Although invented by Ernest Hemingway, the champagne and absinthe cocktail was a staple of goth brunches everywhere. "Okay, okay. I came here with a guy."

He was disappointed to hear that. "So you're not here for the skiing."

"No. I tried, but it didn't turn out well." She took another drink.

"I can't help but notice you're alone in this bar in the middle of a beautiful afternoon. Did the guy not work out either?"

She shook her head. "Coming here was a stupid decision. I met him at a New Year's Eve party. He seemed edgy and exciting. I went back to his place to hook up. Turns out he's a real powder monkey. He invited me skiing in February, and I said yes. Come to find out he's a typical narcissistic millennial. He acts like, when he was born, his mom sprinkled gold dust on his ass so his silk diapers wouldn't chafe. Looking back, I should have seen that he had an abusive personality. In fact, he's probably a sociopath."

"Oh, I'm sorry."

"Nah, it's a minor. There are plenty of other bats in the belfry."

He blinked as he processed the conversation. "You don't speak like anyone I've ever known."

At that, she slid over her napkin doodle. It was a circle with a plus sign that divided it into four quadrants: ⊕ "D.S. al Coda, my friend."

"Come again?"

"Replay our conversation from the beginning. It turns out I'm a beta tester for English 2.0. It's mostly bug fixes, but the update hasn't been pushed yet to the general user base."

"I'm glad to see that it's backward compatible…for the most part."

"Hah! You haven't seen the power user features yet."

He extended his hand. "Well, I'm pleased to meet you. My name is Niels, by the way."

She shook his hand. "Nice to meet you, Neal."

"Not Neal," he shook his head. "Niels. As in Danish physicist Niels Bohr."

"Really? You're named after a physicist?"

"Ah, not really. You know how some Americans just love Monty Python?"

She nodded.

"Well, my parents were the same way about American telly and film. They were barmy about the *Planet of the Apes* films and named me Cornelius. It became shortened to 'Neil,' and when I got older to make it more exotic I settled on 'Niels.'"

"Can I call you Corny?" She smiled.

He shook his head. "No. Definitely not."

"I suppose it could have been worse."

"Oh?"

"At least they didn't name you Doctor Zaius."

He raised his glass and clinked it against hers. "You are *so* right."

She smiled. "Well, Niels, I'm *definitely* happier sitting here in a bar talking to a British nerd."

Belanger had never felt so comfortable with another human being before, let alone while chatting up a woman. Although they had just met, he felt an uncanny connection, as if she had been a lifelong friend with whom he was catching up. Or maybe it was just the beer. But with her last line, he felt emboldened to make a move to kiss her. He leaned in closer.

Beer. It was definitely the beer.

Before he could plant a sloppy, ill-considered kiss somewhere on the face of a total stranger, the mirror behind the bar mercifully shattered and dropped shards of broken glass to the ground.

Someone cried out, "Gun!" There was shrieking. Everyone began running. Alarms sounded from the emergency exits opening. All was chaos.

"Aw, hells no!" the bartender shouted in protest. Bending over, he reached under the bar, produced a shotgun, and cocked it emphatically. Scanning the bar for the perpetrator, he blurted out, "Enough is enough! I've had it with these motherfucking snipers in my motherfucking bar!"

Confronted with another outbreak of panic in a crowd, Belanger exclaimed incredulously, "Balls! This is the second time in two days!"

The doodler's head snapped quickly in his direction with a scowl. "You lied. You are *so* with the mob!"

With a supremely indignant expression, he asked, "Why does everyone think it's me?!? Listen, I'm not in the mob, but the bloke with the gun may be. We need to run. Now."

The nearest exit was the hallway leading to the hotel lobby. They headed in that direction along with a dozen others. When the hall ended in a T intersection, the pair halted for a moment. As they did so, the rest of the crowd rushed past them.

"Much as I'd love to continue our chat, we'd best split up," Belanger suggested. "Just in case this guy is after me, I'll draw him away from the lobby." Convinced that this assured he would never speak to this woman again, he headed down the arm of the T that took him away from the lobby.

As he vanished around the corner, she prepared to run to the now-crowded lobby. She halted, however, at the sound of a small, frail voice calling out "Miss?"

A hunched elderly woman doddered down the hall away from the bar and in her direction. She was squat and pear-shaped, an impression encouraged by a full-length Anjou-colored dress dotted with a pattern of small white flowers and finished with white lace trim. Her hair was an unruly mass of silver. Between that and her bent posture, her face was hard to make out; but she wore gigantic glasses with especially thick lenses. Over her shoulder hung a white vinyl purse densely printed with colorful butterflies. The bag was large enough to double as a beach tote and undoubtedly contributed to her pronounced stoop. As she shuffled her feet, pink flats poked out from under alternate sides of her hem.

"Why is everyone running? What's going on? Can you help me?"

Looking around and seeing no signs of a gunman, the younger woman replied, "Yeah, sure. Come this way." She pointed toward the lobby and waved the little old lady toward her. Together they turned to head down the hallway.

Without warning, Belanger rushed up from behind, grabbed a planter from a glass-topped table along the way, and smashed it over the old woman's head. She crumpled to the floor in a rain of dark soil while the young woman jumped back a few feet and looked on in horror.

"Are you on bath salts?!?" she cried out. "You just killed Miss Daisy!"

Belanger looked down at the prone figure to make sure there was no movement. "That's not Miss Daisy."

"It's a *metaphor*, you psycho!"

"I know what you mean, English 2.0. But Miss Daisy doesn't have arms like that."

On closer inspection, she noticed that the unconscious figure had unusually muscular arms for an elderly woman. They were also hairy. One had a tattoo of an anchor.

"And do you smell that?" Belanger continued. "It's pipe tobacco."

Nodding her head, she remarked, "I kinda thought she was dressed in her Monday worst." She knelt and rolled this person over. She noticed five o'clock shadow. Muscular and hairy legs sticking out of the dress. A neck tattoo that spelled "Grandma." And a gun barrel protruding from the top of the handbag.

"So this is the shooter," she realized. Then she looked up at the man who had just saved her life. "Your hands are trembling. Are you all right?"

Belanger looked on blankly as the adrenaline and cortisol cocktail of the fight-or-flight response flooded his system. His pupils were enlarged, his chest heaved from rapid breathing. He had never done anything like this before. Never lifted a finger against another human being. "I'm not trembling," he mumbled absently.

"All right, Princess Leia. As you wish." Belanger's accidental companion pulled out her smartphone and began typing.

"Are you calling someone?" Belanger asked.

"No, I'm posting." She showed him the app she was running. The screen read *Worst cross-dresser* EVAR *makes Tim Gunn cry.*

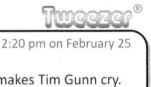

NunMoreDark		2:20 pm on February 25

Worst cross-dresser *EVAR* makes Tim Gunn cry.

+3　　♥　　✎ Followers: 3,059　　🌐 Devils Tower, WY

Concern spread over Belanger's expression. "You posted that on Facebook?"

She laughed. "No, grandpa. It's on Tweezer."

"Tweezer?"

"Yes. Here, let me teach you a new trick. Have you heard of microblogging?"

"That's like Twitter, where you're limited to 140 characters. Right?"

"Right. Well, Tweezer is about nanoblogging. All the ADHD kids are using it. I have over three thousand followers."

"You know that many people?"

"No, but they know me. Being an early adopter has its advantages. But I have to keep the posts interesting if I want my numbers to grow."

"Listen, that's very interesting and all, but someone hired this fellow and we don't want to tip our hand by posting things online. It wouldn't be safe." He looked again at the unconscious figure sprawled in the hallway. "Speaking of safe: if we're not out of here before he wakes up, there'll be the devil to pay."

She grabbed Belanger's sleeve as he began to step away. "Did you graduate *Summa cum risu*? We need to hold this guy's face to the tanning booth and find out what he knows."

"I'm not sure that's a good idea."

"Yeah, well, *I* rush in where fools fear to tread. This fucktard was coming after *me*, and I want to know why. Now don't just stand there: Grow a pair and grab two limbs." He did as he was told, and once they had the assassin off the floor she paused. "I think I put the pope before the bodyguard here. Where should we take him?"

Belanger thought for a moment then said, "The business center. No one will be there during all of this. I have an idea."

CHAPTER

14

BELANGER DEPOSITED the unconscious transvestite in the hotel business center, then said, "Stay here with him. I need to grab a few things."

She looked back askance. "You're off to grab another cold beer, aren't you?"

"Things would have to get *much* more desperate for that."

"And what about him?" She indicated the man sprawled on the floor.

"If he moves…" Belanger turned his head toward the vase on the side table, looked back at her, and nodded. "…you know what to do."

In the moments after he dashed off and left her alone with a killer, English 2.0 gave her failed assassin a long, hard look. Upon closer inspection, she was shocked by how easily she had been fooled. No woman would pair that purse with that dress. His flats were easily the ugliest shoes ever made. And why did guys always have such dorky tats? "I think I'll get an anchor or a dragon holding a skull," said no hot piece of man flesh ever. Finally, those gross, hairy arms weren't part of *any* of her strangulation fantasies.

After only two, maybe three, minutes, Belanger burst breathlessly back into the room and dropped a collection of seemingly random objects on the desk. There was no time to explain. He scanned the room, grabbed the desk telephone, and ripped the cord out of the wall with a hard yank. Disconnecting the base, he tossed her the cord. "We need to secure him before he wakes up." Next he grabbed the unconscious man under the arms and said, "Help me get him on this chair."

As they sat their attacker in the chair, she asked Belanger, "Can give me the speed-dating version of what's going on?"

He held the man's hands behind the chair while she kneeled to tie them with the telephone cord. As she wrapped and knotted, Belanger answered, "I'm a college professor, and one of my students is trying to kill me. Or, in this case, has hired someone kill me."

She looked up from her binding job to catch Belanger's eye. "Wow. I'd hate to see your student evaluations."

Belanger sighed and reiterated emphatically, "It's not me."

She kept her eyes down as she tightened the final knot and replied, "Yeah, that's what my last boyfriend said."

Belanger next grabbed the complimentary packing tape and wrapped it around the shooter's arms and torso, binding his hairy arms to his sides as well as to the chair. "This student of mine is completely mental. He's obsessed with acting out contemporary legends. And that includes how he's trying to kill me." Having completed eight revolutions of packing tape, he tore the dispenser free.

"Contemporary legends?"

"Yes," he said, now binding the killer's ankles to the chair with the tape. "They're modern folk tales that have been repeated so many times that people often mistakenly believe that they're true. For instance…um…we're in ski country." He switched to binding the other leg. "I'll bet everyone in this hotel here has heard the story of Miss Jones, who decided during a ski outing that she needed to use the loo. Since there were no toilets on the slope, she sneaked behind a bush, only to wind up accidentally sliding downhill backward with her trousers around her ankles."

She shook her head emphatically and sighed, "Oh my God, don't remind me!" Catching the dispenser that Belanger tossed to her, she bound their captive's wrists for extra measure.

His eyes lit up. "So you've heard that story too."

She kept taping to avoid eye contact. "You might say I know who it happened to."

"*Exactly,*" he said excitedly, now in full professor mode. "You see, that's the thing about urban legends. The belief that this happened to a friend gives these stories a false sense of verisimilitude."

This time she stopped taping and met his gaze. "It didn't happen to a friend."

"Well, to a friend of a friend. That's actually the most common scenario."

"No, it happened to *me.*"

Full professor mode switched instantly to maximo confuso face. He rose to his feet. "What?"

She stood to meet his gaze. "Remember when I told you that skiing didn't work out so well for me? Well, that's why. Now all the other skiers have a nickname for me."

At that moment, a handsome man with brown hair, brown eyes, and a red ski suit poked his head into the room. "Hey, Snow Cone! How's it hanging?" She gave him a withering look of derision and flipped him off. He nervously withdrew his head from the room and closed the door.

"'Snow Cone'?" Belanger asked, incredulous.

She nodded her head. "I hate it. Before this trip, I had no idea how many guys were into golden showers. And thanks to you, now I know that everyone in the whole world has heard about this. I'm so embarrassed! I wish I was undead."

"But…but that's impossible. The story is a myth."

She walked around the chair, stepped up to Belanger and, before he knew what was happening, slapped him across the face. Hard.

"What was *that* for?" By the time he finished the question, she was looking away nonchalantly, her arms folded.

"What?"

"You hit me."

"Did not."

"You did so! You just slapped me across the face!"

"Nope. Never happened. That's just a myth." Next she pulled out her telephone and began typing.

"What are you doing? You're posting something *now*?"

She showed him her phone:

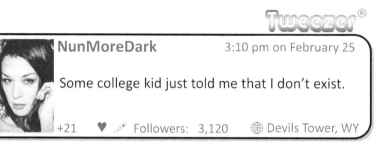

NunMoreDark 3:10 pm on February 25

Some college kid just told me that I don't exist.

+21 ♥ ✎ Followers: 3,120 ⊕ Devils Tower, WY

"Hey, that's not fair! I'm not a college kid. I'm junior faculty."

"Oh, sorry, junior." She typed some more and showed him her latest post:

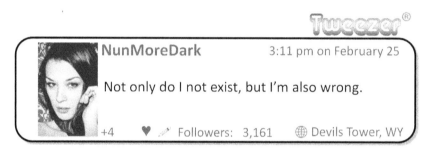

NunMoreDark 3:11 pm on February 25

Not only do I not exist, but I'm also wrong.

+4 ♥ ✎ Followers: 3,161 ⊕ Devils Tower, WY

"Satisfied?"

"Okay, okay. Point taken. Please bear with me, I'm feeling a bit as if Laurence Fishburne has just slipped me the red Mickey. Yesterday morning, I was nearly murdered by a guy with a hook. This parallels the story of a lover's lane predator that has circulated in the United States since at least the 1950s. It was thoroughly documented by Linda Dégh in 1968. It's even turned up in places as far away as Bloemfontein, South Africa.

"Tonight we have a killer dressed as a little old lady. That's the hairy-armed hitchhiker story that sprang up in Yorkshire around 1977 during the ripper scare. The little old lady was originally an hairy axe murderer, though. The story made its way to America in the 1980s and has gone through various face-lifts ever since."

She stared at him, incredulous. "You're a regular walking Wikipedia. I take it back: there's no way a dork like you works for the mob."

"Hey, I have a mind like a steel trap."

"It snaps bones?"

"Even your unfortunate ski accident is a story that has circulated for years."

"It's definitely the most embarrassing thing that's happened to me. At least since that time the meter-reader found me in my apartment building's laundry room wearing nothing but a motorcycle helmet."

His jaw dropped. This story—with a football helmet instead of a motorcycle helmet—dated back to the 1960s.

"It's a long story," she changed the subject. "Never mind."

He shook his head as if erasing a mental Etch-a-Sketch. "After all this, I realize I don't know your name, Miss…"

"You already know my name. You even said it: Miss Jones."

"Oh, right." He thought to himself, *Of course. How apropos: a completely generic name for an urban legend in the flesh.*

She continued, "But you can call me Destiny."

CHAPTER
15

"**W**ERE YOUR PARENTS HIPPIES?" Belanger asked.

Destiny Jones scrunched up her face. "Why would you ask that?"

"Your name. Or were they fans of Destiny's Child?"

"No and no. My parents shared the same birthday. When I entered the family as a birthday present, they felt that it was meant to be. Plus, like I said, my mom's a painter."

"Aha," he said, touching his nose. "Hippies!"

In response to a rustling sound from the corner, Destiny advised, "Heads up, Muad'Dib. It looks like the sleeper is about to awaken." Sure enough, hairy grandma began to groan and move.

"Showtime," Belanger said, pulling his lips into a thin line. He uncapped a black marker, hastily wrote something in large strokes on a fresh sheet of paper, then placed it on the photocopier's plate.

The words "Where am I?," deep and rough, issued from the hapless assassin. Still groggy, he looked around and recognized his two targets in the otherwise empty room. He strained to stand up, to attack them and wring their necks, but gradually realized through his failure to do so that he was emphatically bound to a chair. Tug as he may, his restraints did not yield or loosen. Something was on his head: although out of his sight, it was in fact a colander with a set of jumper cables connecting it to the photocopier. All the killer could see was wires from his head running to the machine beside him.

He suspected he was in trouble but tried to hide it by looking even meaner. "Lucky break, Belanger. But dis won't hold me fer long."

Assuming his role, Belanger glared back, uncharacteristically resolute. "It will hold the likes of you long enough."

"You won't git away. There're more where I come from."

"Right. And that worked out so well for you, didn't it?"

He didn't have a threatening comeback for that. "Whaddaya want wit me? Why am I here?"

"We want information."

"I'll talk ta *youse* when hell freezes over, bub!" He turned his head and spat on the ground.

Belanger adjusted the overturned colander on the man's head. "You may not *want* to, but you have no choice." He tapped the colander emphatically. Then he got into the killer's face and looked deeply into his eyes. "And don't you try to lie, either. We'll be able to tell."

For the first time, the killer looked worried. What was this device he was attached to that would force him to speak against his wishes?

Belanger began simply: "What is your name?"

He sneered. "Popeye."

Belanger rolled his eyes and pressed the big green button on the photocopier. It spit out a piece of paper which Belanger held up for the killer to see. In big black letters, the piece of paper read "LIE."

"Fuck me!" Wide-eyed, he realized that Belanger wasn't kidding.

"Let's try this again: What is your name?"

"It's Ben. Ben Tucker. But my bubs call me Bruiser."

"Of course they do. I suppose that's because you're such a big, bad fighter, right?"

"Naw, that ain't it." He proceeded matter of factly, "Ever since I was a kid, I bruised real easy. My bubs tink dat's funny."

"You said others were after me. How many?"

He shook his head, obviously resisting. But he felt compelled to speak. "I don't know."

Belanger pushed the button, and out came another piece of paper reading LIE. "I told you we'd be able to tell if you were lying. How many others?"

"All right! There's five, including me."

That was an unsettling thought. The first two came very close to killing him. How long would it be until one of them succeeded? "Does that include the French Quarter shooter, the Hook?"

Bruiser nodded. "Yeah."

"So, three others."

Bruiser nodded.

"Why does Nicholas Young want me dead so badly?"

"He can't stand da way ya smell."

Belanger pressed the button again and produced another piece of paper that said LIE.

"Jeebus! Stop doin' dat! Da boss's afraid you're gonna get in his way, mess wit his plans."

That was interesting. Here Belanger thought that killing him *was* the plan. He simply wanted confirmation that Nicholas was playing out an urban legend tableau. "His plans? What are his plans?"

"I dunno."

Belanger reached for the big green button again.

"Please don't! You're gonna suck out my brains! And I ain't got dat many. I'm bein' strait witcha: I got no clue what his plan is. No clue at all. He just axed me ta take care of youse. Dat's all I know."

"Where is he?"

"He's prob'ly checked out by now. Puttin' some miles between him an' you."

"Where is he going?"

Bruiser winced really hard. Practically pleading, he said, "I dunno."

Belanger hit the button again. Bruiser cried out as the photocopier cycled. Belanger angrily thrust the paper in his face and shouted, "You're lying!"

"Goddammit!"

"Try again. The truth this time: Where is he going?"

"Colorado. He's goin' ta Sidewinder, Colorado."

That was surprising, given that he had just sent his transcripts to Wyoming. "Colorado? Why is he going there?"

"He says he wants ta see da Overlook Hotel before he destroys da world."

CHAPTER

16

NICHOLAS YOUNG *means to destroy the world.* That was a major interrogation killer. *It's hyperbole, of course,* Belanger told himself. *Or he's completely delusional.* Regardless, Nicholas was nonetheless dangerous. What had he gotten himself up to? Did he plan to barricade himself in a mall, offing people until the police shot him, thus ending his world and immortalizing himself in cable news legend? Or something worse? Everything that happened lately was so unlikely, so impossible, that Belanger worried he had unconsciously dismissed some angle as too far-fetched. Was there a fatal scenario that he simply wasn't seeing? Octiana Martens's voice again echoed in his ears like the incorporeal counsel of a deceased Jedi master to his padawan: *Get your head out of the ivory tower and see the world the way it really is.*

Bruiser detected Belanger's tough-cop act unraveling before his eyes and grew unruly. "Yo, doc!" he called out to rattle him further. "Are we tru here? I gots a poker game ta catch!"

Belanger no longer paid any attention to the killer. He was completely absorbed in his thoughts, his attention turned inward. "Hm?" he responded absently. "Aye, sure, we're finished."

Bruiser wrestled with his packing tape straps and shook his head, sending the colander to the ground with a rattle. From the side table in the business center, Destiny grabbed the vase and crashed it down upon his head. The sound of dozens of shards of falling ceramic brought Belanger back. He watched his odd new acquaintance wave her hands in front of Bruiser's unresponsive face. Then she looked up with a huge smile and eyes lit with wonder. "That is so *cool!*"

Belanger responded, "This was my first knock-out too. You know what they say: Practice makes perfect."

"Which makes pretentious."

He thought for a moment before nodding. "Yes, there is that."

"What was that voodoo shit you just did? It was totally cool bean soup."

"These urban legends are clearly part of Nicholas Young's M.O. So I thought, why not use an urban legend to *our* advantage? A story dating back to 1977 claims that police in Radnor Township, Pennsylvania, extracted a confession from a suspect using the same setup that we just used. There's actually reason to think this one really happened: a story in the *Philadelphia Inquirer*, picked up by UPI, reported that the confession was suppressed in court after the trial judge ruled that a photocopier cannot legally be used as a lie detector."

"You are hotter than your cooking temperature," she said. "It's like, ask a stupid question, get a stupid answer. But ask a *crazy* question, oh, that's the ticket!" Destiny laid out the colander, jumper cables, and marker on a table. Then she snapped a picture with her cell phone and began typing.

"What are you doing now?" He peered over her shoulder to see:

"Is that necessary?"

"Have you ever heard the saying 'pic or it didn't happen'?"

"No."

"Of course not. Look at it this way: Post some clever words and you'll get a couple dozen likes or shares. But post a *picture*—it doesn't matter if it's cool, or artsy, or the crap breakfast burrito that you just ate—and you're guaranteed four times as many likes."

"And that's important why?"

She sighed at him. "What are you, forty? If a tree falls in the forest and nobody likes it, it doesn't make a sound. It doesn't rank high enough to show up in anyone's news feed. It may as well never have happened. The tree may as well never have existed."

"So, the more likes and followers you have…"

"The more noise I make!" With a giggle, she pranced across the room where another vase sat on a table across from where the other one had been. She took another photo with her cell phone, tapped a few times on the screen, and remarked, "Oh, people will love this!" She showed the screen to Belanger:

"I'm so proud." He was being sarcastic, but something about this quirky woman was undeniably endearing. "You realize, don't you, that the Knockout Game is another urban legend? There's no evidence that it's actually a 'thing.' Most cases reported as instances of the game turn out to be either random assaults, or isolated incidents."

She looked at him incredulously. "Are we really going to do this again? Because my hand isn't even tired."

He changed the subject before she decided to land another blow on his face. "So why don't you just cut to the chase and post a photo of Bruiser?"

Now she was just appalled. "It's not cool to post photos or tag people without permission. Once it's on the Internet, that shit is forever. Standards, Neal!" she lectured while slapping the back of her left hand into her right palm. "For those kinds of photos we use SnapChat."

"I see. And it's Niels."

She held up the thumb and index finger of both hands and crossed her thumbs. "Whatever."

"Speaking of Bruiser, we have to figure out what to do with him."

Belanger caught a devious glint in Destiny's eye. "Leave that to me."

When Ben Tucker came to, it was because of the cold water thrown in his face. So cold, in fact, that he quickly realized he was outdoors. His hands and feet were still bound, and Belanger was holding him upright. Now awake and able to stand on his own, he pulled free. He had nowhere to go, however, because Destiny blocked his path.

Staring deep into the eyes of her would-be killer—seemingly fierce and unfazed, but masking fear and panic just below the surface—she grasped the contents of his soul and understood what she was dealing with. Bruiser fit the profile of a classic serial killer. He came from a broken family—and before it reached that point, his abusive father had broken bones in Bruiser, his sister, and their mother. Those daily verbal and physical assaults had filled Bruiser with cowering rage in search of an outlet. He was unable to strike back at his father, of course. And he couldn't best the children in school, as he was the omega male: frightened, a quiet and withdrawn loner, physically smaller and weaker than other boys in his class. Girls ran when they saw him, not even trying to conceal their repulsion at his sadistic Georgie Porgie. At first he poured his frustration upon his little sister. But the one lesson that his father beat thoroughly into him—before mom burned down the house while dad slept inside—was this: you don't hit girls. With his sister off the menu, his only available victims were neighborhood cats who made the mistake of getting too close.

On the day that the house burned—he still recalled watching it from the sidewalk, mother's arms around both him and his sister as the fire engines summoned by the neighbors arrived too late—the one emotion that overshadowed all the others was Bruiser's feeling of relief when he realized that mom would never discover that he had wet his bed again, thus escaping another thrashing.

That one lesson that his dad taught him—aside from the unintended moral to never keep gasoline in the house—in later years inspired a new tack: masquerading as a girl. It didn't always work, in which case the bullies would have beaten him up that day anyway. But on those rare occasions that the masquerade succeeded, people would let down their guard. And they'd never know what hit them. Literally, they would never know because Bruiser would brutally beat them to death.

They say you never forget your first time, and that was especially true for Bruiser. In the ninth grade, he had shadowed upperclassman Frank Scotus—that asshole bully who used to beat him up in the school bathroom, pelt him with snowballs on his walk to school, and slash the tires on his bicycle—and determined that after school the bully regularly took a shortcut home through the woods. This discovery earned young Bruiser a black eye and cost him his school books, which Scotus tossed in the creek; but the price was well worth it. One spring day, Bruiser waited in the woods dressed in a blond wig with two ponytails, a pretty sundress, white socks, and black patent leather shoes. He stared forlornly at the ground (thus disguising his face) and sobbed. When Frank the Skank arrived with a half-interested "Yo, wuzzup," she pointed at the pummeled and broken cat that lay dead at her feet and choked out the words, "Look what someone did to my kitty." She had, in fact, done this herself but minutes earlier. The grotesque scene, however, completely distracted the smelly jockstrap: he didn't notice for a moment that the little girl was actually his punching bag, or that she was bringing down on the back of his head a rock still wet with fresh cat blood. Having tried and failed in his youth with several cats and dogs, Bruiser knew how hard he had to hit: basically, with everything he had. The hard crack and the instant stream of blood from Frank's skull were far more satisfying than any other animal he had killed. "*That*," he said, "was for pulling down my pants in the middle of the hallway yesterday." Scotus, his head reeling, dropped to his knees. This gave Bruiser the advantage of height to bring the rock back down repeatedly. "*That* is for shoving me into a locker and breaking my nose. And *that* is for stealing the action figures out of my back yard." Although he had no lack of justifications, the blows came more fast and furious than the reasons, spattering blood and teeth everywhere in a moment of extreme catharsis for the years of bullying that he had endured. In that moment, Ben Tucker took "the Scott Farkus Incident" to an extremely dark and brutal place. And he liked it. After wiping his bloody hands and face on the dress, he changed back into his regular clothes and hurried home with the costume and weapon in his backpack. He would bury these behind the tool shed in his yard, the first of many keepsakes of his scott-free predations. Since everyone knew that he was one of several who had been bullied for years, no one considered even for a moment that he was capable of such an act of retribution.

The thrill of that first kill was such a rush that, when he was old enough, Bruiser got himself an after-school job with a municipal construction crew: it was work that paid him to build his muscles. His grades suffered, but it wasn't like he was college-bound before starting his life of crime. Hard labor was its own reward, and the fact that he was paid enough to maintain a meager existence—along with the luxury of buying new dresses from the second-hand shop when his old ones were blood-stained—was enough for him. When he joined a national construction company, he traveled around the country enough that his occasional exploits did not draw police attention to his home turf. A voice in his head egged him on in these crimes by convincing him during the act that every blow landed was one on his despised father. The day that Nicholas Young called him with a mission, it was like the voice in his head had taken physical form.

Bruiser's primal psychology was well understood by primatologists, thanks in part to Barbara Smuts. While studying chimpanzees in the 1970s at the Gombe National Park in Tanzania with venerated scientist Jane Goodall, Smuts found herself stalked by an adolescent chimp named Goblin. At first he just glared at her through bushes and trees. This soon escalated to incessant bullying. He would run by, slapping her as he passed; or he'd rush up from behind, punch her, and run away. He even began to ambush her, jumping on her back and sending them both tumbling downhill as an intertwined ball of hairy and hairless ape. Hearing of this increased bullying, Dr. Goodall advised her research assistant to ignore it, convinced that Goblin would grow bored of the game. In actuality, Goblin, as a young male in the troop, was working his way up the dominance ladder. The first step was to assert his dominance over all the females. Only two remained, and Smuts was one of them. Since she ignored him instead of submitting, this forced Goblin to ramp up his domination attempts. So it went until he tried to steal from Smuts' belt her rain gear, a precious commodity to the researchers in the changeable Tanzanian forest. A ferocious tug of war ensued, and in that moment of struggle Smuts ceased to be a scientist and Goblin was no longer a subject. She punched him in the face as hard as she could. She had never in her life struck anyone before. Afterwards, she stood there shaking, and realized that she would be cleaning the Great Ape House at the National Zoo if Dr. Goodall ever found out that she had just gone apeshit on one of the chimps. Once she came to her senses, Smuts became terrified that the adult males would come to his defense. But they merely watched with bemusement. Goblin, meanwhile, lay there on the ground howling histrionically. He never bothered her again.

Although Destiny didn't know all this, she instinctively understood that Bruiser was exactly like that. Give him a chance and he'd beat you to death. Punch him in the face to remind him of the hierarchy, and he'd leave you alone.

"You listen to me," Destiny said, poking a finger into his chest. "I don't have a cock in this fight, but I'll be damned if I'm going to let some sociopath frat boy intimidate me. That is *so* four boyfriends ago. I'm warning you, I used to be a cutter, so don't think I won't cut you too. And you can tell your big fucking gouda that he has a play-date with Destiny!"

She pulled the back of his dress over his head; yanked down the bicycle shorts he wore underneath; and gave him a push, sliding him downhill backward on a pair of skis. As she watched, she noticed as someone returning for the day on the ski lift rubbernecked to look, until he fell out of his seat and hit the snow.

"Yes!" she high-fived Belanger. "That was Mark, the douchebag I followed here." She pulled out her phone and posted again.

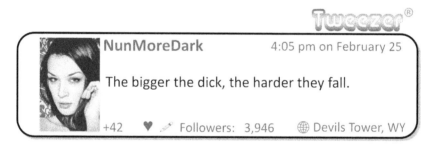

Tweezer®

NunMoreDark   4:05 pm on February 25

The bigger the dick, the harder they fall.

+42   ♥ ✎   Followers: 3,946   ⊕ Devils Tower, WY

As they walked away, Belanger rolled his eyes and remarked sarcastically, "Wicked burn there, Snow Cone."

"Hey," she mock-winced. "That's punching the camel toe. So, Corny, what's our next move?"

"*Our* next move?" He stopped in his tracks. "I appreciate that you've had your fun and games today. But this fight is between me and Nicholas. And he's proven himself to be a very dangerous fellow. I don't want to see you put in harm's way."

"Listen, Nancy. For one, getting shot at is *not* 'fun and games.' And believe me, since earning the name Snow Cone, I've heard of some sick-ass fun and games. Second, whether or not I put myself in harm's way is *my* decision, not yours. Finally, this isn't just between you and Nicholas any more. That fucker," she pointed down the hill, "was coming after *me*. Now *I* have this dog on my leg too. I'll be damned if I'm going to just sit back and wait for someone to pick me off. To the loser goes the sloppy seconds. Our only chance to survive is to take the fight to them. Or at least give it the old community college try."

Belanger nodded. "Fair enough. If we're going to chase them down, at least we know where they're going next: the Overlook Hotel."

She shook her head at him. "Oh, sweetie, I don't mean to take the helium out of your zeppelin, but you *do* know that's the hotel from *The Shining*, don't you?"

"No, I don't. So?"

"The story was inspired by Stephen King's time at the Stanley Hotel in Colorado. When Kubrick made his film adaptation, he filmed exteriors at the Timberline Lodge in Oregon, while interiors were filmed on a London soundstage, modeled on a bunch of different places like the Ahwanee Hotel in Yosemite and the Biltmore Hotel in Arizona." She became aware of Belanger's smile at her own nerdy recitation of facts. "What? All right, so I'm a big old Kubrick geek. I mean, hello, *Clockwork Orange*? Best movie ever. God, don't you know anything about popular culture?"

He laughed. "Who's the walking Wikipedia now?"

"Hey, when everyone hates you, TV is your friend. I even tried being a film major before I gave up on college."

"Sounds more lucrative than being a folklorist."

"I also considered porn, but who wants to watch a pale, tattooed goth chick with pierced nipples and labia?" Belanger opened his mouth to speak, but before he said something that he'd regret, she pressed on. "Anyway, the tall and thin of it is that the Overlook Hotel is fictional. The first thing Stephen King tells you in the book is that the place isn't real. Even the city of Sidewinder doesn't exist."

Belanger nodded to acknowledge that he understood. "Then that's definitely where we should go next."

CHAPTER

17

A BRIGHT YELLOW LAMBORGHINI Diablo VT hurtled down the highway at dusk. A sharp-sloping hood and windshield gave the berlinetta its distinctive acute silhouette, and, just behind its scissor doors, the chassis opened to reveal air intakes for cooling the brakes and an elevated carbon-fiber spoiler over the rear engine. A Mount Rushmore window flag rustled from the front passenger side, where Nicholas Young sat sporting his new Devils Tower sweatshirt. "Dude," he remarked while flipping aimlessly through the latest issue of *Where Wyoming*, "that was *so* worth it just to see the look on the nurse's face."

Behind the wheel of the car, Bruiser gave an embarrassed grin. "I'm glad ya waited at da clinic fer me."

"And *I'm* glad that you're able to drive with a broken leg."

"No problem. I just wish ya stole an automatic."

Nicholas tilted his head sideways toward Bruiser. "Now where would the lesson be in that?"

"Ya ain't mad that I spilled da beans ta Belanger?"

"No, I'm mad because you're such a lousy shot. But, knowing what you all discussed, we'll be ready for them."

"I hope I made up fer it by takin' ya ta Mount Rushmore."

"Yeah, that was great!"

"What was your favorite part?"

"I dunno, let me think. The drive? No. The lines? Not really. The cold?" He closed the magazine and scowled at its cover. "Aww, who am I kidding? It sucked big time." He rolled down the window and pulled the flag loose so that he could wave it and the magazine at his driver. "This is just crap for the masses, tourists who travel the world and stand in line to see a big-ass sculpture of some dead guys. And they take the exact same photo snapped by millions of people before them; only the stupid expressions have changed." He cast the flag and magazine into the road with disgust. "This must be what God and Abraham felt like trying to find ten righteous dudes in Sodom."

"Which one am I?"

"Huh?"

"God or Abraham?"

"Talk about being between the devil and the deep blue sea! You can be both for all I care."

"Excellent, I'm God!"

"It's a dubious honor, I assure you. And don't pat yourself on the back too hard: remember, you also dislocated your shoulder."

"Right," he grimaced as he downshifted the sports car with his bad arm.

Nicholas shook his head and remarked to no one in particular, "Give me one good reason to spare this shithole."

Bruiser looked at him out of the corner of his eye and smiled. "We ain't stolen a Porsche yet."

Nicholas Young's demeanor brightened immediately, even unnervingly, as if someone had flicked a switch in his brain. "Vary your trespasses. I like it!" He nodded with satisfaction. "All right, let's have some fun."

Bruiser punched the accelerator and the car roared down the highway at two hundred miles per hour.

"…while we still can."

CHAPTER

18

Destiny Jones 2:17 pm on February 26

Come play with us!

+64 ♥ ✍ Followers: 4,093 🌐 Sidewinder, CO

Welcome to Sidewinder

N AQUAMARINE COMPACT CAR rolled down a barren stretch of County Road 103 under winter's cool midday sun. Niels Belanger and Destiny Jones had been on the road for seven hours since leaving Hulett, Wyoming, early that morning. Destiny initially objected to such an early departure on the grounds that "every cat has its nap," but it was roughly four hundred miles to where they estimated the fictitious town of Sidewinder to be, and they agreed that they needed to arrive as soon as possible if they hoped to head off Nicholas Young. They had stopped along the way only for a quick lunch and occasional bathroom breaks. And also cigarette breaks, because Belanger wouldn't let Destiny smoke in the rental car.

Upon entering Colorado's Larimer County, they delighted not only to see the town of Sidewinder on the mileage signs, but to learn that they were mere minutes away. "No way!" Destiny exclaimed with child-like disbelief. Belanger just kept driving, a smug smirk on his lips. Although he didn't understand how it was possible, he gladly welcomed vindication of his crazy hunch to drive here.

When the music station they were listening to broke at the top of the hour for a news update, they were so close to their destination, and so excited to be there, that neither of them bothered to change the channel. The announcer continued to jabber as they entered the town limits: "We now bring you the latest developments on the horrific shooting in New Orleans' French Quarter. Surveillance camera footage and witness testimony have confirmed that Corporal Michael Powell, the U.S. veteran and local painter who was dragged to death at the scene, was also the shooter responsible for two deaths and one severe injury mere minutes before. Investigators have no motive for the crime, nor an explanation for his death, although they have ruled out suicide." This was some relief to Belanger, who now suspected that rather than being jailed for accidental manslaughter when he finally turned himself in, he just might be hailed as a hero.

"In other news: After a previously unknown Shakespeare work rocked the literary world earlier this week, WikiBard further stupefied scholars by releasing in eBook format what they are calling *Hamlet Special Edition*, a hitherto unknown revision by Shakespeare written some twenty-five years after originally penning his beloved classic. This new version features improved iambic pentameter and restores scenes that had become possible due to advances in the technology of dressing squires as women. Most controversial is a revision to the famous scene where Hamlet stabs Polonius through a curtain. In the *Special Edition*, Polonius initially attempts to stab Hamlet but misses, and the Prince of Denmark kills him in retaliation. This change has enraged scholars, who have spent their entire careers studying, analyzing, and memorizing the original. An especially vocal group of professorial protestors have had t-shirts printed with the motto 'Ham Stabbeth First.' They swear that they will keep their original editions of *Hamlet* and never read the new one again."

Belanger switched off the radio as he pulled off of CR-103 into the Sidewinder Service Station. It was located right where Overlook Road terminated in a t-intersection perpendicular to the highway. Their destination was a long, slow drive up that treacherous mountain road.

"Since we'll be far from town, we should gas up," Belanger explained.

"Sounds fine by me," Destiny quipped, pulling out her pack of cigarettes. "Gives me time for another fix."

Belanger rolled his eyes.

"Yes, dad, I know they're bad for me. I'll quit when this is over."

As he walked into the service station, Belanger felt as if he had stepped decades back in time. From the dusty, long-unused cigarette machine next to the entrance to the fact that the attendant sat at a counter conspicuously lacking in bulletproof glass, the station looked like it had been plucked straight out of the 1970s. Even the attendant—a wizened and stubbly fellow dressed in blue slacks, a black baseball cap with the station's logo, and a purple-and-white pinstriped shirt bearing an embroidered patch that indicated his name was Lloyd—looked like a throwback to a bygone era. The only thing about this station not stuck in the era of eight-track tapes and disco was the price of gasoline.

Belanger laid his credit card on the counter, smiled, and spoke cheerfully to the attendant. "Hello. The sign on the pump advised pre-paying for fuel. I'd like to fill up my tank. We haven't seen many service stations on this stretch of road, and don't imagine we'll see others between here and our destination."

Lloyd took up the card with his cigarette-stained fingers and swiped it to pre-authorize the gasoline purchase. Handing the card back, he asked, "Where ya headin'?"

"The Overlook Hotel. It's down Overlook Road here, am I right?" Belanger pointed to the rough road that ran off of CR103.

"Yep," he nodded. "Just keep on that road 'till it ends, about twenty-five miles as the crow flies. It'll take ya a spell to get there, though. The road winds and is pretty rough in spots. More often than not, I reckon."

Belanger nodded back. "I'll keep that in mind. Thank you for the advice."

Lloyd nodded back. Just as Belanger began to turn away to pump his gas, the attendant continued, "Yer lucky, ya know."

Belanger looked at the attendant. "Oh?"

"Time was the hotel closed from November to April 'cause the road would get snowed over so bad. Couldn't nobody get inner out. But with global warming, these past few winters ain't been so bad. Been great for business. The hotel done made enough extra scratch to renovate. Now it looks same as it did the day they first opened."

"Well, cheers. I look forward to seeing it."

When Belanger returned, he mused that the sight of Destiny—puffing a long, thin cigarette, leaning against the car, and and contemplating the mountain trail across the road—was a stark contrast to the retro vibe of the service station. She was out of place as much as Lloyd fit right in. It wasn't that she had left her coat in the car while stepping out for a cigarette. It was the full ensemble of black corset, matching corseted fingerless gloves of stretch lace and criss-crossing satin ribbon, silver-studded leather belt, black tulle skirt, and Fluevog combat boots laced to her knees. At least basic black was a good look for winter.

As Belanger unscrewed the cap from the gas tank and began filling, Destiny rhapsodized. "I can't believe I'm actually going to see this hotel. Do you have any idea how many times I've seen *The Shining*? Fifty or sixty. No lie. I never get tired of that movie. It beats the crap out of all the vampire and zombie love stories these days. I just don't understand that trend, it's all L33T to me. I mean, sure, I love the undead too, but that doesn't mean I want to *marry* them. Ewwww. I'd be satisfied with a one-night stand. At most an open relationship. You know, one where I'd keep it interesting by bringing home one of my girlfriends for him now and then, and sometimes he'd introduce me to one of his freaky ghoul buddies. It's all good."

"Well, if there was ever a point on this trip where you were likely to get your wish," Belanger mused, "this is the place."

Unbeknownst to them as they bantered, a dirty hand emerged from under the car near Destiny's heel. Its fingers gripped an opened straight razor. With a quick snap, the hand drew the blade across the back of both feet, just above the heel.

And nothing happened.

The blade merely scratched the heavy leather of her boots, but for the most part it bounced off their substantial heel caps. The hand clenched the razor, made a frustrated gesture, then tried again. And again. And again.

"Hah," Destiny—oblivious to the failed assaults on her Achilles tendon—responded to Belanger, "don't get my hopes up." She puffed on her cigarette again. "Still, my followers will freak out when I post some pictures of the place! I'm up to four thousand now." She began to type on her phone. "Once I hit that number, I changed my Tweezer handle over to my real name. Who knows? I may be famous some day."

She finally scowled as she became faintly aware of a repeated tapping at her heels. Looking down, she saw the hand and the razor flailing impotently, and realized what was happening. "Goddamned motherfucker!" she exclaimed, stomping aggressively on the hand and its fingers with her thick heels. "These are my favorite Fluevogs!" When the pummeled hand released the razor, she kicked the weapon clear of the car.

Belanger's brain quickly processed the fact that Destiny was having an encounter with the infamous "slasher under the car." Since at least 1984, rumor scares of an ankle-slicing predator appeared—typically around the busy Christmas shopping season—in cities as widespread as Birmingham, Winston-Salem, Tacoma, and Phoenix. The motive for this crime varied with the telling. In some cases it was to steal holiday purchases. In others it was to rape the immobilized victim. Some claimed that it was part of a gang initiation. A more benign variant, sans razors, purported that a local fraternity house with a foot fetish was stealing ladies' fine footwear.

In the instant that these facts flooded Belanger's brain, the car heaved unexpectedly. Then it flipped and rolled over several times as the person underneath sprang into a full upright position, arms triumphantly overhead. It was almost as if the figure had simply jumped out of a cake. A two-ton cake. It all happened so quickly that the professor was still holding the gas nozzle, filling nothing in particular.

Niels Belanger and Destiny Jones faced the biggest Mexican they had ever seen. His defiant and angry expression deepened the lines in his craggy face, lines exaggerated by his long stringy hair and bandito moustache. Although it was February, he wore no shirt. His tremendously muscular arms were as large as telephone poles, his pecs hard as armor, and his abs resembled a package of heat-and-eat dinner rolls. Black hair covered his arms, chest, and back. Two bandoliers, one over each shoulder, criss-crossed his naked torso and hung down to the opposite hip. Instead of carrying bullets, however, his bandoliers were filled with straight razors. He wore tight black pants with military stripes down the sides, which suggested that he may have made the Kessel Run in under twelve parsecs.

Having pulled off his dramatic entrance, the Slasher stared stony-faced at Destiny. He shook the bloody hand that she had so thoroughly stomped. Then he grinned.

Crossing and then uncrossing his arms with a fluid motion that comes from years of practice, he drew a razor out of each bandolier, held both hands at ear level, and with a flick of his thumbs simultaneously opened both razors. A beat later and he flung his arms straight out, releasing the razors and sending them flying toward each of his targets.

One razor glanced off Destiny's shoulder, sliced the strap on her purse, and sent it falling into her hands. At the same instant, the other razor flew past Belanger's arm, sliced through his puffy winter coat, the insulation beneath, and even his shirt, and drew a slow stream of blood from his shoulder. It all happened so fast that neither had time to react.

Like the well-practiced killing machine that he was, the Slasher took a step closer to his two defenseless targets while simultaneously drawing two more razors. These he kept in his hands, the better with which to slit their throats.

From her hyperaroused, adrenalized state—heart racing in her ears, pupils dilated—Destiny watched these events unfold as if in slow motion. The Slasher advanced on them menacingly with blades in hand. Belanger stood frozen with his mouth agape, the still-running hose in his right hand making him look more than a little like a tacky fountain statue of a boy peeing. With a sigh, she rolled her eyes and shook her head.

She calmly took a deep drag on her cigarette.

Then, as the Slasher advanced into Belanger's golden stream, with her middle finger Destiny flicked the glowing butt onto their assailant while simultaneously giving him the finger. The sight of the killer bursting spectacularly into flames snapped Belanger out of his torpor. He dropped the nozzle to the ground and pulled Destiny away from the pump and toward the highway. "Run!" he cried out.

The flaming Slasher waved his razors like a crazed chef in a Japanese steak house. He roared like a wounded animal. And, as his intended victims put some distance between themselves and their assailant, the gas station exploded into a giant fireball. Because that's what gas stations do.

The pair dove into the grassy shoulder on the far side of CR-103 just as the station blew. Then they crawled on their knees and elbows to road level and watched the conflagration. Through the flames, they could see the remains of the Slasher's blackening body. Fortunately, the town was remote enough that no other customers were present when the station went up.

Staring in astonishment, Belanger mused, "I can't decide whether that was incredibly badass or completely batshit."

Destiny shrugged. "Why choose only one?"

Sure that they were now safe, they crawled out of the shoulder and onto the road. As they did, their aquamarine rental car—its roof a little worse for wear, and with no one in the driver's seat— creaked and rolled slowly down the road in their direction. Niels and Destiny, still on all fours, stared incredulously until it came to a stop against the shoulder right in front of them. And it just sat there. They rose cautiously to their feet and brushed the gravel and snow from their clothes. Peering around the back of the car, they spotted old Lloyd, the gas station attendant, pressed against the rear bumper. When he noticed them looking, he explained, "I thought y'all might be needin' this."

"Cheers," Belanger stammered. He was multiply stunned: by another attack on his life, by the pants-shittingly scary assassin, by the fact that he now had the beginnings of a "list of people we've killed," by the realization that they just blew up a gas station, and by the miraculous survival—and arrival—of his rental car from the conflagration. He absently reached into his pocket, pulled out a coin, and tossed it to the station attendant. "Sorry about the mess."

"Are you kidding? Bein' down the road from that thar hotel, this is only the third most dangest thing I seen this year."

Tweezer®

Destiny Jones   2:31 pm on February 26

Maybe I won't quit after all.

+56   ♥ ✎ Followers: 4,285   ⊕ Sidewinder, CO

Chapter
19

Earlier that day...

Pete's Roadside Diner hadn't changed much since the 1950s, retaining its original chrome architectural details, large windows, and neon lights. Its customers represented a cross-section of rural middle-America. At one table sat an elderly couple, engaged in their daily ritual of discussing the firmness of their poached eggs and the consistency of their oatmeal. At another table sat two young men in varsity jackets accompanied by two pretty young women made up to look older than high school age; they had stopped on their way to class for breakfast milkshakes (for him) and yogurt (for her). Three middle-aged women in traditional and conservative flowered dresses discussed the upcoming church social. Two clean-cut men in suits and ties conducted business over a greasy-spoon power breakfast. A stubbly man in flannel, on his way home after finishing the night shift at the factory, sat at the counter sipping his coffee and staring stonily into space. Three stools down, another similarly dressed man was on his way to start his shift at the same factory, working at his breakfast while skimming over the newspaper unfolded on the counter in front of him. Behind the counter, the rotund fifty-something fry cook in jeans, white t-shirt, and a hair-net—the eponymous Pete—tended to hash browns and bacon on his grill, three orders written on small sheets suspended just overhead. The waitress wore a pink and white uniform, a white apron, and a nametag that identified her as "Meg."

If all eyes turned fleetingly to Nicholas and Bruiser as they walked in, it was only because Pete's Diner attracted very few passers-by. New faces were always notable. The sight of Bruiser hobbling on crutches and a cast naturally contributed to the rubbernecking. And while Nicholas attracted admiring glances wherever he went because of his good looks, the fact that he was visibly tense this morning only added to his distraction value. Nevertheless, if everyone noticed when the two of them walked in, they soon went back to what they had been doing before. Pete said hello before returning his focus to the grill. Meg, all smiles, grabbed two menus and an orange-handled carafe of coffee on her way to the span of counter where they chose to sit.

"Howdy boys," she said, placing a menu in front of each of them. "Can I get you something to drink while you look at the menu?"

"I'll have coffee, black," Bruiser, seated on the left, replied then overshared, "I'm lactose-intolerant."

Nicholas followed with his sullen request. "I'll take a café au lait."

This puzzled the waitress. "Coffee olé? Is that some kind of Mexican coffee?"

"No," he explained, "it's just coffee with milk."

"Oh, right," she said. She turned the pre-set coffee cups to sit rim-up on the saucers beneath them, and filled both cups with coffee from the orange-handled carafe. "That's good, because all we've got is regular and decaf." Between them she slid a small, rimmed cereal bowl, plain beige in design, mounded with assorted non-dairy creamers.

Nicholas sneered at the steaming beverage before him. "Do you have coffee with chicory?" His French Quarter was showing. Bruiser rolled his eyes and shook his head slightly.

"You want licorice in your coffee?"

"No, *chicory*. It adds flavor."

"I've never heard of that." She rotated the bowl of creamers for Nicholas's benefit. "If you want flavors, I think we have French vanilla and probably hazelnut in here."

He eyed one of the creamers suspiciously. In very small print, its label read: *Water, corn syrup solids, partially hydrogenated soy-*

bean oil, and less than 2% of maltodextrin, sugar, modified cornstarch, dipotassium phosphate, sodium caseinate, artificial flavor, distilled mono and diglycerides, polysorbate 60, sodium stearoyl lactylate, acesulfame potassium, carrageenan, cellulose gel, salt, betacarotene, artificial color. "Never mind the chicory. Can you just bring me some steamed milk? Something without all the chemicals."

Her eyes lit up and she nodded knowingly. "Ohhhh, you're one of those vegans I've heard about, ain't you?"

Bruiser guffawed at the thought, but Nicholas merely sighed wearily. "If I were a vegan, I wouldn't be asking for steamed milk."

"We aren't set up to do steaming here, mostly frying. But I can bring you a glass of fresh milk."

"Sure, I'll rough it." His elbow on the counter, he rested his forehead in his hand. "And while you're at it, can I get some beignets?" Bruiser grimaced and frantically waved his hands, crossing and uncrossing his forearms in a vain effort to dissuade Nicholas from this line of inquiry.

"BEN-yays?" Meg asked. "What are BEN-yays?"

Nicholas lifted his head again and rolled his eyes. "Ben-YAYS. It's kind of a French donut served with powdered sugar."

"I'm pretty sure our only French dishes are fries or toast. Our donuts are one hundred percent American, made fresh in a bakery just down the road."

Slamming both hands on the counter, Nicholas sprang to his feet, the vein in the middle of his forehead bulging, and leaned in toward the now-intimidated waitress. His voice quaked with the effort of containing his rage, and he paused every few words as he shouted, "Is IT TOO MUCH. TO ASK. FOR SOME *FUCKING* BEIGNETS. AND A CAFÉ. AU LAIT?!?"

Bruiser yanked at Nicholas's sleeve, gesturing for him to sit down. With a tug of his head and a shift of his eyes, the assassin indicated that everyone in the diner was staring at them. Meg assured him, "I'll find you something, hon. Don't worry." Then she scampered off to the dessert case.

They leaned toward each other. Bruiser whispered, "Dis ain't wort gettin' so upset."

Nicholas whisper-shouted back in a Batman-like voice, "I don't care, I want a goddamned beignet!"

"Do ya hafta attract so much attention?"

"They don't have fucking beignets. Everyone should know how much this place *sucks*! Just wait until I get on Yelp."

"Ya really needs to git out and travel more, boss. Da rest o'da world ain't like da Quarter."

"She called me 'hon.' That's a Quarter thing."

"Naw it ain't. I once iced a dame in Bal'more who called me 'hon.' She had da biggest fuckin' hair." Bruiser looked up, past Nicholas, then advised, "She's comin' back."

They both sat up and tried to look pleasant: Bruiser exaggeratedly so, with a stiff back, bright blinking eyes, and forced smile, while Nicholas utterly failed to disguise his glowering expression. On average, they were two reasonably complacent men.

Meg set a plate and a glass of milk down in front of Nicholas. "Here you go, hon." He turned toward the counter and looked down. On the plate was a pale brown-yellow donut covered with an unnatural hot pink icing that matched Meg's uniform. Multi-colored sprinkles dotted the icing.

Nicholas stared at the abomination before him and raised an eyebrow, which caused his opposite eye to squint. His upper lip curled. He stared back at the waitress and remarked in flat and measured tones, "It has a hole."

By this point, Meg was tired of trying to please a customer who would obviously never be satisfied. Nodding, she replied in equally flat and measured tones, "That's so you have someplace to put your finger."

With that, Nicholas lost it. The stress of dropping classes and changing schools; Belanger getting nosy and asking questions; the epic fails of his legendary killers; the unforeseen appearance of this Destiny Jones woman, whoever she was; no café au lait; no beignets: Everything that ever bothered him in his life boiled over in that instant.

Nicholas turned to his left, pulled back Bruiser's coat, and reached inside with his right hand. Rising to his feet, he drew Bruiser's pistol, a Springfield XD(M) 9mm compact with a nineteen round flush-fit magazine. He released the grip safety, straightened his right arm, and trained the gun directly at the speechless waitress's chest. Without hesitation, he pulled the trigger and shot Meg at point-blank range. The impact knocked her backward into the wall that just an instant before had become splattered with her blood.

Nicholas leaned over the counter, glared at where her life-less body had fallen, and bellowed, "Try putting your finger in *THAT* hole, bitch!"

Turning his head to the left, he noticed a shocked Pete watching from the grill.

"And *YOU!*" Nicholas pointed and fired two shots into the cook, dropping him to the ground. "Get some goddamned coffee with chicory!" Or maybe not.

As he turned away from the counter, he noticed every eye in the room upon him once again. The patrons' faces were aghast as they sat immobilized with fear. Nicholas slowly swaggered over to the door, twisted the lock, and declared theatrically, "Ladies and gentlemen, please allow me to introduce myself. My name is Nicholas Young. Unfortunately, all of you are witnesses to a horrible double homicide. To make matters worse, you know my name. So sad. But look on the bright side: everyone in the world is about to die anyway so, by dint of eating here, all of you are lucky enough to avoid the rush. I hope you enjoyed your last meal."

For what seemed like an eternity, shots and screams rang out in the small diner as people ran for cover, ducked under their tables, made a break for the door, or simply sat and prayed. The chaos continued until everything—and everyone—fell silent.

Satisfied that he had murdered everyone in the diner, Nicholas walked back to his seat at the counter. He used a napkin to wipe his fingerprints off the gun. Then, holding the weapon with the napkin, he placed it into Bruiser's bare hand. Even for a seasoned killer like the Hairy-Armed Hitchhiker, this incident was the most brutal and beautiful thing Bruiser had ever seen. He sat there in silence, as if admiring and lingering over an amazing performance art installation. *Should I applaud?* he wondered.

Nicholas took one last drink of warm milk before heading toward the exit. "Let's get out of here," he declared. As he unlocked the door and pushed it open, he looked back at his companion and indicated the red pools all over the floor. "Be careful that you don't slip on the blood."

CHAPTER

20

OVERLOOK ROAD was as rugged a stretch of mountain passage as promised. Its serpentine path cut through steep embankments on one side, with frightening drops into the Laramie River on the other. Mile after mile in every direction was devoid of houses or other structures: nothing but rock, snow, and evergreens ringed by mountains that penetrated the clouds. Their twenty-five-mile traverse into the Colorado Rockies was slow going partly because its stone enforcements ruled out higher speeds, and partly because the snow—despite being far less than the impassible norm of years past—nevertheless left slick and treacherous patches. Neither of them wanted to plummet into the Laramie, especially at this time of year. Their poor rental car had been through enough already.

The crawl finally ended when they pulled up to the hotel's three-story façade, accented by the large mountain behind it. Despite boasting over two hundred rooms, the hotel's wooden architecture made the building's sprawl look more like a cabin, or a lodge cum chalet. Well-groomed topiary sculptures on the front lawn testified to the gardener's caring hand even at this time of year. Perhaps three dozen cars occupied the guest lot, a small population for a place this size, but nevertheless good for an off-season weekday.

Destiny fidgeted restlessly in her seat as they coasted into temporary parking for registration and unloading. She had already snapped a picture of the exterior when they first pulled up.

141

Belanger expected her to leap from her seat at any moment. Indeed, once the car stopped moving, her seat belt was off and she bolted out the door, prancing past the bellman and into the foyer. Belanger followed several steps behind at a more restrained pace.

Destiny peered with wonder at the familiar sight of the immense hotel lobby. Its double French doors—leading into both the lobby and adjoining areas—had generous sidelights and transoms that created visually spectacular glass thresholds triple the size of their doors. Round chandeliers hung from the ceiling on three chains, with several faux white tapers rising from the brass circle and terminating in light bulbs; altogether it created a fire marshal-pleasing crown of candles befitting a safety-conscious St. Brigid. To either side of the mosaic entry aisle sat inviting upholstered sofas and modern-looking chairs. On various of the adobe-colored support pillars around the room and over various doorways, black-lettered gold signs pointed the way to familiar places like the Colorado Lounge, Dining Room, Games Room, and Gold Ballroom, as well as the croquet field and hedge maze out back. She took another photo and posted it.

When Belanger finally made his way into the lobby, Destiny ran up and pulled his wrist in order to get his attention. She pointed to a wall of old portraits across the room. "I'm going to go look for Jack Nicholson's photo!" Before he could nod in acknowledgement, she had already rushed off.

Belanger had more practical matters to attend to. He followed the mosaic floor tile to the registration desk, its dark wooden panels sur-mounted by a russet marble top. Behind the desk rose an immense old-school pigeonhole rack for keys and mail. This piece of furniture was mostly for historical interest, as the counter supported an LCD monitor and computer keyboard to register guests and issue key-cards. Behind the desk a perky blonde, who was neither creepy nor deranged, smiled and asked him, "Are you checking in?"

"Actually," he lied, "I'm meeting a friend of mine. We all planned to go skiing together. I wonder if he's arrived yet?"

"I can look that up for you," she offered. "What's the name?"

"Young. Nicholas Young."

She made a few mouse clicks, and typed and tabbed around a bit. "I'm sorry, it doesn't look like we currently have a guest under that name. We don't seem to have a reservation for him tonight, either."

"Then it appears we got here ahead of him." That was a relief to Belanger. All they had to do was wait for him to show up. "He may be counting on vacancies when he arrives."

"That's a pretty safe bet," she remarked as she kept on clicking. "Oh, wait."

That didn't sound good. "Yes?"

"It looks like we just had a guest by that name. You said 'Nicholas Young,' right?"

"Correct."

"Yeah, he checked out early this morning. I'm sorry, it looks like you've missed each other."

"Oh, too bad," he utterly failed to disguise his disappointment. This was much worse than too bad. It threw a spanner into the works. They had no idea where Nicholas was heading next. The trail had gone as cold as the mountain road that they had just spent an hour traversing.

"Since you've come all this way, would you like a room for the night?"

"Yes!" a woman's voice cried out from behind Belanger. He turned to see Destiny leaping up and down. "Yes!" It was quite unbecoming for a goth to act up so. "Is room 237 available?"

The registrar again took her computer mouse in hand. "I'll check." A few clicks later, she responded, "Yes, suite 237 is vacant."

Destiny looked at Belanger with the pleading eyes of a desperate child. "Oh my God, we *have* to stay here. Please? It would be like a nightmare come true!"

"A suite? Are you sure?"

"Yes! It will be more fun than a box full of ferrets. Pleeeeease."

The front desk clerk offered, "Since you missed your friends, I can offer you the suite at the same price as a regular room."

He resigned himself to the idea with a shrug. "Sure, why not? We have no place else to go, and it will be dark soon."

Destiny squeed, hugged Belanger, and did a slight happy dance. It was a respectable happy dance for a goth, so if you weren't watching you might miss the brief wrist shake and momentary hip swing. But there was no hiding her smile, despite her best effort to appear grim.

"Heavens," he noticed wryly, "this has made you one happy camper."

Destiny pretended to stiffen at that remark. "I am *not* happy. That's a vicious lie. And don't even get me started on all the weird things that have happened to me while camping."

CHAPTER
21

"**T**HIS SUCKS!" Destiny grumbled. She was lying on her back across the sofa in room 237, a suite whose double doors opened into a sprawling sitting area with a fireplace, large picture window, and a corner desk. Three carpeted steps led up to the bedroom which, with its king-sized bed and adjoining bathroom, was a suite unto itself. Mortified, she just stared at the ceiling of the sitting area. Her calves dangled over one arm of the sofa and she kicked its side with the heels of her boots.

Her outcry wasn't over the room's flat-screen television, which was a reasonable nod to modernization. Nor was it the scary curtains, which were scary mostly because their horrible and matronly flower print was the exact opposite of spooky. It wasn't even the computer desk with an Ethernet cable for complimentary in-room Wi-Fi. Although none of these were present in Kubrick's film, she accepted such continuity errors. The real problem was, as she finally put it, "We've been here for three hours and *nothing* has happened!"

"What do you mean?" Belanger asked.

She sat up and stared at him as if he were a freshly thawed Neanderthal. "Hello? Where are the tidal waves of blood? The freaky twin girls? Or the spectral writing on the walls? There isn't even a crazy lady in the bathtub!"

"You do realize," Belanger noted wryly, "that you have it within your power to change that last one."

"I just don't see how, with this place turning out to be real, there hasn't been any phantom gunfire, shrieks, or scuffling sounds. There should be knocking on the door with no one there. A ghost sighting. Or at least the inexplicable lingering scent of perfume. But no. I feel like I've missed my connecting flight."

"Haven't you had enough excitement for one day?"

"Nah. The night is still young. But since the gas station, it's been ever a dull moment."

He paused for a moment to think, then offered, "Surely two adults in a nice hotel can think of something to make the night more exciting."

Destiny sat up, mildly amused. *Did he really just say that?* She wondered if Belanger actually intended the innuendo that she read into his remark. But then again, maybe he *wasn't* all that different from other guys. She decided to call his bluff. "Watcha got in mind, sailor?"

"What?"

"Are you thinking of a little roleplay?" She sauntered over and rubbed against him while gasping breathlessly, "'Oh, professor, I'd do *anything* for an A in your class!'"

Belanger's eyes and pupils grew noticeably larger. "No!" he protested. Well, maybe. Actually, yes: exactly that. "I would never proposition…I mean *propose*…I would never presume to…" He sighed. "That's not how I grade my students!"

Destiny plopped back down on the sofa wearing a triumphant smirk. "So what *did* you mean?"

Belanger had no reply, only the expression of a deer caught in headlights. Even Bree never left him this tongue-tied.

"What's the matter? Slasher got your vocal cords?"

He scowled. "That is *not* funny!"

"Sure it is. Now chill already. No doubt we could both use a stress release right about now."

Belanger nodded. "Agreed." He wasn't entirely sure what he was agreeing to, however.

"Why don't you go see if the concierge can scare us up an axe? Meanwhile, I'll lock the door and wait for you to come home."

"How can you even joke about that after the gas station?"

"Listen, Niels: This…quest, manhunt, whatever this bullshit is that we're doing. No one ever promised it was going to be a bathtub of Cristal. So don't be so glum. That's *my* job."

Belanger sighed and told her, "The front desk said that Nicholas has already come and gone." This fact had been deviling him ever since they checked in.

"Ouch. So our marshmallow has fallen off the stick and into the embers."

"Which begs the question: What do we do now?"

"For starters, I never beg. But come on, doc, you must have something in your utility belt of batarangs."

He shook his head remorsefully. "I've got nothing. All we have to go on is a burned pile of shaving kit. And we very well can't use the colander and jumper cables in the boot of the car to interrogate the remains."

Destiny raised her hand proudly. "I'd say 'my bad,' but who are we kidding here? That was totally my *awesome*." She held up her hand for a fist bump, but Belanger simply kept talking.

"Be that as it may, we are presently clueless. So you're right: we may as well just muck about here until we've gone barking mad. Perhaps I'll go down to the lounge and see if the imaginary bartender will pour me a Jack Daniels."

"Let's not be too hasty." She was serious now. "Think, what do we know? Nicholas left New Orleans, went to Devils Tower, then to the Overlook Hotel. What do these have in common?"

"Nothing that I can see."

"All right. Then Bruiser said Nicholas wanted to see this hotel before he destroyed the world. He can't really do that, can he?"

"No, of course not!" He paused for a moment to ponder her question. "At least, I don't think so."

"Niels, you do realize that those are two opposite ends of the comfort scale."

"I know, I know. Of course he can't destroy the world. No one can. It's impossible. But these past few days I've seen so many impossible things come true. I just don't understand it."

"You mean that urban legend stuff you keep talking about?"

"Exactly. My department chair inherits a fortune from Nigeria. Nicholas Young is a serial urban-legend recreator. I'm not entirely sure why I became a target, but I've had attempts on my life by the Hook, the Hairy-Armed Hitchhiker, and the Slasher under the Car. A hotel that doesn't exist suddenly does. And—I'm sorry, Destiny—but your ski accident has been talked about since the winter of 1979."

"Are you fucking kidding me? I wasn't even born then! How weird is it that it happened to me too?"

"I don't know what to make of it. Had it been just one or two coincidences, I'd chalk it up to the law of large numbers. In a big enough world, given enough time, *anything* is possible. But even that can't account for all the fictional events that have come true lately. What's most interesting is that none of these are obscure legends. There's no story about the Peg-Legged Pirate and the Woodpecker. No Bishop and the Cheesemonger, and certainly no Narcoleptic Brain Surgeon. That's to say nothing of the Exceptionally Gullible Prison Guard."

"And yet you *are* saying something of it."

"The thing is," he continued undeterred, "what we've seen come true are the most popular urban legends. Virtually *everyone* has heard of them. Virtually *everyone* in the world believes that they happened to a second- or third-hand acquaintance."

"Well, that kind of fucks consensual reality in the ass without a condom."

His expression warped with what resembled confusion; or maybe he was grasping at a straw. "Come again?"

"If what is real is based on what we generally agree to be true, then what does it mean if the majority of people believe something that's false?"

Belanger's eyes lit up. "That's it!"

"It is?"

"Yes, I think so. Or at least I have a hypothesis." He grew noticeably excited. "Have you ever heard of the Hundredth Monkey?"

She rolled her eyes and sighed. Despite knowing him for only twenty-four hours, she could already tell that he was winding up for a lecture. "Unless it's a goth band, then probably not."

"To set the story up, let's begin with the proposition that ideas and beliefs can affect the real world. This is neither new nor controversial. In the fourth century, Plato argued that everything that exists is but an ersatz copy of their perfect, ideal form. Later, the kabbalah—which syncretizes a lot of Neoplatonism anyway—taught that before anything has a physical existence, it must first pass through the creative and formative realms. And in 1889, Oscar Wilde coined the anti-mimetic maxim 'life imitates art.' More recently, in the field of mass communication, Cultivation Theory predicts that overexposure to television's peculiar version of reality—from soap operas to talk shows—cultivates in viewers an unrealistic perception of the world. This is where we get the idea of the 'mean world syndrome,' wherein little old ladies who watch too many reruns of *Murder, She Wrote* believe that Maine is a much deadlier place than it really is. Baudrillard likewise coined the term 'hyperreality' when he introduced the same concept in semiotics.

"But what if the imaginary can do more than merely inspire or influence us? What if it can spontaneously become real? Turns out that isn't such a new idea, either. A thoughtform or idea that has become tangible is called a *tulpa* in Tibetan Buddhism. Thoughtforms also turn up in Western occultism, where they are called *egregores*. The term is complete bollocks, as it's been hijacked from an ancient Greek word for the fathers of the Nephilim; we can thank Victor Hugo for raising *that* zombie from the dead. Nevertheless, this is where the monkeys fit in.

"In the 1950s, Japanese researchers were studying macaque monkeys on the island of Koshima. These researchers began to leave sweet potatoes on the beach as a treat for their research subjects. The only problem with this good deed was that the potatoes became covered in sand, rendering them unpleasant to eat. Eventually, one monkey discovered that immersing the potatoes in water removed the sand and rendered them more palatable. Slowly but surely, the other monkeys on the island learned to do this too, either by watching the first monkey or by being taught by others. After a while, every monkey on the island knew how to wash the sand from their sweet potatoes.

"When the researchers visited a neighboring island and left their customary offering of sweet potatoes, the monkeys there inexplicably already knew to wash them. There was no months-long learning curve like the one observed on the first island. How was that possible? People have since speculated that after a critical number of macaque monkeys learned this behavior, it stopped being learned and somehow became a species-wide instinct. The term 'hundredth monkey' is a metaphor for that tipping point where the behavioral repertoire of a species changes.

"The British biologist Rupert Sheldrake made this story famous in his 1981 book, *A New Science of Life*. He proposed the existence of morphic fields, which determine the biological structure of a species. It was his way of explaining how the dividing cells of an embryo know whether to become muscle vs. skin vs. bone. He did not believe that this information was encoded in DNA, but rather dictated by a force that spans all members of a species. Furthermore, he extended his theory beyond mere morphogenesis. He argued that it also applied to behavior: the more often a behavior occurred, the more probable it became in future generations. His book basically drew a line between Lamarckian inheritance, Jung's collective unconscious, parapsychology, and mysticism. *Nature* magazine dubbed *A New Science of Life* 'a book for burning.'

"However, there might actually be something to it. Sheldrake pointed to a variety of phenomena that supported his theory: from dogs who know when their owners are coming home before they're within hearing distance, to the fact that some difficult crystalline structures become easier to grow in the lab the more that scientists manage the task.

"For the sake of argument, what if he's right? What if there *is* a hundredth monkey that changes the look or behavior of a species? If that's true, might there then be *another*, larger tipping point—a thousandth monkey or something? The human population is growing at a ridiculous rate: five billion in 1987, six billion in 1999, seven billion in 2012. What if so many people believe these stories to be true that the human race has hit its billionth monkey? Maybe we are consensually changing reality, causing these legends to become real.

"Destiny?" Having by this point realized that he was thinking out loud more than having a conversation, he noticed that his companion had left the living room and gone into the sleeping area.

"I'm in here watching TV," she called out. "Sorry Dr. B., I got bored of the lecture and ordered some gay porn."

He turned his head toward the bedroom, incredulous. "Seriously?"

"*Yeah.* Watching two dudes do it is the name of the app. But this has got to be the worst porno ever. The guy is cute enough, but he still has all his clothes on and he's just talking blah blah blah. Kind of like you. This is supposed to be porn! Where's the beefcake?"

"Well, what is he talking about? Maybe it's relevant to the plot."

"Plot? Stop pulling my dick. I had pegged you as being more into the cinematography of porn. Anyway, I turned the sound off after a while. And check it out, the set is *so* cheesy! I mean, it looks like it was filmed in this exact room."

Belanger's bemused expression suddenly vanished. He leapt to his feet, ran into the room, and looked at the screen. "That *is* our room. And *that's* Nicholas Young!"

"That hottie is Nicholas Young?!? The evil beagle who's trying to kill us?"

Another urban legend was materializing before their eyes—or at least a variation on it. In the most common version, a couple revisits the famous resort where they spent their honeymoon. In the Northeast, it is typically somewhere in the Poconos. In the west, it is Las Vegas. Location notwithstanding, the couple orders an on-demand adult video and is horrified to discover that the poorly made movie is of their own love-making, secretly taped by a hidden camera during their newlywed visit. Often associated with these legends is the equally bogus warning to avoid discount coupons or room specials, as these hotels make their money back by selling adult videos of their previous clientele. This tale had circulated ever since the dawn of home video, but earlier variations dated to the birth of motion pictures and involved an unfaithful spouse being secretly filmed at a brothel or other compromising location. No lawsuits, hidden cameras, videotapes, or even silent movies have ever turned up to substantiate these tall tales.

But now it was really happening—fortunately, in Belanger's opinion, without the sex.

"Turn up the sound. I want to hear what he's saying," he said.

She pointed the remote control at the television and tapped the volume button with her thumb. "Good luck with that. I turned off the sound when he started a monologue about whether he should risk the complimentary breakfast buffet, or order something custom from the kitchen."

Belanger leaned in toward the television and scanned for anything that might be a clue. Aside from some luggage and a handbag on the bed, nothing—at least nothing visible in the shot—appeared different from how the room currently looked. In the video, Nicholas faced the right side of the screen and held up two fingers. "Two words," came a barely audible off-screen voice.

"Great," Belanger deadpanned. "The man who means to destroy the world is playing charades."

Nicholas held up an index finger then tugged his ear. The off-screen voice followed along. "First word sounds like…"

A knock at the door interrupted the videotaped guessing game. Nicholas turned and looked at the left side of the screen. "Room service," announced a different voice, barely audible through the door.

"Ah," Destiny quipped, interested again in the video. "So they're going with the old 'pizza delivery boy' shtick. Not exactly a daring choice—pretty cliché, in fact—but it's a step in the right direction."

The off-screen voice implored, "Make sure da toast is gluten-free likes I asked."

Nicholas rolled his eyes.

"I'm tinkin' of goin' paleo, though," the voice continued.

"I'm sure that will make life on the road with you *much* easier," Nicholas snorted. He walked off screen. Following the sounds of the door opening, Nicholas returned and instructed, "You can set the tray anywhere."

Into the frame entered a burly young man carrying a covered serving tray and a folded tray table. Despite the hotel uniform, the man was edgy by Rockies standards. His head was buzz-cut. He had a stud in one ear and another through the center of his lower lip.

Turning his back to the camera to set up the tray table revealed an Egyptian winged disk tattooed in thick black lines on his nape.

"Oh *hells* yes," Destiny cheered on the video. "Now we're getting somewhere!"

After placing the tray on its table, the server removed its silver domed lid. Nicholas leaned in to inspect what appeared to be eggs, hash browns, a pot of coffee, and some steamed milk. He looked at the server with a concerned glance. "Where's the hot sauce that I ordered?" he asked. A dire expression spread over his face. "Don't tell me you forgot the hot sauce."

Destiny guffawed, then cat-called in her deepest and most masculine tone, "'*I've got your hot sauce right here, fella.*'"

To her disappointment, the server reached into his pocket and pulled out a bottle and showed it to Nicholas with a smile.

"Good man!" Nicholas exclaimed with relief.

"I'm afraid it isn't terribly exotic, but it's all we had."

Nicholas nodded. "I'll make it work." He reached into his pocket, pulled out a bill, and pressed it into the server's hand. "Thanks for bringing it."

Destiny shook not only her head, but her entire torso. "No, no, no! That's not how it goes. He's supposed to say, 'I'm afraid I don't have any money. Maybe I can give you a different kind of tip.' Geez, who wrote this crap?"

"Destiny," Belanger finally brought her up to speed, "this isn't an adult video."

"You mean your student *isn't* paying his way through school by doing porn?"

"No."

"Wow, then he really *is* dumb. It's like the world's shortest novel: 'For sale: man's brain. Never used.'" She sighed wearily. "This whole side-trip is turning out to be one big disappointment. All I can say is that they better not charge us for this movie at check-out."

"Shhh, I want to listen. There may be a clue here."

After escorting the server from the room, Nicholas re-entered the frame, rubbed his hands, and enthusiastically said, "All right, so where were we?"

"Do we hafta do this?" groaned the off-screen voice.

"Yes, we bloody well have to do this. I'm fucking bored out of my skull and the pool is closed. Now: Two words, first one sounds like…" Nicholas laid both index fingers on the right side of his cheek and pressed the tips together. Suddenly he splayed out his fingers while moving both hands away from his face.

"Zit?" guessed the off-screen voice. "Acne. Pop. Zombie."

Nicholas shook his head and made an erasing gesture with his hand. He held up his two right fingers.

"Second word…"

He pantomimed leaning over something in front of him and, holding his right hand level with his temple but about two feet out, made a cranking motion.

"You're startin' a Model T!" Nicholas kept going, so that was clearly the wrong answer. "You're drillin' a hole in the side of yer head! No, yer punchin' a midget."

Nicholas stood up straight with an annoyed expression.

"Sorry, I meant 'little person.'"

Nicholas shook his head. "I give up. Let's try twenty questions."

"Awwwww," the other voice complained.

"I said *Let's try twenty questions!*"

"All right. Is it bigger'n a breadbox?"

Nicholas sighed and rolled his eyes. "It's a *city*. Of course it's bigger than a breadbox!"

"Is it animal, vegetable, or mineral?"

He threw up his hands. "Oh, for fuck's sake, you're hopeless." Grabbing the ugly purse off the bed, Nicholas produced Bruiser's tube of lipstick. He turned his back to the camera and started scrawling on the wall. Moments later, he stepped back and gesticulated. "Last try. Can you figure this one out?" After a pause, Nicholas sighed again. He grabbed a brochure from the desk, waved it at Bruiser, then stuffed it between the mattresses. "When you get tired of thinking— or of trying to think—the answer is here. I'm going downstairs to the goddamn buffet." He began to walk off, but paused, turned around, and snatched the hot sauce from the serving tray. Then he was off again, as evidenced by the sound of a slamming door.

Once Nicholas stepped out of the shot, Belanger could see what had been hastily scrawled on the wall in big red sloppy letters. "Llewsor. That sounds Welsh, like Llewellyn, or the Welsh hero Llew Llaw Gyffes. Are they going to Wales next? It doesn't sound like any city I've ever heard of, though. Where's my phone?"

He turned his head and started to look around the room. Then he abruptly froze. His eyes grew wide with shock. He grabbed Destiny, pulled her close. This prompted her to look at him quizzically. She raised her index finger as if to interject something, but before she did so, Belanger placed his hands on either side of her head and directed her gaze toward what he was seeing: the bedroom mirror. In the mirror was the reflection of the television. And on the television was the scrawl on the wall. There, in clear but chilling childish handwriting was the answer:

Roswell.

As the video played on, Bruiser hobbled into the frame and sat on the bed. He regarded Nicholas Young's abandoned breakfast with disdain. "'Let's try twenty questions,'" he said mockingly. Taking a quick look around, he shrugged his shoulders, pulled a girlie magazine out of his luggage, undid his pants, and reached inside.

"*Aggh!*" Belanger exclaimed with urgent disgust. "Change the channel!"

Destiny concurred. "That is the *last* dude I want to see spankin' the Frankenstein!"

She frantically pushed a few buttons on the television remote until the video was thankfully replaced by a cable news channel. "We bring you breaking news this hour," reported the familiar talking head with round glasses and salt-and-pepper hair and beard. "The text of *The Phantom Menelaus*, heralded by scholars as a previously unknown work by William Shakespeare, has been traced by the hacktivist group Pseudonymous to a Chinese Internet server. Within the past hour, the group has uploaded to WikiBard a thousand pages of documents allegedly proving that the play is not the work of Shakespeare after all. According to the data dump, in September a group of escaped laboratory apes from Guandong Province broke into an iPad factory in Shenzhen and made off with a gross of tablets.

Back in the wild, the apes began playing with the touchscreens, when they accidentally composed the play and serendipitously uploaded it to the Internet. Once-vocal scholars were tight-lipped regarding this development, although we did reach a few for comment. Professor Estrus Mandrell of Oxford chattered, 'O! I am Fortune's fool!' Doctor Savanna Gibbons of Cambridge howled, 'Sod off, I have tenure.' And lecturer Simeon Nichols-Woking of the Central University of Newcastle-upon-Tyne simply grunted and said, 'Oops.'"

By this point, Destiny Jones's attention had drifted back to her smartphone.

Destiny Jones	6:45 pm on February 26
Less talk, more man-on-man action.	
+104 ♥ ✎ Followers: 4,923	⊕Sidewinder, CO

Belanger meanwhile, having regained his composure, retrieved the remote control and switched off the television. "Roswell," he remarked. "Yes, that makes sense. It's home to the biggest conspiracy theory of them all." Then—on fire with new inspiration—he pulled up the corner of the mattress where he was sitting and found the glossy brochure left behind by the room's previous denizens. It was for the Roswell UFO Museum.

"Pennies from heaven!" Belanger remarked.

Destiny, disappointed with the lack of activity in the hotel—either paranormal or pornographic—looked up from her phone and muttered morosely, "More like wooden nickels from hell."

CHAPTER

22

NICHOLAS YOUNG was like a kid in a comic book store. No, really. He was literally in a comic book store. Stanley's Marvelous Comics in Santa Fe, New Mexico, is a Mecca for comic enthusiasts everywhere, and Nicholas insisted on a pit stop at the legendary shop. His eyes lit up before he ever walked through the door, indeed from the moment he opened the Ferrari's door in the parking lot of the free-standing shop.

As every collector knows, the owner's grandfather was Stanley Kerbie, proprietor of Stanley's Smokes, a Santa Fe tobacco store and newsstand. He opened his shop in 1937 and meticulously saved a file copy of every periodical that he carried, including comic books. By the time he retired in 1971, his storeroom was packed with what he considered to be nothing more than business records. His grandson Stanley III, then only eighteen, took over running the shop for his grandfather. When the founder of Stanley's Smokes died in 1987, he left the store to his grandson. Only then did Stanley III, forced to sort through his grandfather's belongings in that impassible storeroom, discover a perfectly preserved trove of comic books dating back to the 1930s. He kept the choicest titles in his private collection—some of which he displayed in the shop—but changed the name of the business to Stanley's Marvelous Comics and put the rest of the books up for sale. This news caused a sensation in the collectors' community, as a large stockpile in such pristine shape from the original owner was unheard of. The Santa Fe trove became the most celebrated pedigree collection in comic collecting, and a legendary destination for enthusiasts worldwide.

Thirty thousand square feet of showroom was too much for Nicholas to take in all at once. Floor-to-ceiling shelves lined the walls, stocked with new and vintage comic book-themed toys, action figures, lunch boxes, trading cards, movie memorabilia, mini-busts, porcelain statues, and other collectibles. The walls also displayed movie posters, lobby cards, and original art from the days when comics were hand-drawn on 11 x 17-inch card stock rather than rendered on computers. Dozens of display tables occupied the wide-open center of the space. Each held divided bins, filled to capacity with comics in their protective bags. Signs hung from the ceiling identified the tables by publisher: D.C., Marvel, Gold Key, Charlton, E.C., Timely, and so on. At the back of the store—behind glass-fronted display cases and the cash register—the Wall of Fame held the most valuable books, available for closer inspection by special request only.

Nicholas made a beeline for the Wall of Fame. This was more a museum visit than a shopping trip for him. And he was not disappointed. There he saw legendary issues like *Amazing Fantasy* #15 with the first appearance of Spider-Man; *Avengers* #4 with the first Silver Age appearance of Captain America; *Brave and the Bold* #28 with the debut of the Justice League of America; and so on. There was even a copy of *Detective Comics* #27 with the first appearance of Batman in 1939. This was one of the most expensive books on the market, worth over a million dollars.

But the book that caught Nicholas Young's eye was the 1939 issue of *Marvel Comics* #1. This was the first book published by Timely Comics, the company that more than twenty years later would be renamed Marvel after this very title. Although books like the first appearance of Superman and Batman fetched much higher prices, Nicholas had heard that *Marvel* #1 was the Holy Grail for many collectors, the rarest of the rare. Its cover depicted a man in flames from head to toe, in mid-leap through a melted hole in a bank vault door. On the other side, a man who was clearly not a banker but a robber turned back toward the vault, firing his gun at this Human Torch only to have the bullet melt on contact. Nicholas was mesmerized by the igneous figure.

"Can I help you?" Stanley III, now in his late sixties, offered from behind the counter.

"Can I have a look at *Marvel* #1?" he asked, awe in his voice.

"Sure thing, but it has to stay on the counter. No looking with your hands." He took the book down from the wall and placed it upon the glass-topped counter between him and Nicholas. The comic was encapsulated in a rigid plastic shell along with a banner that scored the book 9.4 on a ten-point scale. Nicholas leaned over the counter to get directly above it and peered down.

"That's so awesome. How much is it?"

"Five hundred thousand dollars."

Nicholas's eyes widened in disbelief. "Half a million?"

"It's the best copy known in existence."

"Wow. Can I look inside?"

"No sir. Once it's been graded, registered, and encapsulated, you can't open the book."

"Why not?"

"Once you open it, it's no longer in the certified condition. It immediately drops in value, at least until you have it re-certified."

"Why would anyone pay that much for a comic book and never read it? That's like stealing a Ferrari and never driving it!"

"Whoever buys the book can line their birdcage with it if they want. But until then, it stays wrapped up exactly how I first found it."

Nicholas nodded. "Cool. I'll just take a look around, then."

As he wandered among the aisles of comic books, he stopped at bins where the title on a divider caught his eye. Then he flipped through the issues until he found a cover that appealed to him, and set it aside in a growing stack. The first issue of *John Constantine: Hellblazer* showed the blond and scruffy face of its titular antihero—portrayed by actor Keanu Reeves in the film adaptation *Constantine* and more recently by Matt Ryan in the TV show of the same name—superimposed over an inner cityscape, while a black five-pointed star filled the lower left quadrant of the cover.

Next he came upon the first issue of *Ghost Rider*, whose masthead trumpeted the character as "The Most Supernatural Superhero of Them All!" The cover portrayed a man clothed in black leather, a blazing skull where his head should be, popping a wheelie on his motorcycle as he barreled through a police barricade; meanwhile three stunned officers drew their guns. The comic recounted the story of stuntman Johnny Blaze, who became the avenging Ghost Rider after he sold his soul to the devil to save the life of his mentor. Blaze was portrayed in two movie adaptations by Nicholas Cage, himself a comic book fan: it was his copy of *Action Comics* #1, the first appearance of Superman, that fetched over two million dollars at auction.

To his stack Nicholas added a trade paperback that collected together and reprinted several issues of the series *Hellboy*. The title was based on the fictitious demon Anung Un Rama, or Beast of the Apocalypse, who was summoned to Earth as an infant by Nazi occultists but was ultimately liberated and raised by the kindly Professor Trevor Bruttenholm. In an effort to blend into normal society—an impossible task given his huge stature, red skin, cloven hooves, stone right hand, and long tail—the earthbound demon kept his horns filed down to two circular disks that protruded ever so slightly from his forehead.

Wandering a little further, Nicholas came across a box of comic books not in the ubiquitous protective Mylar sleeves. This caught his attention, so he began flipping through them. Before long, he came across a pinch of issues that made him grin broadly. They were for a character called the Son of Satan, whose solo debut was in *Marvel Spotlight* #12 and then in a short-lived series under his own name. Son of Satan was a muscular blond young man sporting red boots, red spandex pants, a wide yellow belt, and a flowing red cape with a cowl. His bare chest was emblazoned with a circumscribed pentagram, and his blond bangs curled upward on either side of his head in a suggestion of Aryan horns. As a weapon he wielded a golden trident or pitchfork. In one issue—the "ominous origin issue"—he held a swooning woman on one arm as he steered a flaming chariot drawn by three infernal horses. A distraught man in the foreground proclaimed, "He—he ain't human!" while the hero vowed, "You rose against me—all of you! But now you'll pay!" The title splashed across the bottom of the cover was *From Hell He Came*. "Dude," Nicholas mused, "this rocks!"

On another—titled *When the Devil Stalks the Earth*—Son of Satan raised his pitchfork commandingly while surrounded by demons in the background, and proclaimed, "Father! Stand you back! You shall not invade the Earth—except over the body of *your own son!*" Yet another cover depicted him at the reins of his hellish chariot, his cape rustling in the air behind him, as he announced, "The time has come, my father—for our final confrontation! The battle only *one* of us will survive!" This issue had the caption "Down into the depths of Hell he rides—to face the Devil himself!"

Nicholas flipped through a few of these unbagged issues, smiling more and more as he did. *Daimon Hellstorm*, he mused over the Son of Satan's mortal name. *What a fucking cool name. I wish I thought of that.* Satisfied, he added these issues to his stack then returned to the counter where he again encountered Stanley. "How much are these? They weren't in bags with a price tag."

Stanley glanced down for but a moment, recognizing the books instantly. "Oh, those came out of the bargain bin. These days, that character is undesirable. So the books aren't all that valuable. Nobody really collects them. Normally I charge a buck apiece for the bargain bin, but if you buy these other books I'll toss in the *Son of Satan*s for no charge: my gift to you."

It turned out that was exactly the wrong thing to say. *Undesirable. Not valuable. Bargain bin.* A bilious rage welled up within Nicholas. He had spent the past three years trying to fit in, like Hellboy grinding down his horns. All that time he denied who he was, rather than being authentic about his true nature. And for what? To be treated as though he were as undesirable and valueless as a bottom-tier comic book. *What am I so afraid of? Is this piece of shit rock in space worth what I've put myself through? No more. I am so through. From now on, I'm going to be honest about who I am.* Nicholas glared at Stanley with unspeakable rage burning in his eyes.

Stanley blanched.

A few moments later, Nicholas Young walked out the door and across the parking lot to the waiting Ferrari. As he did, the windows of the store behind him blew out from the force of a giant fireball consuming everything within. Under his arm were a copy of *Ghost Rider*, *Constantine*, the *Hellboy* anthology, assorted worthless copies of *Son of Satan*, and the best known copy of *Marvel Comics* #1 with the Human Torch on the cover. Once he got into the car, he was going to tear apart its plastic sleeve and read the hell out of that comic book.

CHAPTER
23

Destiny Jones   3:33 pm on February 27

Aliens abducted my milk and mutilated my cheese fries.

+87   ♥ ✎ Followers: 5,385   ⊕ Roswell, NM

Welcome to...

ROSWELL

Dairy Capital of the Southwest

"WELCOME TO ROSWELL: Dairy Capital of the Southwest" proclaimed a roadside sign at the city limits. The surrounding area was indeed renowned for its farms and dairies: taking these properties into account, by some estimates there were 1.5 cows for every resident of this small city of forty-eight thousand. Here on the outskirts, there was no hint of Roswell's claim to fame as the historic location of a purported UFO crash.

On July 8, 1947, public information officer Walter Haut of the Roswell Army Air Field issued a press release—to the great excitement of the media—which stated that the 509th Bomb Group had recovered the remains of a crashed "flying disc" from a Roswell-area ranch. The very next day, Commanding General Roger M. Ramey of the Eighth Air Force clarified that what had actually been recovered was a radar-tracking weather balloon, and effectively closed the case. Thirty years later, one of the men who originally recovered the debris, Major Jesse Marcel, came forward and claimed that the United States military had covered up what was actually the crash of an alien spacecraft. From that day in 1978, the dairy capital of the Southwest became home to the most famous and controversial UFO cover-up conspiracy theory of them all.

As Niels and Destiny drove south along highway 285—North Main Street within the city limits—indicators of Roswell's more ignominious heritage emerged. As they crossed West Pine Lodge Road near the outskirts of town, a Walmart Supercenter caught their eye. The familiar blue façade was, in Roswell, painted an unearthly green and sported graphics of a UFO and of a smiling alien head. Three miles later, as they approached the heart of the downtown area, they encountered a pair of extraterrestrial-friendly fast-food restaurants. The local franchise of Arby's roast beef sported signage both on the building and under its trademark neon cowboy hat, with bright green lettering reading "Aliens Welcome" and a silhouette of a large-headed alien that could have been used inside to identify the little green men's room. Three blocks later, at Eighth Street, they passed a McDonald's restaurant in the shape of a UFO: red and yellow strips of neon lights on the exterior added to the fun and otherworldly feel of the building.

Finally crossing Third Street, they entered ET central. UFO-themed shops dotted the next two blocks of road: The Alien Zone gift shop boasted an expansive back room called Area 51 where for a mere three dollars countless photo ops awaited in its various staged sets, from a simulated crash site to an alien in an outhouse. The handle of a giant mug extended from the exterior of the Not of This World Internet café, just above a metal awning, and its starry sign advertised their "heavenly" espresso. Next door, the Roswell Landing gift shop sold every conceivable UFO souvenir, from t-shirts to plastic inflatable aliens. Past Second Street, the International UFO Museum and Research Center occupied a converted theater, with its name emblazoned upon both a horizontal and a vertical marquis. The Starchild gift shop had a disk-shaped UFO parked on its roof, slightly overhanging the front of the shop, and another crashed halfway through its storefront. The spectacle concluded with the Crashdown Café—immortalized on the television show *Roswell*—whose blinking neon half-UFO protruding from its façade resembled a carnival merry-go-round more than a space ship. Throughout this stretch of road, the post lights lining the street sported lamps shaped like alien heads, glowing green except for a pair of large opaque oval "eyes" to complete the illusion.

Following a hand-painted sign that read "Alien Parking," Belanger pulled into the next motel they came upon. After he switched off the engine, they both heaved sounds of relief and gratefully stepped out of the vehicle to bend and stretch. Destiny pulled out some matches and lit the cigarette that was already in her mouth. If the trek from Hulett to Sidewinder the morning before had been arduous, then their seven-hundred-mile journey to Roswell was even worse. Not only were they already tired from the previous day's drive, but this one took ten hours. And, like yesterday's road trip, today's required a wake-up call for an hour at which Destiny would have preferred an axe to her skull.

Tossing the ignition keys to his passenger, Belanger said, "I'll get us a room. Stay here and watch the car. If you see any trouble, or anything the least bit suspicious, lean on the horn and I'll come running."

She nodded and pulled out her smartphone—the exact opposite of keeping an eye out. Before she finished her third update, Belanger returned with a key attached by a ring to a large diamond-shaped piece of orange plastic.

"What now, doc?" She clicked on her phone, then exclaimed, "Hey! I've hit five thousand followers!"

"I'll alert the Beeb," Belanger acknowledged, hardly impressed. "Let's go back to that Walmart and get some supplies. Given that someone has tried to kill us at the last two places we've been, we have no idea what may await us here…but I want to be ready for whatever it may be."

"We survived both times. I kind of like those odds."

"Well, let's be sure that we maintain that track record."

"Like they say in English 2.0, an ounce of prevention is worth a can of whoop-ass."

Its extraterrestrial-friendly exterior notwithstanding, Roswell's Walmart was much like any other. A greeter at the entrance welcomed them. A colorful cast of customers perused the shelves. And its big-box interior provided aisle after aisle of anything a shopper could possibly want. Combing through the entire store for emergency provisions would take more time than they had, so Belanger suggested, "Let's split up and meet back at the register in ten minutes."

As he turned to march off, Destiny saluted and remarked, "I copy, Gold Leader."

She had no idea where her traveling companion was headed. Perhaps he would look in kitchen wares for a better colander. Or maybe he had an ingenious ploy that involved a casserole dish, garden hose, and paper shredder. But she was certain of one thing: *her* destination. She went straight to sporting goods, and from there to the area where a locked cabinet behind the counter displayed a selection of hunting rifles. Two sales associates stood vigil at their post, guarding the firearms and waiting to be of service. One of them was in his early forties, a mildly rotund, long-haired man with a closely shorn and well manicured beard and moustache. She didn't need to see the *Fantastic Four* t-shirt under his uniform to know that he was a fanboy. He just had the look. Plus, his *Watchmen* wristwatch kind of gave it away. The second salesperson was less than half the other's age and fresh out of high school, his face freckled and pimpled. His red hair was cropped short. His thick plastic-rimmed glasses gave him a look of intelligence, but his awkward mannerisms suggested that his intelligence was mitigated by a withdrawn life. His name badge identified him as Wesley and indicated that he was a trainee. The other man's nametag read Simon and identified him as the manager.

"Hello, gentlemen," Destiny said as she approached the counter. "I'm in the market for a firearm. What have you got for me?"

The manager swaggered closer to the counter, as much as possible in a single step. While he might ordinarily have been intimidated by such a beautiful and unusual-looking woman, in this setting he comfortably felt himself the master of his domain, as if she had asked him to recommend an action figure. By her own admission, he knew more than she did, just as he knew more than his trainee. In this situation, he was happy to elucidate and establish himself as the alpha nerd.

"That depends on how big a thing you reckon on shooting," Simon began. "If you hit a squirrel with a big shotgun, there won't be anything left to eat. But if you shoot a deer with too small a shell, you won't kill it and it will just suffer. You always want to go for a humane kill."

Wesley, the more earnest of the two, blurted out, "What are you hunting?"

"Uh...I'm not sure." For starters, she very well couldn't say "people." Besides, she honestly had no idea what new threat might accost them in their pursuit of Nicholas Young.

"Are you thinking maybe the size of a capercaillie?" Wesley followed up.

"Son," Simon interjected derisively, "does this young lady look like she's going to Sweden to hunt a heather cock?"

Wesley shook his head in acknowledgement. "Naw, she don't look Swiss to me."

"Swedish."

"No, not that either."

"Let's go with something more obvious." Simon turned to face Destiny. "Are you maybe fixing to shoot something the size of a merganser?"

"Oh!" Wesley piped up. "It's a majestic creature."

"Lovely plumage."

"And tasty, too."

"Did you know," Simon asked Destiny, "that while common and hooded mergansers nest in trees, red-breasted mergansers nest on the ground? No matter whether it's marshes, rocks, or piles of driftwood."

"I hear tell," Wesley added, "that they can lay up to eleven eggs."

Destiny held her hands palms forward in a "stop" gesture. "Guys, no. It'll be bigger than a duck."

Wesley was quick with another suggestion. "Well, then, how about a pine marten?"

Simon scowled. "That's a good guess...except that we're *in the middle of the gosh-danged desert!*"

"I'm not suggesting that she's literally going to shoot a pine marten in Roswell," Wesley reasoned. "I'm just asking whether she intends to shoot something the *size* of a pine marten."

The manager nodded to indicate that his trainee's explanation was acceptable. "All right then. Carry on, soldier."

Wesley turned back to Destiny. "How about a pine marten?"

"No," she remarked without a pause. "Bigger."

Wesley scowled and snapped his fingers once. "Rats!"

"That would be smaller," Simon corrected.

"It's just an expression. Although capybaras *do* get pretty big."

"You've got a point there, son. But while rats are members of the genus *Rodentia*, what is their superfamily?"

"*Muroidea.*"

"And the superfamily of the capybara?"

"I don't know."

"You damn well do know, soldier! How many times have we drilled this?"

"Yes sir! *Hystricomorpha*, sir!"

"And that means?"

"Capybaras are not rats, sir!"

"Right. So where were we?"

"Something bigger than a pine marten."

"Perhaps an ibex?"

"Or a mouflon?"

"Maybe even a chamois."

Destiny rolled her eyes. "Bigger."

Wesley raised his brows in disbelief. "Bigger? Like a bear?"

Simon scoffed audibly. "*That's* a bizarre suggestion!"

"Sorry, it's the first thing that sprang to mind."

"I'll let it slide this time." The manager squinted suspiciously at his trainee. "But I'm gonna keep an eye on you."

Destiny waved her hands. "No, not as big as a bear." *At least I hope not.*

"Hmmm, let's see now." Simon thought hard, stroking his closely cut beard. "What's bigger than an ibex but smaller than a bear?"

"A wisent," Wesley proffered.

"A European bison?" the manager challenged his trainee again.

"Well, she's more likely to encounter an American bison."

"Plains bison or woods bison?" Simon interjected quickly, pointing his finger to challenge the young man's suggestion.

By this point, Destiny had had quite enough. She leaned on the counter to draw nearer to the salesmen. Eyes widened, they turned to listen as she spoke so softly that only the three of them could hear. "Listen, I didn't want to come right out and say this but…" She paused dramatically, then glanced around to make sure no one was nearby. "It's an *alien.*" That was at least in the ballpark for size, and more acceptable than saying "*you guys,*" which was how she felt at that moment.

Their eyes lit up knowingly, and they nodded their heads. "I see," Simon remarked sagaciously. "An alien is definitely bigger than a capercaillie."

"I tell ya," Wesley started in, "those critters ain't nothing but trouble. They're brave, too. They'll wander right into your yard at night and eat your rose bushes."

Simon shook his fist in agreement. "If I *ever* catch the one that keeps getting into my trash at night…"

"Or that one that keeps giving me an anal probe."

Simon paused and stared at him for a long moment. "You ain't from around here, are you?"

Wesley looked back at Destiny. "Are you sure these are bad aliens? Like *ID4*, *Mars Attacks*, and *Battle: Los Angeles*? Might they be good aliens like *E.T.*, *Close Encounters* or *Contact*?"

With the puffing up of his chest and a gesture of his hands, Simon entered into his best imitation of professorial mode. "Everyone knows there ain't been no friendly aliens since the late 1970s. In 1980, the UFO literature shifted from 'friendly observers' to 'evil motherfuckers conducting sick sexual experiments on our ladyfolk.' Either that or they're space Hannibal crying out *Terra delenda est.* Just look at *Resistance: Fall of Man* and *Half-Life.* People on their PlayStations and X-Boxes these days just ain't interested in helping ET phone home."

"All right," Wesley held up his hand in defeat. "But even if they *are* bad, what kind of alien are we talking about: your classic gray Zeta Reticulan, a Hopkinsville goblin, a Flatwood monster, or an old-school little green man?"

"What difference does it make? Whatever it is, she'll want to blast the fuck out of it." The manager turned back toward his customer and assured her, "Ma'am, never mind what I said before. You want the biggest gun you can get. It ain't like you're gonna eat the alien—I hope." Then he looked over to his trainee to prompt him. "And that gun would be…?"

"An AR-15 style semi-automatic assault rifle, sir!"

"Specs?"

"Made of lightweight aluminum and synthetic materials, 5.56 millimeter with magazine feed, rotating-lock bolt, actuated by direct impingement gas operation, weighing approximately ten pounds."

"Stock number?"

"5509873957295." Wesley pulled a gun out of the display cabinet and handed it to his manager.

"Good man!" Simon replied, and placed it on the counter between him and Destiny. A little over three and a half feet in length, the gun was matte black with a pistol grip and triangular shoulder stock. "This one has the optional optical sight, recommended if you want to pick them buggers off before they get too close."

Wesley followed by producing a box of bullets. "I recommend these for a clean kill. These are *Ich luge* bullets. My grandfather snared a shitload—"

"Oh, now you're just making stuff up!" Simon interrupted, outraged. "We ain't got no stock number for that." He pulled out a different box of bullets and handed her one. It was longer than a double-A battery, and slightly thinner. Two-thirds along its cylindrical length, the bullet narrowed sharply, and from there tapered to a tip. "Fuck the humane kill. Fill up your magazine with these bullets and blow the bastard back to Mars. If you wound the alien without killing it, it never ends well. Do you remember *The Day the Earth Stood Still*?"

Wesley interjected, "The original or the remake?"

"Don't blaspheme, boy!"

"Yes, sir. But what if she runs into a giant alien along the lines of *Cloverfield*, *Super 8* or *Starship Troopers*?"

"Duh. Obviously she'd need a tactical nuke. But she can't buy one over the counter...because?"

"It's a special-order item. But we *do* offer free shipping to the store."

Simon nodded. "Correct. I'm proud of you, son."

"And what if the aliens are tiny, like the *Andromeda Strain*?"

"I don't think this young lady would be coming to buy a gun from us if she was fixing to kill a virus. Use your head, boy! She'd be over in pharmacy."

"Right, right. But what if the aliens look like us humans?"

"You mean like *Invasion of the Body Snatchers* or *The Thing*?"

"Or maybe *Species*."

"Now you're talking, son! While I reckon this gun would lay waste to Sil right handily, it ain't exactly sportsmanlike to shoot a naked lady."

"She ain't a naked lady, boss," Wesley protested. "She's an alien."

"Well, technically she's an alien-human hybrid."

"But still—"

"Don't sass me, boy! When all you're getting from aliens is anal probes, I don't reckon you'd kick Sil out of bed."

Wesley hung his head. "You're right."

"Damn straight I'm right!" The boss sighed wearily then returned his attention to their spooked customer. "There always has to be two: a master and an apprentice."

Destiny raised her eyebrow and tapped his name badge. "Don't you mean a manager and a trainee?"

Simon's eyes widened as if he had unintentionally divulged the launch codes for America's entire nuclear arsenal. "Yes," he nodded. "That's, um, exactly what I meant."

"He's also my C.O. at the local militia," Wesley volunteered, eager to rejoin the conversation with the pretty lady. "And he's the dungeon master at our weekly gaming night."

"Shush, boy!" Simon snapped. "That group is invitation only!"

"Oooookay," Destiny commented, at a loss for words. She picked up the gun and examined it to see how it felt in her hands. "I'll say this much: You guys sure know your aliens."

"Well," the manager met the compliment with cocksure candor, "you have to know these things when you work in Roswell, you know."

Holding the rifle to her shoulder, Destiny compared the experience of looking directly at various objects in the store versus peering at them through the scope. The latter soon felt comfortable, so she practiced sweeping the store with the weapon while looking through the scope. Its magnification accentuated the movement of the gun, so she had to pan slowly to prevent losing everything in an indistinct blur.

In that moment, as she pointed at the entrance, she saw through the scope the most surprising sight: a clown walking into the store. From the white cake makeup and red bulbous nose to the ruffled collar, oversized polyester/lamé jumpsuit, and exaggerated shoes, it was everything one would expect from a self-respecting clown. On closer inspection, however, something about this buffoon wasn't quite right. The halo of red hair around its bald white head was matted and bedraggled. The eye makeup looked angry, sinister. And despite a broadly painted red smile, the mouth was full of pointed teeth. In fact, at this distance, she wasn't sure if that smeared-on smile was makeup, blood, or the remains of a hastily eaten jelly donut. In all, he was worn and disheveled, like a homeless clown who had just awakened from a park bench and staggered into the store to warm himself. In one hand he carried a bottle of seltzer water. The other gripped a unicycle.

A woman ran up to him. Destiny was too far away to hear what she said, but through the scope she clearly saw the woman's lips form the words "A clown!" He bobbed his head around in acknowledgement, which drew her even closer. Next the clown held up the seltzer bottle and sprayed her. Even at this distance, Destiny heard the woman's screams. The bottle was apparently filled with some kind of acid, and the doused woman clutched her face and dropped writhing to the ground. The clown stepped over her body and pummeled the people nearest him with his unicycle.

"Shit," Destiny whispered, lowered the gun, and looked around. This trouble was definitely headed their way. *Where are you, Niels?* She saw no sign of him in the big-box store. Turning urgently to Simon and Wesley, she found them immersed in a debate about the best *Alien* movie and whether or not *Prometheus* counted as part of the canon. They were oblivious to the commotion at the front of the store.

Spotting the clip of .223 Remington cartridges that the manager had placed on the counter, Destiny popped it into the rifle. She looked again through the scope. The marauding jester was too far away, his unicycle mayhem too kinetic, and panicked retreaters too unpredictable for her to confidently fire a gun for the first time in her life. Plus, she had no idea how this thing worked. Instead, she pointed it overhead and fired a few rounds into the ceiling. As the echo of the gunshots reverberated through the store, everyone stopped and fell silent—even the clown—all eyes now on her.

"Niels!" she bellowed, loud and commanding.

Much to her surprise, everyone within shouting distance dropped to their knees. This included the argumentative salesmen. The only exception was a tousled-haired professor in housewares who stared flabbergasted. At least she didn't cry out, "Hey, Monkey Boy!" in a room full of his colleagues. Belanger's stunned expression was only partly due to her firing an assault rifle in a crowded store. For the most part it was because she had just brought to life yet another urban legend. In the story's original form, which plays on racist fears, a large African American man enters an elevator with a leashed dog. When the owner barks the order "Sit!" the other elevator passengers—all of them middle-aged white women—drop to the floor assuming they are about to be mugged. In its various permutations, the African American is identified as a celebrity such as Eddie Murphy, Reggie Jackson, Lionel Richie, or Mike Tyson, and the incident frequently takes place at resorts like Las Vegas or Atlantic City. It was immortalized in pop culture in a 1973 episode of *The Bob Newhart Show* when a black client arrived with his dog, Whitey. And now it was happening for real.

Belanger rushed over to Destiny, his eyes wide with anger. "Have you gone mental? That stunt might have hurt someone! Do you know how many times someone has shot at me these last few days? I'd *really* fancy a break from that. I ought to give you a piece of my mind!"

"Yeah, well, make it the amygdala, because you're totally jacked." She pointed across the store to the clown, who had by now risen back to his oversized feet and was mowing through kneeling shoppers like a Grim Reaper with a one-wheeled scythe. "We have company."

"Ah, bugger. So it begins. And I didn't even get to cash out."

Since the clown was between them and the main exit, Niels and Destiny ran in the opposite direction. They ducked into the storeroom, and the clown picked up the pace in pursuit. They ran and weaved through tall aisles of industrial shelving until they saw light from the parking lot streaming through a loading bay. They charged in that direction and burst through a pair of double metal doors on the adjoining wall. This put them in the parking lot on the side of the store. They dashed across the asphalt to where their rental car awaited, not bothering to look back at their pursuer who was a good hundred yards behind.

As they approached the car, déjà vu swept over Belanger. *I'm damn well getting it right this time!* He pulled out the key fob and unlocked the doors in advance so that the car's flashing light would help them spot the vehicle—which faced them—and immediately get inside. Once they jumped into the car, they locked the doors. With the frenetic, frothing carnival horror nearly upon them, Belanger started the engine and did not wait to see what would happen next. He threw the car into drive and punched the accelerator. The tires squealed and burned, but soon they gained enough traction to propel the car out of the parking lot.

Waving the seltzer bottle of acid over his head, the clown hopped onto his unicycle and tried to pursue them. But it was hopeless, and the car quickly sped out of sight.

CHAPTER
24

"**W**HAT THE HELL WAS *THAT?!?*" Destiny asked as they pulled into their motel parking lot, a good four miles from the site of the attack.

"I don't know," Belanger confessed. "I've been running through all the clown-related urban legends I can think of, but none of them fit. There's the one about a babysitter who phones her clients because she doesn't fancy the clown statue in the living room...except it turns out they don't own a clown statue. What we saw was definitely no statue." It was a busy night in Roswell, and the only empty parking spot at the motel was between a Mini Cooper and a Chevy convertible with its top down. Seeing no signs of the killer at this distance from the store, he pulled in. "There are various myths about Bozo the Clown: cursing on-air, tots telling him to shove it, him being drunk, and so on. And there's even one about Ronald McDonald getting arrested. I can't see any connection here."

They got out of the car and stepped up onto the sidewalk. Belanger reached into his pocket for the key to their room. "The nearest clown legend that I can think of sprang up in 1981 about the kidnapping and murder of children, inspired no doubt by John Wayne Gacy. However it wasn't a single clown, but a *gang* of killer clowns."

At that instant, the door to the Mini Cooper opened and out stepped Poundfoolish, the clown from the store, except this time he wielded a long chain instead of a unicycle.

From the passenger's side emerged Roland MacPoland, a demented mop-topped clown in a bright lemon-colored jumpsuit and armed with a cleaver.

Amazingly enough, yet another clown emerged from the driver's side. Loonibelle wore a jester's hat with jangling bells on the end of its green and purple tendrils, colors that matched the rest of her harlequin body stocking. She operated Punch and Judy hand puppets, while the Punch puppet operated a full-sized club with multiple nails protruding from the end.

From the passenger side next emerged No-No, who sported a rainbow-colored fright wig and the most garish fluorescent purple and cyan-colored tuxedo known to man. His poofy white gloves made his hands look swollen, and he threatened them with a rubber chicken with a saber thrust lengthwise through it, threading the poor fowl like a worm on a hook with the blade protruding from its inanimate mouth.

Then Pogo appeared from the opposite door. His red tufted hair curled up on either side of his head into a semblance of horns. He wore a boldly striped red and yellow shirt, and extra-wide suspenders held up his oversized argyle pants. Where he should have been juggling rubber balls, he instead juggled running chainsaws.

Finally, out stepped a ghoulish clown with the same big red nose as the others. A much-too-small derby rested on top of his head. Fuzzy balls filled in for buttons down the front of his baggy jumpsuit, red with blue polka-dots. Enormous bright red shoes adorned his feet. After he stretched to his full six-and-a-half-foot height, Pagliouchie sat down on his tricycle and began to make hideous non-Euclidean balloon animals.

Niels and Destiny looked at the gang of six darkly malevolent buffoons. The buffoons sneered back. Niels held up and jangled their key and the big plastic holder to which it was attached so that Destiny could see their room number—lucky thirteen—and once she nodded, they sprinted in that direction. The clowns moved to pursue, but on both the driver's and passenger's side they advanced simultaneously and clumped together so that none could pass. After some hand waving, head slapping, and clown horn honking, they broke through their self-made logjam and followed in hot pursuit.

This clusterfuck bought enough time for Niels Belanger to open the door to their room. Destiny entered right behind, then hastily closed and locked the door. For good measure she also set the safety lock. As soon as she did, someone on the other side jiggled the handle. This was followed by the sound of a shoulder slamming into the door. When that failed to allow entry, the heavier kicking sound of an enormous shoe shook the door, and its frame began to yield. The kicking continued, but its progress was not fast enough for some of these jokers; and with comedy, timing is everything. A wooden club shattered the window beside the door. Loonibelle used her club to knock out the glass shards that protruded from the frame, then stepped through and announced herself, "The call is coming from inside the room!"

A frighteningly jolly voice from outside added, "The rest of us will be inside in *jester* minute." This threat was punctuated by the menacing portamento of a slide whistle.

"Into the washroom!" Belanger suggested, and they dashed in that direction. As before, Destiny locked the door, then grabbed a metal-framed chair from the corner and propped it under the knob. Soon the sounds of pounding against the door from the other side echoed off the bathroom tiles.

"Shit, there's a whole gang of them!" she exclaimed.

"This is not good."

"'Not good' is just a pussy way to say 'bad.' What now?"

He looked around the narrow rectangular space. *Washroom*, he thought to himself. *Washroom*. The vanity, sink, and mirror sat directly across from the door. The toilet rested on one side. The other end of the small room housed the combination tub and shower enclosure. Their only weapons were white towels, a spare roll of toilet paper, a shower cap, a miniature bar of soap, and samples of shampoo and conditioner intended for travelers with very little hair. They were doomed.

Glancing at Destiny's purse, he recalled something that he had seen in a movie. His eyes lit up. "Have you a lighter and a can of hairspray in there?"

"What is it with you and fire? Were you a pyro as a kid?"

"You'll recall that fire worked pretty well against the Slasher."

"Sure, I just thought that if you led a secret double life as a pyro, that would make sense of a lot of things."

Belanger did a double take. "What exactly does that make sense of?"

"Never mind. Here." She reached into her purse and pulled out a box of matches.

He scowled at the small cardboard container in her hand. "That isn't a lighter."

"Do you have any idea how many of those plastic carcasses a smoker puts into landfills? I'm being kind to the Earth."

"Your carbon footprint is going to get much smaller if this doesn't work." Hands shaking, Belanger slid open the matchbox. Meanwhile, the assault on the door became louder, the knob rattling more intense, the horn squeaks angrier. Fumbling with a match, he struck it across the box, but in his haste he barely contacted the striking surface.

Someone began to kick the door with their huge clown feet.

Belanger tried again—a better strike, but no luck. He tried quickly twice more, unsuccessfully. If he survived, perhaps he'd take up smoking.

"Do you want me to do that?" Destiny offered.

"No, I have it."

"This isn't the time to be stubborn."

Belanger paused and glared at her like an overly nagged husband. Then he struck again, and the match lit. "See? I told you I had it." Meanwhile, the drywall around the bathroom door cracked from the relentless assault. "Now give me the hairspray."

His plan was simple. He would ignite the hair spray's propellant and turn the can into a blowtorch. Those garish costumes certainly weren't fire-retardant. And with all that greasepaint, he imagined the whole gang would light up like a hilarious powder keg.

Belanger's expectant expression evaporated when Destiny produced from her purse a small plastic bottle of pump hairspray and handed it to him.

Crestfallen, he stared at the container and asked, "What the hell is this?"

"It's hairspray, just like you asked. The only thing a goth uses more than hairspray is black eyeliner."

"It has no propellant!"

"I happen to like the ozone layer. Dude, you are an ecological Jeffrey Dahmer."

"I can't use this!"

"Do you want some black eyeliner instead?"

He shook out the match and gave an exasperated sigh. Meanwhile, the door frame began splintering.

"We're going to die, aren't we?" Destiny asked.

"There's a good chance," he acknowledged with a nod.

"Damn, this isn't how I planned to die. I thought it would be at an awesome rave."

Belanger looked around the bathroom again. *Shower. Window.*

"Stand aside, you bozos!" a gruff and goofy voice ordered from the other side of the door.

Towels. Sink. Mirror.

The head of an axe split through the center of the bathroom door.

Toilet. Tissue paper. Samples.

The axe disappeared, then split through the door again, widening the hole.

Mirror, he thought again. Then Belanger pointed firmly at the sash above the tub. "Climb out the window. I have this sorted."

"What?" she asked incredulously. The axe broke through the bathroom door a third time.

"Get that window open, I'll be right behind you."

On the other side of the door, a chainsaw motor revved. He had seconds to act. Belanger stepped up to the vanity and looked deep into the mirror. He took a deep breath, opened his mouth, and spoke.

"Bloody Mary."

The head of the chainsaw pierced the door just above the knob and rotated around it.

"Bloody Mary," he repeated. *This had better work or I'm totally stuffed.* The chainsaw completed its cut around the doorknob and withdrew.

"Bloody Mary!" he cried for a third time, then dove into the tub.

Gray mist filled the bathroom, and in front of the vanity stood what might best be described as a ninja Annie Oakley. She had a wide stance, her shoulders slightly hunched. Dirt and blood matted her hair, with occasional strands straggling down her face. A cocked eye patch encircled her head and covered her right eye. A long scar ran along her left cheek. She wore a threadbare red dress with white polka dots, the seam split where its short right sleeve met the shoulder. White lace that had seen better days circumscribed the sleeves, neckline, and hem, except for random spots where it dangled loosely. Mud and dried blood spotted the fabric. The brown leather belt that cinched her waist also held a holster, six-shooter, and hunting knife. Matching cowboy boots, heavily worn and soiled, covered her feet.

She crossed her arms over her shoulders and from the dual holsters strapped to her back she drew a scythe and pitchfork. Their metal was dirty and their handles broken short, turning them into makeshift spikes.

A firm kick from outside flung open the bathroom door.

Interposed between Belanger and the clowns, Bloody Mary turned into the onrushing gang and easily impaled the first charging clown on her pitchfork. With a single smooth motion, she dropped her pitchfork arm to the side and Poundfoolish slid limply off the tines, motionless, and landed beside the toilet in a pool of his own blood. Simultaneously, Bloody Mary swung her opposite arm. The scythe sliced open the next clown, Roland MacPoland, from the right shoulder to below the left hip, spilling his entrails over the floor. The pitchfork then swung up from below, scooped up Pagliouchie just under the ribcage, lifted him over Mary's head, and tossed him against the vanity mirror. A smear of clown blood ran from the impact point to the place where the body landed on the sink, just beside Poundfoolish.

Belanger had no intention of sticking around to watch this play out. He was unsure if even Bloody Mary could hold off all of them. Neither was he sure, if she *did* successfully kill all six, that she wouldn't come after both of them next. He helped the rest of Destiny through the small window, which overlooked the dumpster in the alley behind the motel. As she dropped from the escape hatch, she remarked, "I wish you had said 'Beetlejuice' instead. That would have won best of show!"

Destiny Jones   4:47 pm on February 27

Michael Keaton would kick Annie Oakley's ass.

+131   ♥ ✎ Followers: 5,718   ⊕ Roswell, NM

CHAPTER
25

OT TORMATO was a Yes tribute band comprised of forty-something weekend warriors. Their keyboard player, surrounded by an arsenal of synthesizers and laptops, had thinning hair tied back in a pony tail, plastic-framed glasses, and a white short-sleeved dress shirt with a tie that matched his black slacks and shoes; in honor of the Yes keyboard maestro, he also sported a red cape, which made him look not so much like a synthesizer wizard as Clark Kent caught mid-costume change. Both the bass and lead guitarists wore wide-sleeved silk shirts that resembled the unexpected consequence of a drunken tryst between a kimono and dashiki. And the drummer sat behind a kit with so many toms and cymbals that he was invisible.

"Thank you," the bass player said into the microphone as the band concluded an instrumental number. When a synthesizer began to burble sawtooth sample and hold tones, he continued, "We are Hot Tormato, and this next song is a deep cut from 1978 called 'Arriving UFO.'"

The lead singer stepped out of the shadows and revealed himself to be a stocky man with long blond hair and a clean-shaved face. His stomach peeked out below his well-loved and slightly shrunken *Drama* concert jersey, the spillage accented unfortunately by his tight—and even tighter-belted—blue jeans. He grasped the microphone on its stand with his right hand, a tambourine in his left, and with an unexpectedly high and pure alto tenor, launched into the song:

I could not take it oh so seriously really
When you called and said you'd seen a UFO,
But then it dawned on me the message in writing
Spelt out a meeting never dreamed of before.

The band was very good, and faithfully reproduced the original recording that caused fans to debate passionately Yes's move toward shorter and poppier songs.

Hot Tormato had but a small cadre of fans, mostly family members and fellow musicians, all of them male. Only a handful of other people were in the bar, which was decorated with vintage 1950s science-fiction movie posters. In a corner near the entrance sat Niels Belanger and Destiny Jones. The latter was clearly miserable.

"Why are you so down?" asked the professor. "After that close call with the clowns, it was your idea to come here." Indeed, the assault on their lives had come and gone some five hours before. Neither Bloody Mary nor any clowns seemed to be in pursuit. If history was any indication, Nicholas would have fled town by now. The downside to this was that, once again, they were without a clue where to go next. All they knew was that they couldn't return for a good night's sleep at the scene of a mass murder.

"Yes," she admitted, and then the dam burst. "When I saw this place was called the Men in Black Club, I expected it to be a goth club or a leather bar, not another alien-themed dive. What is it with this town? And what is it with this friggin' music?"

"'Friggin'?" he asked, bemused by her circumspection.

"Yeah, friggin'. My e-meter isn't quite hot enough yet to drop the f-bomb. But I tell you," she pointed at the band, "I'm just about ready to unpack my adjectives. I mean, what's with this music?"

"The style is called progressive rock. Bands in that genre were known to push the boundaries of traditional blues-based rock and bring in elements of psychedelia, folk, classical, jazz, and experimental music. They often composed large-scale conceptual pieces. It was popular in the days before television and music were digital."

"I swear to God, Niels," she looked him in the eye, "if you wax rhapsodic about the days when MTV used to play music videos, I will punch you in the throat."

"No worries. Classic Yes pre-dated MTV."

"Why does it sound so…*happy*? This doesn't sound anything like rock!"

"In their heyday, Yes was actually one of the most successful bands in the world. Arguably the third biggest, after Led Zeppelin and the Rolling Stones."

She stuck out her pierced tongue. "You mean you *like* this music?"

"I'm just playing devil's advocate. I mean, I don't *dis*like it. It's refreshing to hear a band sing things other than cliché love songs."

"Hey, goth isn't about love songs either. It's about suffering and dark emotions. And the singers actually sound like dudes. You should check it out sometime."

> *So look out, in the night*
> *Once they arrive*
> *On that perennial light*
> *Impress a bolder empire of energy*
> *In the ships we see*
> *The coming of outer space.*

Destiny knocked back her drink then rose to her feet. "Order me another one, I'm going to need it. Meanwhile, I'll be returning that last one back to the cosmos."

She headed past the stage toward the rear of the bar and located the restrooms. The two doors had silhouettes of male and female aliens. Destiny muttered under her breath, "Somebody get me back home to New York." She pushed open the door and stepped inside.

The bathroom was deep and narrow, with stalls running along the left-hand side, sinks and hand dryers on the right. At the end of the room, two men with their backs to her were talking. The blond one emphasized, "That's why Area 51 is so important to our plans."

"*Yo, fellas!*" Destiny shouted to get their attention as she took several domineering steps forward. "This is the ladies' room."

"Sorry," the blond one apologized as he turned around. "We thought the ladies' room at a prog rock concert would be the perfect place for a private meeting."

It dawned on her that she was face to face with Nicholas and Bruiser. "Hey," she blurted out with the realization. "You're the guy from that porno!"

Her remark puzzled Nicholas momentarily, but he neverthe-less stepped forward to stare into Destiny's eyes and intrude on her personal space. She stiffened her back and glared back. As they paced around one another, he observed, "And you must be Destiny Jones."

She blinked, and stopped circling. "How do you know my name?"

"Oh, I'm sorry. Did I catch you with your pants down?" He smiled and gestured toward Bruiser, who had just hobbled over on his crutches. "Rest assured, I've heard all about you." This wasn't his usual patter. He had taken on a character, affected a more refined vocabulary, attempted to sound more menacing. Then he produced his smartphone. "Since then I've become your biggest fan."

Her eyes lit up. "Really? Did you see that I just passed six thousand followers?"

"Yes," he remarked drolly, "you're practically trending on Twitter."

By this point, Destiny realized that Nicholas had interposed him-self between her and the exit. She reached into her purse and assert-ively brandished her eco-friendly pepper-spray keychain. "Don't try anything, or I *will* fuck you up."

For a moment he leaned back and sniggered at her threat. Then he smiled charmingly. "From the shape of poor Bruiser here, I don't doubt it. But why do you immediately assume that I would 'try any-thing'? After all, *you* followed *us* into this bathroom, just as you've followed us ever since Devils Tower. But I've never raised a finger against you. In fact, I've never met you before. And you know abso-lutely nothing about me, either. Yet, you've cast me as the villain of the piece. You just assume that I'm evil or dangerous, with no basis at all for that conclusion. I mean, ask someone who knows me." He put his arm around Bruiser's shoulder for emphasis, pulled him close, and locked eyes. "Am I *really* such a monster?"

Bruiser looked at her. Turning up his palms, he made a dunno face and shrugged his shoulders.

Destiny looked back at Nicholas, who continued. "Well, I've got news for you, little sunshine." In an instant, his charming smile flat-lined. His expression turned cold, lifeless—she kind of liked that. And his eyes burned with a darkness that made even a goth like her flinch. He licked his lips, then answered his own question. "I am."

His grip tightened around Bruiser, shoving him hard. Destiny tried to dodge, but in such tight quarters she had nowhere to go. The unbalanced brick house that was Bruiser fell backwards into her, knocking her face-down on the floor. Adding insult to injury, Bruiser landed on top of her, pinning her on the ground while his crutches clattered to the floor. By the time Destiny realized what had happened, Nicholas was dashing out of the bathroom.

"Get back here, goddamn it!" she cried, flailing her arms and legs. "I'll kick your pussy little ass, you chicken shit!"

"Lady," Bruiser said as he stared at the ceiling, "please just don't pull my pants down again. I only gots one good leg."

Unexpectedly an amorous couple, entwined face-to-face, burst into the bathroom. She was very attractive, a tall slender Asian woman in a white blouse, belted black pencil mini-skirt, and high heels. She pushed back and down the tailored jacket of her date to expose his merlot-colored silk dress shirt. He was fit and trim, and his short, neatly-groomed brown hair matched the immaculate styling of his Italian suit and shoes. He shoved her against the wall, causing the hand-dryer to turn on and blow hot air down the open back of her too-short skirt. He then pressed his body and mouth against hers. In response, she wrapped her arms and left leg around him.

As his oral attentions moved down her neck and approached her cleavage, she ran her fingers through his hair, briefly opened her eyes, and then suddenly stopped moving. "Um, Mike," she said as her oblivious lover pulled open her shirt to expose the lacy bra beneath, burying his face in her chest, "it looks like another couple got here ahead of us."

"Ew!" Destiny cried out and flailed against the weight of the man lying on his back on top of her. Bruiser was doing his best to sit up and release her. This was definitely not Shakespeare's beast with two backs. "We are *not* together!"

"I'll say!" Bruiser replied, annoyed by the vehemence of her denial. "She beats da crap outa me."

She harrumphed loudly. "It was only that one time."

Bruiser raised his eyebrow.

"Okay, twice. But you were trying to murder me, you jerk!"

"I'm sorry, I was just doin' my job. Ya don't know my boss like I do. I'm da victim here."

Destiny was incredulous, outraged. "When the person you're trying to kill fights back, that does *not* make you a victim!"

"Then how come I gots two casts an' a concussion?"

"Because you deserve it!"

"Oh, sure, blame da victim. *'He was totally askin' for it. Didja get a load of da dress he was wearin'?'*"

"Are you seriously this clueless, or is that the concussion talking?"

"Say whatcha will, but I'm da only one in dis relationship who's said 'I'm sorry.'"

"We are *not* in a relationship!!!"

Bruiser shook his head forlornly. "Ya know, it's da emotional abuse what hurts da most."

Mike finally extracted his face from his lover's bosom. "Another couple? Well," Mike squeezed her breasts with each hand, not even bothering to turn around, "maybe they'd like to join us." The suggestion stoked her passion, and she pulled his face closer to hers and thrust her tongue into his mouth.

Destiny raised an eyebrow. "You two *are* kind of hot."

These negotiations were interrupted by Belanger throwing open the bathroom door. He had—moments before—seen Nicholas Young run through the bar and out the front door. His first instinct was to pursue his nemesis. But given his trajectory, Belanger extrapolated his origin point to behind the stage, where one would find the bathrooms…and Destiny. Thus, he let Nicholas escape and chose instead to run and check on her. From the moment he fully opened the door, they all heard that Hot Tormato had segued into a cover of Klaatu's 1976 classic, "Calling Occupants of Interplanetary Craft." "Destiny!" he shouted over the band. "Are you okay?"

She was still face-down on the floor, but by now she had her chin propped up on her palm, elbow underneath. Bruiser struggled to grab one of his crutches. The couple continued their lovemaking against the blower, unconcerned about the events around them. "Looks like you'd better get in line," she quipped. "There are three people ahead of you."

Belanger stood there, relieved but baffled. "What's going on?"

"I'll push the latest update for you: First but not foremost, Bruiser knocked me down. I'm fine, Nicholas escaped, and I was just about to have a three-way with this nice couple. Now would you please shut that door? If I have to hear any more prog rock tonight, I'm going to let Romeo here beat me to death with his crutch."

Bruiser, who was sitting up by this point, looked mawkishly at her and his face lit up. "Really? Hey lady, I guess I had you all wrong. You're okay."

With an eyebrow raised, she replied, "Watch it. No cat owner has ever said, 'Her meow is worse than her scratch.'"

"Yes, ma'am." Bruiser sheepishly averted his eyes like the omega male they both knew he was. By that point, however, she was already at work on her latest status update.

Destiny Jones   9:46 pm on February 27

Looks like I'm what's for dessert.

+165   ♥   Followers: 6,759   Roswell, NM

Meanwhile, the band played on.

> *Calling occupants of interplanetary craft.*
> *Calling occupants of interplanetary, most extraordinary craft.*
> *Calling occupants of interplanetary craft.*
> *Calling occupants of interplanetary ultra-emissaries.*
> *We are your friends.*

CHAPTER

26

ESTINY JONES WAS NEVER HAPPIER to find herself checked into a smoking room. After attempts on her life over these past days by a butch transvestite, a crazed Mexican barber, and a mob of circus rejects—not to mention a run-in with the man who had sent them all to kill her—she was wound up tighter than her corset. Sitting on the bed, propped upright against the headboard, she reached into her purse and pulled out a lighter, flashed it at Belanger, and smiled. It was brand new. On their way to the Men in Black Club, she had gone into the first service station they saw and bought a metal lighter: one that wouldn't wind up in a landfill, but one that Belanger could use to incinerate clowns. She settled on one painted to look as though it had a bullet hole. She teased him that "It reminds me of the day we met."

From her purse she drew a fresh cigarette, lit it, and took a long, rapacious drag to calm her nerves. Then she stared again at the whiteboard that Belanger had grabbed from one of the meeting rooms. He had written upon it with black erasable marker:

WHAT WE KNOW
Phase 1. Devils Tower → Hairy-Armed Hitchhiker
Phase 2. Overlook Hotel → Slasher under the Car
Phase 3. Roswell → Killer Clowns
Phase 4. ← ???
Phase 5. Destroy the world

She blew a big cloud of smoke toward the open door, then said, "Maybe Nicholas Young will destroy the world by turning all guys into UFO nerds, thus driving away women and causing the human race to gradually die out."

"Hey," Belanger defended his gender. "There are geek girls too, you know. Ever heard of the Estrogen Brigades? Twihards? Cumber-bitches? Beanstalkers? Hiddlestoners?"

She shook her head, unimpressed. "No."

"Bamber Bunnies? Spiner Femmes? Debbie Downeys? Gimli's Girls? Shatnerds?"

"Okay, okay, I get it." She was still unimpressed, but this barrage of names made her head hurt.

"Sereni-T&As? JAG Hags? Hobbettes? Jason Stackhussies? V's for Vendetta?"

Finally, she frowned with well-founded suspicion. "Are you sure those aren't all the same people?"

"Well," he conceded, "there *is* a high degree of overlap in fandom."

"Never mind," she said with a hand gesture for added emphasis. Either that or she was practicing to be an umpire. "That sounds like it's on a 'need to know' basis. And I don't need to know about your D&D conventions."

"Be that as it may, if we can figure out how Nicholas Young plans to destroy the world, it may give us a clue to his next move."

She shrugged. "Your guess is probably better than mine."

"So Bruiser didn't know anything," he said, not so much as a question but as a summary of the ground they'd already covered this evening.

"Nope. When he hit that tree at Devils Tower and broke his leg, he also got a concussion that affected his short-term memory. I guess us using his head as a plant liberation device didn't help. Fortunately, he doesn't remember any of that. Heck, he didn't even realize that I had questioned him three different times this evening before we finally let him go."

That was unfortunate. Even if he had known anything, there was a possibility that he had forgotten it by the time he was questioned. "And you didn't hear them say anything before you spoke to them?"

She closed her eyes and rubbed her temples in an effort to relive that moment. "I'm not sure, it all happened so fast."

"Think. Anything you remember might help."

She took a deep breath and walked through the encounter in her mind. "I remember they *were* talking when I first walked in." Her eyes rolled around while she scoured her memory. Then finally she recalled, "Yes. Nicholas said that something was important."

Belanger sat at attention. "What was important?"

Destiny winced and shook her head. "I don't remember, it was just some number."

"What number?" he pressed her. "This is the only glimmer of a clue that we have."

"It was something like…" She strained to remember the details. "Area 54?"

Although he tried to restrain himself, Belanger let out a short burst of laughter.

"What?" As usual, Destiny was the last one in on Belanger's mental life. And she was weary of the constant need to catch up.

Belanger composed himself. His best way to accomplish this was to enter professor mode. "He probably said 'Area 51.' It's a top-secret military base in Nevada where experimental aircraft are tested. And it makes perfect sense. Nicholas has already been to Devils Tower and Roswell. Now Area 51. You see, conspiracy theorists believe that the government uses Area 51 to test and research captured UFOs. Perhaps Nicholas intends to steal and use some kind of top-secret military weapon." He snickered again, but held in most of his chortle. "On the other hand," he dropped his professorial airs completely, "Area 54 would be the military's top-secret disco across the street." Unable to contain himself any longer, he let out a hearty belly laugh.

"Oh, fuck you," Destiny flipped him off. "It isn't *that* funny."

"Come on," he continued ribbing, "I'm just taking the piss."

"After being nicknamed Snow Cone, I don't want to hear about *anyone* 'taking the piss.'" She took another puff and exhaled angrily. "Goddamn it, Niels, you're so full of yourself." She snatched the cigarette out of her mouth and lapsed into a mock British voice. "*Area 51. Estrogen brigades. Progressive rock. The Hundredth Monkey.* Jesus, you've been lecturing me from the minute we met. People want to kill us, and you still have to explain every single urban legend there is in excruciating detail. All right, I admit it: I'm no expert in folklore. And yes, I've had some unlikely and embarrassing things happen in my life—*believe it or not*. But that doesn't make me stupid. And it doesn't make me one of your students." She grabbed her purse off the bedside table and rose to her feet. "It does, however, make you a complete asshole."

She stuck the cigarette back in her mouth, turned, and stormed out the door, slamming it shut on her way out. Once outside, she paused on the covered cement walkway that ran around the second-floor rooms. The winter night air was much warmer here than in their previous stopovers. It was brisk and refreshing, cool enough to see her breath but not cold. She puffed her cigarette to calm herself. It didn't help. Then she pulled out her phone and typed furiously.

She took another long, deep drag then blew out the smoke. She leaned against the railing and stared at the sky. After another puff, she reconsidered and returned to her phone.

With that, she stuffed the phone into her purse and stomped briskly around the outdoor perimeter of the second floor, hoping to walk off her anger. It always helped her to deal with frustrations over the mean girls in school, especially when she imagined herself stomping on their pretty little heads.

Inside, Belanger stared at the door in stunned silence, chastened by her remarks. She was right. This whole adventure played into his expertise, and because she was unfamiliar with their significance— she was even a *part* of the unfolding urban legends—her naiveté was an excuse for exposition. Belanger recognized how that may have come across as smug, even patronizing. But it was never his intention. He just wanted to bring her fully into the events that had thrown them together. He only wanted to share everything he knew. He wanted to share with *her*.

Finally, in a frustrated display of *l'esprit de l'escalier*, he twisted up his indignation and shouted to no one in particular, "Did it ever occur to you that I have a hell of a lot more experience lecturing to classrooms than I do speaking to beautiful women?" Then he raised his face toward the ceiling, dropped his shoulders, and sighed in defeat.

He debated whether to go after Destiny. Would she be too angry to listen to reason? Would he appear too needy, too clingy, or too concerned for her feelings? Would it push her even further away? He was never any good at negotiating interpersonal relationships, and he disliked confrontations. It would be best, he decided, to let her cool down a bit.

He walked over to his laptop, which was resting on the motel desk. Into the navigation bar of his browser he typed http://www.tweezer.me. A welcome screen loaded with a large version of the nanoblogging service's logo. Ignoring the "log in" and "sign up" hyperlinks, Belanger went straight to the "find your friends" box. There he typed "Destiny Jones" and clicked on "search." In moments, her recent posts filled the screen. From them, he saw that her seven thousand followers now knew what a 8===D he was. He clicked on the comment icon, which resembled a pencil. A blank box with a cursor opened beneath her post. He tapped several keys on the keyboard and clicked "ok."

Destiny Jones   10:40 pm on February 27

Correction: What a total 8=D

+304   ♥ ✎ Followers: 8,179   ⊕ Roswell, NM

Anonymous: I'm sorry. Would you please come dancing with me in
Nevada? You can pick the music.

Next he grabbed the remote control, turned on the television, and flipped mindlessly through the channels. It was just something to release his frustration, something to distract him. When he had enough, he set down the remote, oblivious to what channel he had stopped on. He wasn't even watching. It was merely background noise while he stared at the ceiling and lamented being such a jerk. It would also serve as something for him to look at, nonchalant, when she finally cooled off and walked through the door.

Meanwhile, a television news announcer reported, "After scholars dismissed the purported lost Shakespearean play *The Phantom Menelaus* as the ravings of an 'angry ape,' the collective which authored the play released a terse press release saying simply,

> 'Triumphs for nothing, and lamenting toys,
> Is jollity for apes and grief for boys.'

This has been widely interpreted as the collective flinging poo at academics who have dismissed their work. We reached out to both parties for a comment on this story. The scholars had no comment, as it was still undergoing peer review. The authors responded exclusively to us that

> 'More strange than true: I never may believe
> These antique fables, nor these fairy toys.
> Lovers and madmen have such seething brains,

Such shaping fantasies, that apprehend
More than cool reason ever comprehends.
The lunatic, the lover and the poet
Are of imagination all compact:
One sees more devils than vast hell can hold.'"

Belanger's computer made a chime sound, so he hastily rolled off the bed and to his feet. On the screen, he saw a "+" sign next to his apology. Hovering over it with the mouse revealed that his comment had been plussed by Destiny. He smiled, relieved and reassured that it was now safe to chase after her and try to convince her to return to their room. After all, they had a game plan now. Area 51 was nine hundred miles away, or two long days' travel by car. They would need to get an early start. He put on and tied his shoes to go get her.

Stepping onto the walkway outside the room, he looked in both directions but did not see her. So he walked the perimeter of the second floor, calling out "Destiny?" softly enough not to disturb any of the other guests. Around another corner, and he again saw no sign of her. An overhead light brightly illuminated a spot at the end of this row of motel rooms.

Something small lay on the ground there.

Belanger approached the lighted area, looked down, and kneeled to investigate. Picking the object up and turning it over in his hand, he recognized Destiny's brand new lighter, the one with the fake bullet hole. Slipping it into his coat pocket, his attention turned to where the lighter had been resting on a large powdery pile of...scales? They resembled what was left behind by those annoying moths that he knew all too well from his pantry. *Strange*, he thought. *This is far more than you'd get off a single moth. It's more than you'd get from even a whole closet full. And the size is all wrong.*

In a horrible flash, he understood. There was no body, no sign of his companion anywhere. That left only one conclusion: Destiny Jones had been kidnapped by the Mothman.

Noooo! Why, oh why, did she have to stand under a bright light!?!

CHAPTER
27

B Y THE TIME BELANGER REALIZED that the sudden whoosh-ing sound was coming toward him, something had already grabbed him from above the shoulders of his jacket and dragged him quickly along the motel's second-story walkway. At the point where the outdoor footpath rounded the corner of the building, that something released him. The momentum of his rapid advance sent Belanger headlong into the railing. He struck the wrought-iron barrier so hard that his vision blacked out momentarily, and his head hurt so much that he was unsure if he was bleeding or simply sweating with panic. Pain from the impact radiated from his head and shoulders.

The whooshing sound circled around, then something grabbed Belanger by his belt and wrist, sliding him off the ground and over the edge of the railing. He reached vaguely for the horizontal bar with his free hand—a vain attempt to grasp and hang on—but was too disoriented to put up much of a struggle. Soon he was suspended in the air, then just as suddenly free-falling to the courtyard below. The impact from a story-and-a-half drop knocked the wind out of him and left him gasping vainly for breath. This time he was certain he was bleeding from the body parts that first hit the pavement.

All he could do was roll onto his back and wince. Through squinting eyes, he saw a hovering figure clad in a World War I-era aviator cap with large goggles. Belanger made out a brown leather bomber jacket with a wool-lined collar, and dark olive-green cargo pants tucked into military-style front-laced boots. Enormous brown-gray wings, dotted by black circles with white centers, jutted from slits in the back of the jacket. Belanger got a better look as the assailant descended from above, grabbed him, lifted him just barely off the ground, and rocketed him across the courtyard. He flailed in a pathetic gesture of resistance, but his constant collisions with rocks and shrubs kept him disoriented.

Wait a minute, he asked himself through the sensory barrage. *The Mothman has* breasts?

He didn't get to ponder the question for long. The next thing he knew, he was released again. He had so much speed that when he hit the ground his body bounced and rolled once, twice before he careered involuntarily into a steel table-and-chair café set. Although the furniture had been chained down to prevent theft, the chain was loose enough for this collision to knock over all five pieces. Sprawled motionless on top of the overturned furniture in a semi-conscious daze, Belanger mused that human bowling was far more brutal than human chess.

His mind cleared enough to realize that he was no longer on the ground, but was once again whisked through the air, face up, by two firm hands grasping his belt from above. This time the release launched him into a tree trunk. Belanger marveled at the quietness of such a hard impact. There was no crack of a mighty oak, nor a crack of his spine. He ached from the blow, but it wasn't as bad as the previous three. Maybe he was just numb. He rolled into a sitting position, then kicked against the ground in a lame crab-walk to push himself closer to the trunk.

The tree was small enough that its canopy prevented the Mothman—er, Moth*woman*—from grabbing him from above. The glow of the parking lot lights illuminated his assailant hovering farther back to prepare a diagonal, rather than vertical, strike under the branches. Belanger summoned everything he had in that moment of clarity to crawl behind the tree. Battered, bruised, and bleeding, he used the trunk as a support to grope his way upright. He leaned against the tree, his face pressed into the rough bark, his breathing labored, and kept his adversary in sight.

The Mothwoman maintained her height and distance, but darted horizontally left and right, searching for an optimal attack angle. In response, Belanger kept his eyes trained on her and rotated to keep the tree between himself and his attacker. By this strategy he bought enough time for his head to clear. His diaphragm happily cooperated with his lungs, and despite painful throbbing everywhere, he was pretty sure that he had no broken bones as yet.

His eyes darted briefly from the Mothwoman to survey his environs for a more strategic position. The two-story auto camp formed a large u-shaped battlement around the courtyard. He was too exposed to make a break for his room on the second floor. All the other doors represented locked guest rooms. The only publicly accessible indoor area was the registration office. If he reached it, he could barricade himself inside and call the police. Unfortunately, the office was on the far end of the motel, across the car park and near the road. It was a substantial and unprotected distance to traverse, and most likely tactical suicide. Perhaps the cars would provide enough low cover for him to make it.

Belanger braced himself, took a deep breath, then began the most athletic activity he had ever willingly undertaken: a mad sprint across the motel parking lot.

He nearly made it when a hard kick to the head from above struck him squarely on his right temple and sent him spilling into the driveway. He flipped onto his back to see that the Mothwoman's trajectory had taken her past him. She banked and began to circle around for a return strike. Running was pointless, he realized. The Mothwoman had a clear speed advantage, and would be upon him before he ever got to his feet. Belanger slapped his pockets desperate to find something to use as an improvised weapon. The hotel key and its plastic holder were useless. So was the rental car key fob.

Inside his coat pocket, his fingers closed around Destiny's lighter.

As the Mothwoman swooped toward the professor, Belanger rolled at the last instant, barely avoiding the next punishing assault. This gave him a few seconds to crawl to his feet. Still crouching, he held up the lighter, flipped open its metal cover, and frantically flicked his thumb on the wheel. The flint sparked and the lighter glowed to life. *Much better than a bloody box of matchsticks*, he mused. Its glow was radiant in the dark night.

"Hey Mothma'am," the professor taunted with a wave of the burning lighter.

She froze mid-air, her attention transfixed by the flame.

"Look what I've got. It's a fire. You like fire, don't you? The nice, warm light. The happy light. Do you want it?" The Mothwoman grinned, her eyes opened wide. "It's yours!"

Belanger threw the lighter into the air, down the driveway and toward the street. The Mothwoman rapidly changed course to follow it.

Just then, a pair of approaching hi-beams lit up the darkness. The Mothwoman hovered in place to relish the glorious sight, as if it were the Lepidoptera God itself. She hastily darted toward its source.

It turned out that she was flying directly toward a semi truck and trailer. As the Mothwoman approached, the startled driver swerved to avoid the woman or bird or whatever the hell that thing was in front of him. Unfortunately, the Mothwoman advanced so quickly that no amount of driver maneuvering could prevent a collision with her. Momentum pinned the Mothma'am to the grill like an etymologist's specimen. The swerving truck crossed the double yellow line in the road and collided head-on with another oncoming semi. The sickening sounds of metal scraping against metal, rubber burning on the road, and opposing momentums straining against each other filled the night with their brutality.

Belanger watched the carnage unfold with awestruck horror. When he threw Destiny's lighter, he only intended to buy himself enough time to seek shelter in the motel lobby. He had no idea that the Mothwoman would turn herself into a bug on a windshield. Or cause such a terrible accident.

He also realized that these events played out a variation of an urban legend popular in both Europe and the United States since the 1970s: One day two semi trucks collided so hard that their cabs had to be hauled to the junk yard as one piece. When the vehicles were finally pried apart to reclaim the scrap metal, a VW bug and its passengers were discovered completely flattened between the two trucks. Except in Belanger's version of the story, the bug was the Mothma'am.

CHAPTER
28

"I F THIS DON'T BEAT ALL T'HELL!" the EMS tech exclaimed to a police officer at the site of the truck collision. Red and blue flashers from police, fire, and medical vehicles lit up the night while construction lights pointed at the freak accident to help identify its cause. While the investigation was underway, reporters and camera crews huddled behind crime-scene tape with a line of mobile news vans, the masts of their broadcast antennae raised skyward. The motel's tenants that evening had streamed outdoors at the first sounds of the accident, and they lined the stretch of road immediately in front of the wreckage. Several people in their pajamas walked over to the barricade to speak with the waiting reporters, hopeful that they would appear on television declaring, "Lord have mercy!" or "This is a false-flag operation." If they were really lucky, they might even become the next viral video at Auto-Tune the News.

"Yeah," the officer agreed. He was a large man, with black curly hair and a moustache that framed his no-nonsense eyes. While he may have been overweight, much of that padding was actually muscle. "Between this and the clown massacre earlier today, it's been the craziest weekend I've ever seen on the force. A real corker."

"We see lots of crazy shit in EMS too, but nothing like that last one. Just pieces everywhere. But we'll get 'er taken care of, Josh."

"Thanks, Carlos. You're a good man. I was glad to see you on both calls."

Carlos nodded. "Have the clowns' names been released to the media yet?"

"No," Officer Josh shook his head. "Protocol requires us to wait until we've notified their next-of-harlequin."

"Riiiight," he remembered. "Their circus family. That hasn't stopped social media, though. They're having a field day with this. I've already seen headlines like CLOWN CARNAGE and CIRQUE DU SLAUGHTER. The kooks in the conspiracy meetup at the Crashdown Café are convinced that a top-secret circus convention was in town, and the government was testing weaponized clowns to infiltrate the Middle East. Kind of like *Argo*, except with cotton candy. These guys are claiming that the clowns misfired and now the military-industrial complex is covering up the whole thing by making it look like a harmless mass murder."

"Pffft. People will believe any goddamned thing. But Carlos, between you and me"—the police officer lowered his voice—"you should see the rap sheets on those clowns. They've been taking their show from town to town and really knocking 'em dead. They were *hardened* entertainers."

"Wow, they sound like real cut-ups. Do you think some vigilante killed them? Or maybe a competing act?"

"Possibly. Or it might have been a crazy murder-suicide pact. These *are* clowns, after all."

"Yeah, good point."

"Our main person of interest is the fellow who was registered in the room. We want to find him and bring him in for questioning."

That very person of interest happened to be standing just out of earshot, having inched his way through the crowd of gawkers to the yellow police line. Belanger observed and weighed the official response while trying to remain inconspicuous amongst the onlookers. He was doing a pretty good job of blending in, too, aside from being beaten and covered in his own blood. He didn't need to hear Carlos and Josh's conversation to realize it was only a matter of time before detectives determined that the guest in whose room the clown massacre occurred was also a guest at this motor lodge. From the motel registers they would know the make, model, and license plate number of his rental car: a vehicle that even now sat in the car park just waiting to be identified. If the authorities apprehended him, he would not only have plenty to explain—all the way back to the Hook in New Orleans—but if he was held for questioning he might never catch up with Nicholas again. Or Destiny. In fact, he might never again see the outside of a prison cell. That is provided there was an outside to see at all, should Nicholas somehow successfully destroy the world.

Belanger dissolved nonchalantly back into the crowd. With the authorities on the lookout for him, he needed to leave Roswell immediately.

He hastily limped to his room, gritting his teeth and moaning with every step. He went directly into the washroom and tended to his wounds. They consisted mostly of large scrapes to his elbows, knees, hips, and shoulders. Despite a gash on the bridge of his nose and across his right eyebrow, his head did not seem to be split open. Furthermore, he didn't feel nauseated, dizzy, imbalanced, or unfo-cused: none of the telltale symptoms of a concussion. He was never-theless in severe pain. From his duffel bag he retrieved and swallowed two ibuprofen pills to dull the ache and discourage the soreness that would doubtless settle upon him.

Next he changed into unbloodied clothes. With his injuries, they wouldn't remain that way for long so he made a mental note to stop for elastoplasts once he had put a safe distance between himself and these investigations.

Returning to the main living and sleeping area, Belanger hastily gathered the remaining clothes from the hotel dresser and shoved them into his bag. He returned to the bathroom with the bag and, using his forearms, swept the toiletries inside with a single gesture. A quick zip, and he was ready to go on the lam.

He hit the refresh button on his web browser one last time. It was still pointed at Tweezer, and he hoped for some sign that Destiny was all right. Or even alive. But the only thing that changed onscreen was the number of fans of her page—occasionally ticking up by one or two—and the ads in the right margin which ironically advertised how to get cheap running shoes or a great rate on health insurance.

The uncharacteristic lack of an update indicated that, wherever she was, she was unable to post. He snapped shut the lid of his laptop and shoved it into his bag.

Finally, he scribbled a hasty note on the motel stationery:

> *Dear Destiny,*
> *If you get this note, I've gone to find you. Call my cell, (220)867-5309.*
> *Worried,*
> *Niels*

Stopping by the front desk, he paid cash for one more night at the hotel just in case Destiny showed up there. Then he drove back to the department store. Before long he emerged with his purchases of a handgun, some small butterfly bandages for his nose and eyebrow, and their largest available cup of hot coffee. Popping open the boot of his car, he did a last-minute inventory: *Duffel bag and computer, check. Pistol, check. Duct tape, check. Jumper cables and colander, check.* With that, he closed the trunk and walked around to the passenger door—then remembered that he was in the United States. He went to the other side and got behind the wheel. Maybe his head took a harder beating than he realized.

The car engine roared back to life. Belanger reasoned that if he had to leave town in a hurry, then he may as well begin the nine-hundred-mile trek along westbound I-40, and press on through the night to Area 51. That way he would be there ready and waiting for a showdown with Nicholas Young. And if that murderous frat brat—who had already killed Rusty Piquot in cold blood—had harmed Destiny in any way, Belanger would make Nicholas regret ever registering for his class.

CHAPTER
29

THE CAR STOPPED SUDDENLY. A few seconds later the trunk opened and allowed light to pour inside. Destiny peered out from the cramped compartment and squinted while her eyes adjusted. She recognized the silhouette of Nicholas Young standing at the bumper. He tossed her something cylindrical wrapped in wax paper. She caught it in her hands, which were bound together in front of her. The object was a breakfast burrito. It was warm. And it smelled delicious.

"Dude, you must be a mind reader," she replied gratefully.

"Just a reader," he replied flatly, and flashed his smartphone. Then he pulled a Swiss army knife from his pocket and cut the zip ties around her ankles and wrists.

"Thanks. That will make it easier to eat without getting salsa all over your roadside hazard kit."

He held out his hand. "Give me your phone."

"What?" He may as well have asked for a kidney.

"Give me your phone and I will let you out of the trunk. This isn't a request. I won't ask you again."

She raised an eyebrow. "You do know that 'request' means 'ask,' right?"

He held out his hand and waited. Clearly, English 2.0 wouldn't work on him.

With a defeated sigh, she pulled her beloved smartphone out of her pocket and handed it to Nicholas. In exchange, he gestured toward the empty space outside the rear of the car and, with a raise of his eyebrows, indicated that she was free to exit.

As she stood up and brushed herself off, Nicholas closed the trunk. Destiny remarked, "All I can say is this had better be a damn good drive-in movie." They were actually in a parking structure. Most spots were taken. With no reply from Nicholas, she stretched, groaned, then continued rambling. "Getting up at the ass-crack of dawn these last three days is killing me. It's so early that it's *angry* early. You know, if you look at any zombie movie, the dead don't rise first thing in the morning. There's a reason for that."

Ignoring her comment yet again, he grabbed her arm. "Don't try anything smart. I have a gun, and I'm a *much* better shot than those ass monkeys I sent after you." Nicholas redirected his gaze toward Bruiser, whom Destiny had just noticed behind her near the passenger door. "No offense."

"Oh," Bruiser shook his head, "none taken, boss."

Destiny turned, feigning surprise. "Hey! It's the ol' parole officer and tether!"

"Where?" Bruiser asked, nervously looking around the parking structure.

"I mean *you*, Bruiser."

Nicholas rolled his eyes as he started to march Destiny through the structure. "King of the ass monkeys."

"So," Destiny looked back at the man with the gun, "this must be the grand finale of your buddy film. Soon, Butch and Sundance will part ways, no longer to be caught in a bad bromance."

"Oh, don't worry about Bruiser," Nicholas responded as dry as the desert air. "I'll be sure to give him a nice sundress and box cutter as a parting gift."

Bruiser cooed, "Awww, that's *so* nice of you!"

"My God!" Destiny responded with mock horror. "With his cast and crutches, he'll look just like a little old church lady. Altruists and liberals will be defenseless!"

Nicholas gave her a sideways glance and smirked. He recognized a little bit of himself in her. And he had to like that part, just a little. "You remind me of my sister, Lilith."

She beamed sarcastically. "Lucky me."

"Yeah," he nodded. "She's a single mom. Her kids had massive birth defects. Their dad's a deadbeat, a real dirt-bag. Never paid a cent in child support, and he never visits them. At least not since he dumped her for a younger, hotter model and started a new family. It was like he had no sense of right and wrong. Anyway, ever since then, my sister has had 'anger issues.'"

"Sounds like she has good reason to be pissed. Come to think of it, so do I."

"Yeah, well, I gutted her about ten years ago, but her wisecracks just keep coming."

That pretty much killed the conversation.

They walked—or, in Bruiser's case, hobbled—in awkward silence until they entered New Mexico's largest airport, Albuquerque International Sunport. Its Pueblo-style architecture was a nod to local culture and geography, with a solid, square appearance that almost looked like it was originally designed using wooden blocks. This design, combined with high ceilings and large windows, imparted a light and airy feeling of openness to the interior. Comfort was a clear priority, as the usual black sling-back chairs were absent in favor of more welcoming wooden chairs with brown padded seats and backs; their blocky style matched the design aesthetics of the building itself. As a further nod to local culture, one hundred twenty pieces of Native American, Hispanic, and Contemporary work by New Mexico artists decorated the grounds.

As they entered level three of the terminal, Nicholas directed them to the security checkpoint. He circumvented the line of passengers awaiting screening and led them down the aisle for employees. When he encountered the security personnel there, he raised his left hand and made a single waving gesture. To Destiny's surprise, the TSA personnel waved the three of them through.

After they passed through security in this unconventional manner, Destiny was surprised yet again when they took an unexpected turn away from the main concourse. "Wait," she queried. "Why are we heading in this direction? The sign says these are international flights. We thought you were heading to Area 51."

Nicholas smirked knowingly and remarked, "Exactly." Then he burst into maniacal laughter. Rather than dying out in a quick and appropriate manner—but, then again, what is appropriate for maniacal?—it went on a little too long. It built to a crescendo and sustained like a hug that lingered from friendly to awkward and then finally creepy. People around the concourse stopped and stared, so Nicholas finally checked himself and declared, "Sorry, folks. I just remembered a funny dream I had last night."

He waved his hand again and instructed, "As you were." Everyone instantly returned to their routines as if his outburst had never happened. Even Bruiser's expression went from amused to blank. Then Nicholas continued to lead Destiny through the terminal.

"That's a pretty shiny trick you have there," Destiny noted.

"Thank you."

"Why didn't you just use that on Niels in the first place? It would have saved us all a lot of trouble."

"You mean Dr. Belanger? Yeah, I can only influence the weak-minded. Fortunately, that includes most people. It's a simple trick. But limited, at the end of the day."

"So," she nodded, searching her brain for something to say, "why do you suppose the classic monster movies all involve kidnapping a woman?"

Although Destiny's nervousness was talking, Nicholas wearied of her tangents. "Are you calling me a monster?"

"Think about it: Quasimodo. Dracula. Frankenstein's monster. The phantom of the opera. King Kong. The creature from the black lagoon. It's a near-universal trope among monsters."

"Maybe they are fans of Stockholm syndrome relationships."

"I like Quasimodo," Bruiser piped up, but neither of them paid any attention.

"I wrote a paper about this in one of my film classes. Know what I think?" Destiny asked.

Nicholas rolled his eyes and shook his head. "I'm sure I have no idea, But I get the sinking feeling that you're about to tell me."

"These movies portray the male sex drive as an impressionable and uncontrollable monster—something every guy can identify with, don't you agree?—that objectifies women as the target of indiscriminate desire. I dug up this old paper by an early anthropologist named Staniland Wake on the practice of marriage-by-capture. He said that tribes who ran short on available brides used to steal women from other tribes. Women captured this way always resisted, but Wake claimed that this resistance was traditional and only done for show. He claimed that if she *really* wanted to escape, her pursuers would have allowed it. Do you believe that steaming crock? It's all some macho rape-culture bullshit fantasy. My prof told me that Wake's paper may be outdated, or even junk anthropology. But the point of my essay was that it didn't matter whether or not the scholarship was sound. Wake's piece was published in 1929, and it mirrored a predominant male fantasy at the time these monster movies were first made. You have to admit, the women in those films never struggle very hard. It's as if the director is giving all the guys in the audience a nudge and a wink that she really wants it. I mean, the monster is like all *Arrrrgh!* and she's just all *Oh, I swoon!* and collapses right into his waiting arms. Could anyone possibly write a more obvious rape fantasy?"

"Your professor must have been very proud."

The sarcastic comment reminded her that Belanger had made a similar remark shortly after they first met. She hoped that he was all right. "So can you explain one thing?"

Nicholas sighed. "What's that?" At least it sounded like she was finally getting to the point.

"Well, I've been happy to give both of you enough bath water and a toaster for this scheme of yours. But what do you need *me* for?"

Nicholas stopped in his tracks and tightened his grip on her forearm. He squeezed so hard that it brought her to an immediate stop. Her body curled up—only a little, because she didn't want to give him the satisfaction of knowing that he was hurting her. Although she winced, try as she might she was unable to break free. "You really have a high opinion of yourself, Miss Jones."

"Well, I *am* pretty awesome," she quipped through gritted teeth.

"I hate to burst your bottle—"

"Bubble."

"But you definitely won't find any rape fantasies here." She reminded him of his sister, after all.

"Based on what I've seen of your film work, that suits me just fine. I don't date below my league."

"Let me make one thing perfectly clear: I *don't* need you. For *anything.*" He again burned with anger, with that same startling look in his eyes that she saw at the Men in Black Club. His words flowed with such venom and contempt that they stung her ears as much as they did her feelings. "You are undesirable. You have no value. *Nobody* wants you." It was a striking recap of the words that had set him off at Stanley's Marvelous Comics. "You'll all be dead soon enough. For now, you are alive on my suffrance, and for no other reason than because it amuses me. So I advise you in the *strongest* terms to use all of your well-learned politesse. Or, so help me," he squeezed her arm even tighter for emphasis. She winced and again tried unsuccessfully to pull away. "I *will* lay your soul to waste."

At that, he relaxed his grip and continued to pull her through the terminal.

"Hey, Larry Talbot, look," Destiny blurted out excitedly to Nicholas in an attempt to change the subject to something more comfortable. "Shoe-shine!"

Bruiser replied, "I wonder if he can do my pumps?"

CHAPTER
30

*A*T 6:27 A.M., Belanger pulled into an all-night service station to fill his tank with gas and his bloodstream with caffeine. All night long, the car and its operator had been driven by a mix of determination and dread. He was determined to stop Nicholas, but worried sick about Destiny. Despite these motivations, his car and body needed occasional refueling. He was so stiff and sore from his encounter with the Mothma'am that getting out of the car was painful. He hurt in places that he didn't even realize were parts of his body. But he managed to exit the vehicle and make his way into the shop.

He returned with a steaming cup of coffee from the station's dispenser, and washed down a couple more ibuprofen tablets. Then with his free hand he placed the nozzle into his gas tank and locked the fuel pump trigger in the fill position. While the pump ran, he opened his trunk, fetched his laptop, and opened it. Awakened from hibernation, his web browser still pointed to where Belanger had left it back at the hotel: Destiny Jones' Tweezer feed. He was on the outskirts of Flagstaff, Arizona—the middle of nowhere—with no Wi-Fi signal. But he browsed sentimentally through the posts previously cached to his hard drive. These extended back to their first meeting mere days ago. Aside from the last post, which painfully reminded him of their blow-up, her plethora of other updates elicited a warm and happy smile from him. Despite repeated threats on his life (which cumulatively, no doubt, scored pretty high on the Holmes and Rahe scale of stressful life events), her companionship was a constant bright spot, a reprieve from the incessant barrage. Without her, he doubted he would have been as vigilant, fought back as hard, or gotten as far in his quest to stop Nicholas Young and his plan to end the world.

He marveled at the frequency of her Tweezer updates, and at how quickly her following had grown. As he browsed, he hovered on one of her many recent posts that he hadn't yet seen. It included a candid photo of him fast asleep in the hotel room in Sidewinder.

Given her stand about posting photos of other people only with permission, he was surprised to see himself, albeit unrecognizable, in her Tweezer feed. Yet he also felt privileged—and a little thrilled—to see himself included in this important aspect of her world.

More than ever, he felt determined to stop Nicholas Young, save the world, and show Destiny Jones that he was definitely *not* a dull boy.

The nozzle clicked off to indicate that the gas tank was full. Belanger returned the hose to the pump, sipped his coffee, then lumbered back to the driver's-side door. He had no time to waste, and a showdown to catch.

Destiny Jones slid shut the lock on the airplane's bathroom door and heaved a heavy sigh. She feared for her safety. She was worried about Belanger, and whether he was okay. But most of all, she was angry. Angry because Nicholas Young had given himself a first-class ticket, while she was stuck with Bruiser in the very back of economy class. Angry because up the aisle she could see Nicholas in the lap of luxury, playing charades with the executives and stewardesses. Angry because fucking Bruiser, with his leg cast, just *had* to have the aisle seat, leaving her in the middle next to some seedy guy in a plaid suit who wanted to sell her afterlife insurance. And angry because, while Nicholas knocked back glass after glass of complimentary champagne, she was unable to enjoy even a measly foil bag of fourteen salted and roasteds, because the notorious Hitchhiking Granny had a peanut allergy. For a legendary killer, Destiny mused, he sure was high maintenance.

When the light inside the cramped compartment brightened and the "occupied" graphic in the main cabin lit up, she relaxed just a little. Ironically, the most confined place in the plane was where she felt most free. It was the one place that neither Nicholas nor Bruiser could follow. This feeling was an illusion, of course. She was still trapped in the same aluminum hull hurtling through the sky at five hundred miles per hour: same as all the other passengers, except they were oblivious to the fact that the world was about to end. She relished the lie all the same and wanted to stay here as long as possible.

What to do with her freedom?

The obvious choice was to use the toilet. However, the floor of the bathroom was wet and she didn't want her shorts soaked with water—or whatever it was—when they fell to her ankles. So she lowered the garment halfway, parted her legs just enough to hold the shorts in place, and discovered that in this position she was unable to bend her knees to sit. So she pulled her bottoms back up, willing to hold it until her next freedom break.

Next she washed her hands. While drying them with paper towels, she draped one over her head like a puritan bonnet, looked in the mirror, and contemplated taking some selfies in the Flemish style. However, Nicholas had pocketed her phone. She was unable to post any self-portraits, much less do something useful such as warn Belanger or call for help.

Surely, she thought, she could do *something* proactive about her situation. Her expression brightened with inspiration. She reached into her purse, pulled out her cigarettes, and stuck one in her mouth. Smoking was forbidden in airplane lavatories, so if she set off the smoke detector she might be able to force an emergency landing. But rummage as she may through her purse, she was unable to locate her lighter. This made her angry: it was brand-new. So much for that plan. She returned the cigarette from whence it came.

Next she pulled a tube of lipstick from her purse. She began to write "I've been kidnapped" on the mirror, but then she recalled how easily Nicholas was able to get through airport security and board this plane. He would probably use the same trick on anyone who read the message. What's more, it would piss off Nicholas and there was no telling what punishment he might mete out. If sufficiently provoked, he might seriously hurt or even kill her...or someone else on the plane. With another paper towel, she wiped the mirror clean.

In that moment as she leaned toward the mirror, she recalled the clowns who had broken down the door to the hotel bathroom in Roswell. That moment seemed hopeless for them, yet Belanger bailed them out. Gazing intently at her reflection, Destiny took a deep breath and said, "Beetlejuice." She looked around, but nothing seemed to be happening. She stared into the mirror again. "Beetle-juice!" Still, nothing happened. She opened her mouth one more time, then thought about what actually happened in the movie. It probably wouldn't turn out well on an airplane.

Both her expression and shoulders dropped. She was out of ideas. For now. Surrendering the false freedom of solitary confinement, she headed back to her seat. She took small comfort in the irony that one of the in-flight movies was *This Is the End*.

CHAPTER
31

HAVING DRIVEN THROUGH THE NIGHT and into the late morning for twelve straight hours, Belanger felt like Kiefer Sutherland in the most boring season ever of *24*. Fatigue would do that to a person. But once he ended the US-93 leg of his journey and turned onto State Highway 375, the green road sign reading "Extraterrestrial Highway" made him feel like it was sweeps week. Its retro-futuristic white lettering read "Extraterrestrial" on one line and "Highway" on another. The second word, much shorter than the first, was flanked on the right by a white silhouette of the state of Nevada, the number 375 overprinted in black; on the left was the distinctive triangular silhouette, also in white, of a stealth fighter.

Along this stretch of arid road through sprawling deserts and ranches, Belanger spotted further confirmation that he was on the right track. A yellow diamond-shaped sign with a bull silhouette, warning of an open range area ahead, had been doctored to add an overhead UFO with the bovine captured in its tractor beam. Elsewhere, he spotted a rectangular sign that declared the speed limit to be Warp Seven. Finally, a brightly colored billboard read "Welcome to Rachel, Nev. Humans: 54. Aliens: ?" Rachel was the last outpost before Area 51, the last chance to fill one's tank or belly. As the sign indicated, the little town only claimed some fifty residents and four local businesses.

One of these was the Little A'Le'Inn.

A combination bar and motel, the Rachel Bar & Grill truck stop was rechristened the Little A'Le'Inn in 1990 after Bob Lazar famously claimed that he had worked on alien technology near Area 51. Lazar's claim promptly transformed the sleepy town of Rachel into the symbolic as well as physical epicenter of the UFO community. A pair of attention-grabbing events shortly thereafter cemented Rachel's place in pop culture history: In 1993, Rachel resident Glen Campbell—the other one, not the American country-music star—summarized the phenomenon in his *Area 51 Viewer's Guide* and revealed that the officially non-existent military base was clearly visible from Freedom Ridge, some twenty-five miles outside of town. Then in 1994, a television crew of fifty occupied the town, doubling its population, in order to broadcast CNN newsman Larry King's spectacular special *UFO Cover-Up: Live from Area 51*. These events made Area 51 a go-to destination in Nevada on par with the Vegas Strip and the Bunny Ranch. UFO enthusiasts and conspiracy theorists flocked to the tiny town in a seemingly endless stream. The inn, with its alien-themed t-shirts, coffee mugs, and other souvenirs, was the only local business that catered to these tourists. According to rumor, the bar was protected by Archibald, an alien that only the owner, Pat Travis, could feel or hear.

Housed in a nondescript double-wide that might have been a country store in another life, the Little A'Le'Inn identified itself with a roadside sign that read "Earthlings Welcome." In case someone missed that, there was the reassuring sight of a flying saucer dangling from the hook of a tow truck parked beside the sign. Near the bar's entrance was a time capsule, placed there by the makers of the film *Independence Day* as a testament to the inn's importance in popular culture.

Inside the building, Belanger noticed several tables and a long counter with barstools ready for diners. Customers occupied about a third of them. Meanwhile, a pool table in one corner and a souvenir area in another catered to visitors who preferred other diversions. The latter held the most promise for his mission parameters.

He walked up to the souvenir counter and asked, "Do you sell maps of Area 51?"

"We sure do," said Martina, a cheerful fortysomething woman with a ponytail and white Little A'Le'Inn t-shirt. "If you're interested, we can also set you up with a guided tour of the vicinity."

"No, thank you," he shook his head. "I want to go out there alone."

"Suit yourself. In the meantime, would you like to have a bite? It won't be dark for a while yet, and that's the best viewing."

"Just a coffee, please. I'll be heading right out. I…plan to meet someone there."

"Oh!" chimed in one of the diners seated nearby at the counter. Her expression became animated at the thought of a kindred spirit. She was in her early thirties with a long face and equally long black hair. She wore a button-down denim shirt and a pair of loose-fitting khakis. "Are you a repeat abductee, too? Phil here has been abducted thirteen times."

"Fourteen if you count the time they dropped me into a tree when their tractor beam lost power." Phil was easily twenty years older, yet too young for the severe male pattern baldness that afflicted him. If his friend's face was overly long, then Phil's was overly short, and it had a somewhat hourglass shape where his thick lenses and frames hugged his face. The ends of his moustache curled down and reached all the way to his jaw line. He wore a jacket over his red, black, and white flannel shirt and a well-worn pair of jeans. "While I was falling, the tree snagged my man purse and slowed me down a spell. Probably saved my life. But now my bag is stuck so high up in that tree that I can't get to it and retrieve my medical marijuana card."

"It's true. I saw it happen just the other night."

"Sure enough. But Tammy here has never been abducted. That's because she's an alien herself. Or so she says. Everyone around here knows it, too. Heck, she's even been interviewed in the *Times*."

Belanger raised an eyebrow, piqued. "The London *Times*?"

"Even better," Phil beamed proudly at their local celebrity. "The *Fortean Times*."

"He's right." Tammy stood to reveal the distinctive bump of a woman eight months pregnant. With a rub of her rounded belly through her maternity blouse, she whispered her secret. "It's an alien!"

"She thinks she's from Alpha Centauri," Phil stage-whispered to Belanger. "I think she's a little cuckoo."

"Yet you still listen to me. So who's the crazy one?"

Belanger remarked to the small crowd that gathered around him. "I'm just looking for the best route into Area 51."

A man who had been sitting quietly in the corner, sullenly smoking a long pipe, approached. He wore a dirty old green t-shirt, blue jeans, and a pair of well-worn, mud-caked cowboy boots. He had long, shaggy brown hair, beard, and moustache with hints of gray. Sparkling gray eyes stared from a face that one might describe as weather-beaten, but you should see how the weather looks. He grabbed a map from the counter, then pulled Belanger aside and led him back to the table in the corner. "You draw far too much attention to yourself, Mr. Undercover." He was a lawful good ranger. Either that, or a tour guide.

After they were both seated, the stranger leaned in close and spoke quietly. "So, you want to see Area 51. Dreamland. Homey Airport. Paradise Ranch. Watertown Strip." Disappointingly, in the course of the short walk from the souvenir counter to the table in the corner, this arid Aragorn had transformed into a used-car salesman. He unfolded the map on the table between them to reveal that only a few unpaved roads led to Area 51 and the restricted zone surrounding it. He looked Belanger in the eye and continued. "Area 51 is part of a larger top-secret military facility the size of Connecticut located eighty-three miles northwest of Las Vegas. Smack dab in the middle, on the southern shore of what used to be Groom Lake, is Area 51. It's a military base with a huge airfield: one of its seven runways is the longest in the world, and stretches across the entire dry lake bed. Some people believe that the site is used to test secret military aircraft and weapons. Others claim that the government uses the base to reverse-engineer alien UFO technology. For years, people have seen all kinds of things fly around the area. The base shows up on satellite pictures. It was even visible from nearby peaks. Until the government annexed them, too. Despite all the evidence to the contrary, the government officially denied the existence of Area 51 until 2013."

"Listen," Belanger said with some embarrassment, realizing that this must be how he sounded to Destiny. "I simply want to know how to get there." UFO folklore was outside his area of interest, and he just wanted to cut to the chase.

"It's easy." He pointed to a road on the map. "The back gate is closest to town, down Back Gate Road. Not much to see there, though. But if you continue down the ET Highway past Coyote Summit, you'll reach the famous Black Mailbox."

"Black Mailbox?"

"Yes, except it's white now. It hasn't been black since '96. The poor Medlins, it's their mailbox. They're a ranching family, and their house is six miles off of the ET Highway in the middle of nowhere. The post office won't deliver to their doorstep, so their mailbox is on 375. It's the only thing on that stretch of road for forty miles, so naturally the UFO folks decided it has to have something to do with Area 51. No one could tell them otherwise."

"It's ain't a mailbox," remarked one patron from a neighboring table, overhearing the conversation. "It's a space beacon."

"See what I mean?" He leaned in closer to Belanger and spoke in a quieter tone. "Folks started to open the Medlins' mail, thinking they'd find some classified documents. All they ever found, though, were bills and junk mail. Some numbskulls got so frustrated that they shot up the mailbox. So Steve Medlin swapped the black mailbox for a bulletproof white one. And for the tourists he put up a smaller box with a mail slot labeled 'Alien Drop Box.' Some folks stick in letters to their Space Brothers or Santa Claus or whatever. Others put in money as a thank you for letting them camp there while flying-saucer watching. The point is you can't miss it. Just look for all the UFO spotters camped out around it. None of these roads are marked, so you need to use the mailbox as a signpost for Mailbox Road. Like I said, it's the only thing on that stretch. Watch your speed, and keep an eye out for rabbits, coyotes, antelope, and cattle."

The guide pointed to the map again and continued. "Mailbox Road will take you to Groom Lake Road, which runs up to the main entrance. You can't really *go* to the main entrance of course, because the camo dudes will stop you before you get anywhere near."

"Camo dudes?"

"Yep," he nodded. "They're the security team that guards the outer perimeter of Area 51. They wear camouflage uniforms, drive white pick-up trucks, and monitor all the roads with high-powered binoculars and night scopes. Take one step past the posted warning signs, and they're on you like Nazgul on the One Ring. The land around the base for twenty-six miles has been annexed by the government. It's all restricted. You are technically trespassing on government property before you ever see the first warning signs, and at that point you're still thirteen miles from the base. There are security cameras, motion sensors, and vibration sensors on the road. The whole area is restricted airspace, and the government has F16 fighters to make sure it stays that way. While the folks who work there arrive by bus or plane every day, there's no way for regular folks to get any closer without clearance."

"Well," Belanger mused grimly, "I have to discover a way."

"Mister, I don't know what you're planning, but the camo dudes carry M16s and are authorized to kill trespassers on sight. That place is locked down tighter than Barad-dûr."

"They wouldn't be the first people to shoot at me this week."

His eyes widened at that admission. "Are you a secret agent?"

"No, sir. I'm a professor." With that, Belanger collected his coffee, paid for the map at the counter, and returned to his car.

During his drive down Extraterrestrial Highway toward Area 51, Belanger mused that it would be just like Nicholas, brazen as he is, to try to walk through the front gate. So Groom Lake Road it was. After a seemingly endless stretch of same-looking road, he finally reached the promised mailbox near mile marker 30. Stickers and graffiti covered its exterior, and someone had assembled a circle of white rocks on the patch of clear land beside the Black Mailbox.

The turn-off for Mailbox Road was indeed unmarked. The road itself was bumpy, and Belanger's tires threw up a cloud of dust that must have been visible for miles. The same was true after his right turn onto Groom Lake Road. Its dessicated route was marked only by desert grasses, shrubs, and cacti. Nothing else was visible except for the distant mountains that surrounded the area. Each mile was identical to the one before.

Then he saw it: a white sign with bright red letters that spelled WARNING. He had arrived.

Belanger brought his car to a halt just short of the sign. Putting the vehicle into park and turning off the engine, he emerged with a groan and considered the warning sign. Beneath those bright red letters up top, the smaller black print below read:

> RESTRICTED AREA.
> It is unlawful to enter this area without
> permission of the Installation Commander.
> Sec. 21, Internal Security Act of 1950; 50 U.S.C. 797.
> While on this Installation all personnel and
> the property under their control are subject
> to search.

If that was unclear, red letters at the bottom explained: *USE OF DEADLY FORCE AUTHORIZED.* That gave him pause to consider his next move. He could wait here for Nicholas. Or he could try getting closer. The question was whether the security team would permit either one.

Past the sign he noted several tall hills a couple of miles away. Even at this distance, through the clear desert air, he spotted a white Jeep Cherokee with blacked-out windows perched upon one of them. It was the camo guys, just as he had been warned. They were already aware of his presence, watching and waiting.

Back in the direction from whence he came, he saw a cloud of dust far in the distance. Another vehicle approached his position. *Wow, is this good timing or what?* he thought to himself. But was it Nicholas? Yet another assassin? Or more camo dudes? And how would he respond to each of these? Fortunately, he had time to think about it before the vehicle reached him. Belanger popped open the boot of his rental car, pulled out his newly purchased handgun, and stuck it into the belt area of his trousers. He had never fired a gun before and wasn't even sure if putting it there was smart. But he knew that it was now well past the time to be smart.

As the vehicle drew near, its silhouette became clearer. Belanger knew from its rectangular shape that it wasn't a car, but a delivery truck. And this prompted a deep sense of dread. After the clowns, pretty much anything could be hiding in there: a dancing and wrestling zombie bear, a machine gun-wielding kangaroo, or even two dozen Rockettes come to simultaneously high-kick him to death.

As the delivery truck finally approached and slowed to a halt, Belanger stepped behind the warning sign for cover. He held his breath and prepared for the worst.

A man in a purple uniform exited the truck with a package in his hands.

What's in the box? Belanger wondered.

The driver looked around, spotted Belanger, and walked in a decidedly unthreatening manner straight up to the sign. He offered the package. Belanger took it. Then the delivery person remarked, "I was told to deliver this box here this afternoon." Without another word, the delivery person returned to his truck, shifted it into drive, and headed back up the road.

Belanger looked quizzically at the parcel. *What's in the box?* It was a twelve-inch brown cardboard cube. On each of its sides was a red sticker which read "Please Handle with Care: FRAGILE." The shipping manifest taped to the lid indicated it was from Nicholas Young.

That fact filled Belanger with dread. Cautiously, he set the box on the ground and pulled out a pen knife. His hands were shaking. He was on the verge of panic. *WHAT'S IN THE BOX?!?* Kneeling beside the package, he carefully cut the packing tape on both edges of the top flaps and down the center through the delivery instructions. Then he folded back the top flaps. Wet spots darkened the two inner flaps. From its appearance and smell, he recognized immediately, "It's salsa."

He opened the two inner flaps. Then he peered inside the box. What he saw caused him to gasp involuntarily, and to bolt straight upright onto his feet with horror.

CHAPTER

32

PPREHENDING THE OFFENSIVE BOX which lay open at his feet, Niels Belanger immediately recognized its contents, dreadful and sickening. It had obviously been severed from its possessor after unimaginable suffering and sacrifice. There, nestled at the bottom of a bed of bubble wrap, he distinctly saw the body of a phone. And not just any phone. It was the smartphone of Destiny Jones. It was even now powered up to her last status update.

	Destiny Jones	5:27 am on February 28
	Ridesharing in a lunatic's trunk. What I wouldn't give for a breakfast burrito.	
	+61 ♥ ✎ Followers: 8,398 ⊕ Albuquerque, NM	

This confirmed his worst fear: that Nicholas Young had in fact taken Destiny captive. And worse, he had taken her phone. Belanger stared at the screen in abject dismay.

He was startled when the phone unexpectedly began playing Ministry's "Everyday Is Halloween," and the screen reported an "Incoming Call." With great trepidation, Belanger reached into the box, gingerly retrieved the telephone, and pushed the talk button.

When he did, the smug grin of Nicholas Young appeared on the screen in real-time video chat.

"Hey hey, doc," Nicholas quipped. "It looks like John Doe has the upper hand!"

"You bastard!" Belanger wasted no time unleashing his fury. "If you've harmed Destiny at all, I swear I will hunt you down."

"Oh snap, check out the new Mother Superior. I'm shaking in my crocs!"

"I'm fine, Niels," her voice reassured from off-screen.

"For now," Nicholas warned through gritted teeth, his eyes shifted sternly sideways—no doubt toward Destiny—with a dire, unspoken reprimand.

"Where are you, you ruddy tosser?" Belanger insisted. "I'm waiting for you. Why aren't you here?"

"There?" he laughed. "In the desert a metric fuckton of miles away from civilization?"

"Yes. You said it was important to your plans."

"Right on, true dat. But it was never my plan to actually *go* there."

Belanger's anger yielded to the suddenly more pressing and nauseating feeling that he had been had; that he just spent the last thirteen hours chasing a lie. "But we thought…"

"Turns out you were harder to kill than I expected for some doughy professor. Once I realized that you were tailing me, I thought it would be fun to jerk you around and lead you on a snipe hunt. After Bruiser's run-in with Ms. Jones, her constant status updates made it easy to keep one step ahead of you the whole time. And bonus: I sent you on a wild goose chase into the desert out in the middle of fuck-ing nowhere."

All this time, Belanger had considered Nicholas a dummy, an underachiever, an intellectual child (albeit an evil one). The professor was humiliated that such a person had bested him. "Why?" His voice was the plea of a man defeated, his plans hopelessly scuppered.

"To get rid of you while I went to my real destination."

"So you were never going to Area 51. This whole chase was a diversion." These weren't questions so much as Belanger coming to terms with the bitter truth.

"That's pretty much the definition of 'wild goose chase,' doc. But it wasn't just a diversion. It also provided me with an ass-load of entertainment."

"So while I'm here in Nevada…"

"I'm on the opposite side of the world in Geneva: *way* too far away for you to do thing one about it."

That was the last place on the list of places he expected Nicholas to be, right after "library." "What is in Geneva that's so important to you?"

With grim seriousness, he answered, "Cern. And the Large Hadron Collider."

This puzzled Belanger even more. "I've seen your grades, Nicholas. I know you're not there to do a science experiment."

"No, you dumbass. I'm going to use the lhc to create a black hole to swallow the world."

Belanger rolled his eyes. "That's scientifically impossible!"

"No, it's true," Destiny interjected, again from off-screen. "A bunch of folks back in New York have told me their friend knows a physicist who says it could totally happen."

Nicholas shrugged. "See? It *is* possible."

"But," Belanger argued, "the collider has been operating without incident for years. Why should today be any different?"

"Because *I'm* here. And so is Destiny Jones."

Belanger realized that "impossible" meant nothing in the face of overwhelming popular consensus. This was especially true where either Nicholas or Destiny was involved. Put them together and *anything* was possible. "My God," he gasped. "You're seriously going to do it!"

Nicholas corroborated that statement with a nod of his head. "Yes, yes I am. Any minute now, in fact. Roll credits. Buh-bye, Doctor B. You should've just given me that A."

With that, the screen went blank. Call ended.

Despair, defeat, fear, anger, stress, and exhaustion all mixed in his bloodstream in a sanguinary cocktail of hormones that left his head reeling. He was caught completely unprepared when, an instant after the call ended, someone grabbed him roughly and forced him to his knees. "Down on the ground!" a voice commanded.

Belanger was only vaguely aware of the sound of several rifles clicking, and the barked command to "Put your hands on your head!" In a dream-like state, he complied. His jacket and shirt rode up his torso, and his bare midriff felt the desert air.

"He has a gun!" another voice shouted. Further weapon sounds immediately followed, along with a deep voice like a drill sergeant that warned him, "Move even a finger, and you're a dead man!" Belanger felt a tug at his waistline, which he understood was the pistol being pulled from his pants.

In that swirl of emotions and impressions, Belanger flashed back to his impromptu Tarot card reading from Bree, which now felt like a lifetime ago. "A magician changes the world through sheer will-power," she had explained to him, "bending the universe into line with his intentions." *What a load of New-Age bollocks.* "If the monkey refuses to let go, he's trapped by his own greed." *I must be a very naughty monkey indeed.* "Don't get trapped by the illusion." *In fact, I've successfully done the exact opposite and now couldn't possibly be any more trapped.*

His brain finally assembled these discrete pieces of information into the awareness that things had just gotten about as bad as they possibly could. Looking around, Belanger saw four security personnel in camouflage uniforms beneath their body armor. One scowled at him and shouted orders into a walkie-talkie. The other three trained their rifles on him at point-blank range, itching for any excuse to use authorized force to kill him.

A magician changes the world through sheer willpower, bending the universe into line with his intentions.

From his knees, hands cooperatively behind his head, Belanger peered up the length of the M16 gun barrels, looked the guards earnestly in the eyes, and told them, "You need to do exactly as I say."

CHAPTER
33

THE LARGE HADRON COLLIDER is the world's largest high-energy particle collider. It was built by CERN (the European Organization for Nuclear Research, whose acronym is formed by arranging the initial letters by their atomic weights) in collaboration with eighty-five countries and hundreds of universities with more than ten thousand scientists whose names use hundreds of thousands of characters and whose CVs list terabytes' worth of papers. Completed in 2008—or 22.41 x 10^5 in years Kelvin—its initial launch was delayed after a scientist accidentally spilled his cola on the reactor console. The system finally became operational in November 2009.

Hadrons are particles such as protons and neutrons whose constituent quarks are bound together by the strong force. The by-products of high-energy collisions between these particles help physicists to answer fundamental questions. With the LHC, hopes were pinned on such posers as: confirming the existence of the Higgs Boson particle, which accounts for mass in the universe; reconciling General Relativity with the Standard Model into a Theory of Everything; and identifying the breed of Schrödinger's cat.

Passing through building security using the very same mind trick that got them through the airport, Nicholas Young entered the LHC's control room with Bruiser and Destiny in tow. He took a good look at the open office area filled with fluorescent lights, ergonomic desks, high-backed rolling chairs, telephones, and a computer monitor-to-scientist ratio that was an affront to developing nations everywhere. If one managed to miss the huge sign on the building that read "CERN CONTROL CENTRE," one might think this was a telemarketing company. That no such activity took place here was evident from the fact—obvious to all—that the room was laid out like a quadrupolar magnet. Four horseshoe-shaped consoles with matching curved outer walls, each seating about thirteen operators, opened onto a common area in the center of the room. Each of these semicircles also contained a small round four-seater table in the center for impromptu subgroup meetings, lunch breaks, or watching the latest cat videos on someone's phone. Large flat-panel monitors dotted three of the four blue-gray walls; the fourth wall overlooked the CERN grounds and featured a series of tall, narrow, floor-to-ceiling windows interspersed with equal-sized wall panels, whose combined effect approximated the look of a sideways sheet of tractor-feed computer paper with green bars. The hum of activity—keyboards clacking, papers rustling, and colleagues speaking—filled the air with a background of sound somewhere between a susurrus and a low rumble.

His survey of the room and its activity completed, Nicholas pulled out his pistol, pointed it at the ceiling, and fired. Destiny, standing beside him, cringed at the loud and unexpected bang. Bruiser grinned mindlessly. The room fell still and silent.

"At minimum," Nicholas bellowed commandingly, "how many people does it take to operate this thing?"

An intern who stood nearby with a stack of photocopies nervously answered, "Two, really: a physicist and a technical engineer."

Nicholas nodded and announced, "In that case, I need four operators to stay here. The rest of you, into the conference room. *Now!* There's plenty of coffee and donuts from this morning. No cell phones."

Located near the border of Switzerland and France, the scientists remained neutral and surrendered. They saved their work, locked their computers, set down their projects, and filed into the conference room like photons at the start of a double-slit experiment. Bruiser stood at the doorway to collect their cell phones and wave them through like a cop directing traffic with a gun in his hand. Once all were inside, he closed the door and locked it. Then he hobbled back to his boss.

Nicholas turned to his group of four volunteers and asked, "So, who have we here?" He looked at their PIV badges and sized them up. The two technical engineers consisted of Saraswati Banerjee, dressed in a long blue skirt, cyan and white striped blouse, and a peacock print hijab; and Kan Ji Hee, who looked every bit the engineer in his dress slacks, short-sleeved white dress shirt, black tie, and pocket protector. That left two physicists. Angus MacGregor, with his white hair and bushy eyebrows, was by far the most senior of the pack. Beata Puškarić, meanwhile, was a dark-eyed, bespectacled Croatian in her late twenties.

Without warning, Nicholas turned to the Scotsman and fired two shots into his abdomen. One of the others screamed. As the scientist collapsed on the floor, he groaned in a thick brogue, "Erg, I'm dyne!"

Nicholas calmly replaced the gun in his jacket holster and glowered at the three aghast scientists. Beata wept, despite her best efforts to remain silent. "If you fail to cooperate," he addressed Kan Ji Hee, "that is what will happen to you, and I will replace you with Ms. Banerjee. Got it?"

They were too stunned to reply.

"GOT IT?!?"

This time they all nodded.

"Super," Nicholas replied. "Now crank this bitch up as fast as it will go."

Kan Ji Hee and Beata Puškarić promptly scampered over to two nearby workstations, logged on, and began clacking away. As they did, they communicated in their peculiar technical language.

"The LHC beam event is going online."

"Starting collision sequence in five, four, three…"

"Magnets are fully operational."

"Prepare to inject protons."

"Proton movement confirmed."

While this technobabble was underway, Destiny fixed Nicholas with an incredulous, mortified expression. "You didn't have to shoot that guy!"

Her objection meant nothing, and he responded dismissively, "Actions speak louder than words."

"And thinking is a lot quieter." She tapped the sides of her temples for emphasis.

"*Everyone* is about to die. It doesn't matter who goes first."

"Why didn't you just use the mind trick?"

Nicholas rolled his eyes wearily. "You seriously haven't pieced this together yet, have you? You monkeys really are incredibly stupid. Isn't it obvious?"

Destiny shook her head.

"Haven't you learned anything from all those movies you've watched? I'm *evil*. I mean, look at how Aryan I am. Blond hair, blue eyes, tall…incredibly handsome. It's a rule in movies that the blonder the hair, the more evil you are. Am I right?"

She wondered if this was a trick question, so she hesitated before answering, "I guess."

"'You guess'? Oh, come on, Miss Film Student! Joffrey Baratheon is one blond son-of-a-bitch. How about Draco Malfoy? Blond. Feyd in *Dune*, Roy Batty in *Bladerunner*, Calvin Candie in *Django Unchained*: blond, blond, blond," he counted them off on his fingers. "Let's face it: if you're in a movie and you're Aryan-looking, you may as well be Hitler."

"Okay, okay, that *is* a thing. But wouldn't it be easier to just dye your hair? I mean, my hair isn't naturally raven black."

He looked at her askance. "So what you're saying is that the curtains don't match the carpet?"

"No. But who shoots someone who's helping them?"

He rolled his eyes again. "Do I need to connect all the dots for you?"

Her expression indicated that he indeed needed to.

He started with an easy one. "All right, what's my name?"

"Nicholas Young."

"Riiiight. So if I'm Nicholas the second, then that makes my father…?"

She didn't get it.

"How about Nicholas the Elder," he offered.

She shook her head blankly.

"Old Nick?"

"Are you talking about the men's deodorant?"

"No!" he shouted, exasperated. "I'm speaking of the devil." He really should have gone with Daimon Hellstorm.

"I'm so with you, dude. I hate my parents too."

"I mean he is *literally* the devil."

"For 'literally,' are you using the pre- or post-2013 Cambridge dictionary definition?"

"I mean that my father is Satan. The Great Adversary. The Prince of Darkness. Mephistopheles. The King of Hell. I am the devil's son."

"No shit? Why are you *here*?"

"It was sort of a spur-of-the-moment decision. Three years ago circumstances that I don't entirely understand opened a portal to your world. The fam was sitting around listening to dad get plastered and bitch about his falling out with God…for like the billionth time. *Literally.* So when I saw that portal, I thought to myself, 'Fuck this noise, I'm out of here.'"

"And what?" she reasoned. "You found out that the grass isn't always greener so now you're going to scorch the lawn?"

"It's like this: According to the book of Revelation, Heaven has a sign from the fire marshal that says 'MAXIMUM OCCUPANCY: 144,000.' That's out of everyone who has *ever* lived in the past two thousand years. Think about it. There are seven billion people in the world *right now*. If only 144,000 get into heaven, then that means only one person out of every fifty thousand has a golden ticket. When this world disappears, the rest of those seven billion—and all their ancestors—will be crashing on my daddy's sofa. He will have a virtual monopoly on all the souls throughout history."

"So this is all about you trying to win daddy's love?"

"Daddy's love?" he spat. "Fuck that, yo! I just want him to have someone else to uncork on with his drunken tirades. My uncles— folks like Beelzebub, Mammon, and Leviathan—were all very excited by a new addition to the royal family, someone in line for the crown; but what they were *most* happy about was not having to listen to their God damned brother's war stories any more. Do you have any idea what it's like to be the devil's son? The heir to Hell? Do you have any idea what it's like trying to live up to all the expectations?"

She shook her head.

"I came to Earth to get away from all the pressure, to make a fresh start. But you monkeys have built up an image of me that is larger than life, larger than *any* myth. I mean, there's an entire movie trilogy about me. Except I don't really have a 666 birthmark on the back of my head. And with my grades, there's no way I'll ever make it in politics. Oh, and did I mention that when dogs see me, they just want to bite me? Bastards. And how about *Rosemary's Baby*? My mom ain't no Mia Farrow, let me tell ya! Meanwhile, computer geeks think my daddy is Bill Gates because his name in ASCII adds up to 666. I *wish* my dad had as much money as Bill Gates! Do you know that there's even a superhero called Son of Satan? That's right, I'm the star of a fucking comic book. In the comics, I carry a magic pitchfork and fight crime by shooting hellfire from my hands. Chuh, in my dreams!

"How can I possibly top any of that? Or even live up to it? No matter what I do—either here or in the underworld—I will fall far short of what people expect of me. I just can't win. And I can't die. So the only solution is to destroy the world."

"I get it," Destiny finally understood. "The bar has been set so high that you can't possibly meet it."

Nicholas wrinkled his nose. "Not like I even *want* to." He affected a poor imitation of a feminine voice and continued, "'*As if I cared what the homecoming queen thinks.*' Am I right?"

The sound of her own words from a private conversation with Belanger, now repeated back to her by Nicholas, was very disquieting. Then she reminded herself, *Oh, that's right, he's a* supernatural *douchebag.* Nevertheless she felt a modicum of sympathy for him, even though his coping mechanisms were no brain, no sane. "Yeah, but I didn't try to blow up my entire high school," she reasoned. "Instead of living up to other people's expectations, I just ignored them and did what I wanted to. Maybe you should do the same." He didn't reject the idea, so she kept talking. Maybe if she got him onto a more positive topic, she could talk him down. "So, what *would* you rather do instead?"

"No one's ever asked me that before." His expression and words waxed chimerical at the question and all its possibilities. "I don't really get much time for it, but do you know what I really enjoy doing?"

"What?"

"Cooking."

"No way."

"Way. It's so *creatio ex nihilo*. Give me the simplest ingredients and in a few minutes I'm like 'Fiat lunch!'"

"All right. See? That's something."

He nodded. "I would have totally aced my cooking classes even if my roommates *didn't* commit suicide."

"Maybe you can open a restaurant." *Good*, Destiny told herself. *Keep him talking about happy things.* "Um…what kind of stuff do you like to cook?"

"Anything, really. But I *love* spicy food, especially chili peppers. I have yet to find something that's too hot for me." Suddenly he put out his index finger as if the gesture allowed him to hold that thought. "Ooh, I know."

"What?"

"I would kill to market my own line of spicy condiments."

There you go. Keep it light; talk him down off the ledge. "Oh, you mean like Diablo sauce." She chuckled and slapped her knee.

With that invocation of his accursed father, Nicholas Young's expression changed from playful to furious. Whenever he found *anything* that was exciting, cool, or edgy, Satan was always there first. "*Nooooo!*" He shoved Destiny away, lunged toward the scientists, and pushed the Big Red Button.

The Large Hadron Collider sprang to life, and protons began the process of accelerating toward its twenty-seven-kilometer tunnel. Deep in the bowels of the reactor, hydrogen fed into the Linac 2, or linear accelerator, which stripped the atoms of their electrons and passed the nuclei through an electric field. This accelerated the hydrogen protons to one-third the speed of light and sent them into a successively larger series of rings for additional acceleration: The booster sped them up to nearly the speed of light. Because these protons moved so close to that physical maximum, the energy added to them in the subsequent proton synchrotron—and then in the following *super* proton synchrotron—simply increased their mass until it was seven thousand times greater than their resting state, making these particles ideal to hurl at each other head-on. Only then were they introduced into the collider proper. Here, thirteen thousand amps of current cryogenically cooled nine and a half thousand magnets along the route to nearly absolute zero. These now-superconductive magnets directed the protons and added extra energy to them until they were circulating the twenty-seven-kilometer tunnel eleven thousand times per second. Finally, they were diverted into the detection chamber, where two proton streams crossed and collided with a stream of particles going just as fast but in the opposite direction. This simulated, as much as physically possible, the particles produced at the moment of the Big Bang. At these speeds, collisions occurred extremely quickly, on the order of six hundred million mini Big Bangs each and every second.

When these protons collided at near light speed, they generated and focused enough trans-Planckian energy at their collision points for gravity to leak in from the four-dimensional branes that existed alongside our own universe. In other words, these pinholes in space-time allowed gravity to seep in from parallel universes and collect into miniscule gravity pools. These formed microscopic tidal black holes that evaporated almost instantly. As the collider continued to produce six hundred million collisions per second, more and more of these micro holes poofed in and out of existence until the Law of Large Numbers took hold. The odds of a stable black hole occurring were approximately equal to the spontaneous appearance of a sentient catfish reciting haikus.

> *Higgs Boson in church,*
> *Told to leave, says "Without me*
> *You cannot have Mass."*

Fortunately, just as Nicholas Young had hoped, he lucked out and was spared a painful and unwelcome poetry reading. After enough of these tidal black holes expired, a quantum improbability resulted in a single stable black hole. Rather than consuming an infinitesimal 10^{-22} kilograms of mass in its blink-of-an-eye lifespan, this one survived and began to consume additional subatomic particles created by the billions of collisions around it, thus growing gradually larger. Soon it moved on to the hadrons, until it eventually swelled to a size where it began to draw atoms and molecules from the chamber itself.

This was but the start of its omnivorous lifecycle. Eventually the collision detector began to collapse upon itself, unable to support its own weight due to the immense gravitational pull within its heart. In the end it crumpled like a ball of paper, only to vanish thereafter into a dark spot of nothingness. Then the tubes that carried the protons started to get drawn in like giant straws. And because all this was located more than five hundred feet under the earth, when the man-made structures housing all this technology finally crumbled, the black hole began to suck up the soil and rock that up to that point shielded the countryside from any radiation generated by the LHC's activities.

Before long, wide swaths of land around the black hole gave way and shifted as adjacent parcels began to slide toward the event horizon of the world's largest sink-hole. Black holes are invisible—their gravity traps everything including light—but even at several miles' distance, gravitational lensing around the event horizon of this one caused the countryside to appear unnaturally warped. The phenomenon's devastating effect on the surrounding countryside was obvious: trees fell over, mountains collapsed, and the building itself slid slowly toward the center of the carnage. The control room occupied by Nicholas, Destiny, and the others began to tremble, rotate, crack, and buckle as it came under the influence of the voracious creation.

Nicholas grinned broadly, his wild-eyed gaze transfixed by the sight of his creation, a destructive force beyond reckoning. He had no idea that the end of the world would be this…beautiful. It was only a matter of time before the black hole grew large enough to swallow the entire planet, and then the solar system. Nicholas laughed triumphantly, even excitedly, at seeing his plan come to fruition.

The roof and wall of the complex collapsed. Bricks and drywall rained throughout the room. They assumed at first that this was yet more devastation due to the black hole, but it soon became clear from the gaping hole in the command center's wall that the damage was in fact caused by a huge flying saucer crashing into the building near Nicholas and Destiny's location. The spacecraft was a classic silvery saucer shape, thin along its equator until it rose into domes both above and below the center of the disc. Three latticed legs with large rounded pads on the ends extended from the bottom to provide a level landing position for the vehicle. The saucer was so large that only half of it occupied the once-spacious control room; the back half extended into the grounds outside the laboratory.

A whirring noise escaped the craft, and a thin ramp slowly descended from its underside. Despite its slight appearance, the gangway contacted the ground with a resounding thud that testified to how substantial and heavy just this one portion of the craft really was. Once the plank deployed, brilliant light radiated from the underside of the craft at the top of the plank and refracted off the dust that hung in the air from the saucer's spectacular entry. Its door began to open.

A silhouette appeared at the top of the ramp. Its height was difficult to judge because of the size of the vehicle, its unfamiliarity, and all the dust swirling in the light. However, its general shape was definitely humanoid. Aside from its torso, with two arms and two legs right where you'd expect them, this body supported an oversized head whose cranium was wider at the top and narrowed closer to the jaw. The more it descended, the grayish silver color of its skin became clear, as did its large black eyes and distinctive lack of a mouth.

"Satan on a Saltine, it's an alien!" Nicholas Young exclaimed in awe. In fact, it was the classic gray alien of countless conspiracy theories and junk documentaries. Had Simon and Wesley from the sporting-goods department been here, they would have pointed out that its technical classification was Zeta Reticulan.

Reaching the bottom of the ramp, the alien faced Nicholas and company and held up its right hand. It splayed its five fingers, keeping the index and middle fingers together, as well as keeping the pinky and ring finger together. This W shape was the distinctive and familiar gang sign of the Vulcans. Although the entity had no lips to move, Nicholas, Destiny, and Bruiser distinctly heard the words "May the Force be with you." It was as if this creature communicated telepathically.

"Holy crap," Bruiser panicked. "The alien's inside my head!!!"

Next, it held the palms of both hands to either side of its cheeks.

"Wait a minute," Destiny whispered to Nicholas, "is he doing Münch's *The Scream*? You're up, dude. I think they communicate through charades."

The alien pushed up on its head. Destiny and Nicholas both widened their eyes with horrified disbelief when the head began to separate and lift away from its shoulders. This was clearly no game of charades. It was more like a psychedelic trip gone horribly wrong.

As if they weren't startled enough by this close encounter—of the third kind, Bloecher subtype B, as Simon and Wesley would have pointed out—the distended head popped clean off to reveal in its place a familiar face: shaggy black hair, plastic-framed eyeglasses, and a toothy grin that revealed non-American standards of dental aesthetics. The big-eyed gray alien head was actually a helmet. And the alien wasn't naked, he was wearing a high-tech gray space suit.

"Niels!" Destiny cried out at the sight of his face. She attempted to run to him, but Nicholas restrained her.

At that moment, the floor between Belanger and the rest of them cracked and sagged. Then it broke off and dropped into a deep pit that was remarkable for its darkness. A strong breeze swept through the room, as if a vent were drawing air into a fan in the ground. With the floor between the opponents vanished into a chasm too wide for a doughy professor to leap across, Nicholas released Destiny. There was nowhere for her, or anyone else, to go except into the event horizon.

"You're too late, Doctor Belanger!" Nicholas gloated. "The reaction has already begun. There's no stopping the black hole now!"

Bruiser peered into the voracious darkness swirling below them. "I hope dis is over soon, 'cause I'd like to grab a burger before my blood sugar crashes. I got hypoglycemia, ya know."

Destiny stared at him incredulously. "Bruiser, you realize that when this is done, there will be no more hamburgers. In fact, there will be no more people for you to kill. There will be no more *you*."

Bruiser glanced at Nicholas, his eyes pleading for a response because he was unsure if Destiny had just told a horrible lie, or if his boss had grievously betrayed him. "B-but what about my sundress?"

Nicholas reached over to Bruiser, grabbed both his shoulders, and looked him squarely in the eyes. "You can wear your sundress IN HELL!" While those words rang in Bruiser's ears, Nicholas shoved him away. Already unstable on his crutches, Bruiser toppled into the chasm and, with an inaudible pop, blinked out of existence.

Before Nicholas knew it, Destiny was shouting in his face, "What is your zero-day bug? I have no love lost for Bruiser, but he was your friend!"

Nicholas shrugged. "He was more like a pet goldfish, really."

"*That's* how you treat a pet?"

"What? It's better than how I treat people."

"I'd hate to see how you treat your enemies."

Taking that remark as an invitation, Nicholas grabbed Destiny's arm, reached across his body with his free hand, and pulled out his pistol. He held it to her head and locked eyes with her. Belanger watched helplessly across the chasm as Nicholas released the safety and pressed the gun barrel even harder into her temple. "Allow me to demonstrate." He squeezed the trigger halfway.

And he just stared deeply into her eyes.

Frightened, angry, and fierce, Destiny glared back and waited for him to do something. "Well? What are you waiting for?!? I'm not about to be intimidated by an immature man-cunt like you, and I'm sure as hell not afraid to leave this screwed-up, backwater hate-fest of a world."

Nicholas smiled, let her go, and threw his gun into the black hole. Then he turned his back on her as if to indicate that her existence wasn't even worth acknowledging. "You *do* remind me of my sister," he sighed.

"Hah!" she exclaimed triumphantly. "I knew it: You can't bring yourself to kill me."

"Oh, sure I can," he responded with disturbing coldness in his voice. "But rather than kill you quickly, I'd rather see you suffer for all eternity as your atoms are slowly torn apart across the event horizon of this black hole." He didn't even bother to face her as he spoke. He simply stared into the growing black abyss under his feet. Finally he turned his gaze to Belanger. "Soon, everyone and everything will be sucked in. Game over."

Belanger reached into his suit with his right hand to pull something out. Was the professor packing? Nicholas tensed, glanced at the black hole, and cursed himself for throwing away his gun in a bodacious but reckless gesture of superiority. He also started to have buyer's remorse about killing Bruiser. Maybe he shouldn't have done that either. Bruiser also had a gun.

Even across the pit, Destiny recognized that what Belanger pulled out and held up was her smartphone. He looked at her and winked. She beamed a smile which indicated that, despite their argument, all was forgiven. His hand dropped to his side then swung upward to release the phone in an underhanded pitch. It flew in a perfect arc over the rift and into Destiny's waiting hands.

She looked at the screen and saw that it was powered up to her Tweezer app. Then her eyes popped. Her jaw fell open.

	Destiny Jones	5:27 am on February 28
	Ridesharing in a lunatic's trunk. What I wouldn't give for a breakfast burrito.	
	+897 ♥ .·˙ Followers: 1,239,841,930 ⊕Albuquerque, NM	

She had over a billion followers. 1,239,841,930 to be exact. She looked back at Belanger with a mix of curiosity and incredulity.

"Alien technology," he called across the increasing racket of the room's slow but inexorable collapse. "Everyone on the Internet is now subscribed to you. You know what to do."

Nicholas watched, puzzled, as Destiny began furiously thumb-typing on her phone. *Why would she bother to post about the end of the world?*

She clicked "send."

Tweezer®

Destiny Jones   7:30 pm on February 28

Black holes in a particle accelerator: *SRSLY?*
What a stupid douche.

+1028 ♥ 🖊 Followers: 1,239,841,930 🌐 Meyrin, CH

People around the world immediately began to plus her post. With each plus, even more people saw the post in their feeds. It broke one thousand likes in seconds. And it kept going. Destiny balled her fingers into a fist and drew her elbow to her side. "Yes!"

Then they heard pops and fizzes from deep in the earth below. This was unusual, since sound cannot escape the gravitational pull of a black hole. Nevertheless, as they watched, arcs of electric blue light broke across the surface of the atramentous orb. This despite the fact that not even light can escape a black hole's event horizon. At that moment, Nicholas Young's experiment ceased to pass the duck test: it no longer looked nor quacked like a black hole. The phenomenon was dissipating, the reaction failing.

Destiny began to type again. Before she hit "send," she called across the chasm, "Hey Niels, how's this one: 'American couple puts son of Satan over their knee for a spanking'?"

Belanger's gleeful expression of victory transformed into something more serious and hopeful. *Couple?*

Nicholas's expression, meanwhile, changed from confusion to despair. His victory was evaporating in a cloud of disbelief. What would be left for him then? The smug superiority of Niels Belanger. The incessant gabbling of Destiny Jones. And condescending looks of disapproval from Al Pacino, Robert DeNiro, Jack Nicholson, Viggo Mortensen, Tim Curry, and Elizabeth Hurley, all of whom not only did a better job than he did of being Satanic, but they made it look easy.

"Noooo!" he cried out. He dove over the once-crumbling floor and into the dissipated remains of the black hole, where he vanished into its stygian darkness. Then the whole thing popped out of existence and released a loud and powerful whoosh of air into the devastated control room. It was as if all the air, light, and debris that the black hole had sucked out of the room suddenly escaped and rushed back in, blowing Belanger and Destiny's hair back and forcing their eyes shut. When it ended just as suddenly, they opened their eyes and saw that the room had returned to its original state. Except for the giant UFO that had crashed through the wall.

With the abyss between them gone, Destiny ran over to Belanger and threw her arms tightly around him. The hug was equal parts victory and good-to-see-you. Then she stepped back, looking him over, head to toe in his alien suit. "Wow. You sure are one scrawny dork!"

"Yes, the suit is very…slimming."

"It doesn't leave much to the imagination. Going commando was a very daring choice."

"The suit requires it. Thank you for not pointing and laughing at my camel toe."

Looking closer at his face, she checked out the bandages on his brow and nose. "And what happened to your face?"

"Long story," he said. "But you should see the other…um…gal."

"Wait. You got your ass kicked by a girl? You are such a nerd."

"Hey, she was a pretty tough bird!" he objected. "Also, I nicked your lighter. I owe you a new one."

Destiny shook her head and laughed. "Nah, it's time I quit anyway. Those things'll kill you."

"I think we've had enough of things trying to kill us. At least for this week."

She looked over to where the saucer rested on the rubble of the control center's wall. "Nice parking job there, slick. I didn't know you could fly one of those things."

Belanger put his arm around her shoulder and began to lead her back to the craft. "Oh, I can't. But let me introduce you to my new mates: Ping and Vroom." At the top of the ramp, two silhouettes with big heads waited and waved at them. "At least that's what I call them. We are physiologically incapable of pronouncing their real names. Not without surgically adding a second tongue, splitting open the hard palate, and years of speech therapy. I prefer Ping and Vroom, don't you?"

She held up her thumb to indicate her agreement. "Are they bona fide aliens?"

Belanger nodded his head. "Let's just say they've had their 'little green cards' since 1947."

"That's even older than you!"

"Very funny. Their species is long-lived. Fortunately they don't have television on their homeworld, so that's helped them pass the time here."

"And their heads are just helmets, too?"

"Aye. That's why in all the alien encounter stories, their lips never move when they speak."

"So they aren't really telepathic. Makes sense. So what do they really look like?"

"Just like Cornelius in *Escape from the Planet of the Apes*."

"Oh, they do not!" She poked him in the ribs. They were an easy target since his arm was around her shoulder. She made no attempt to pull away, however. "I'll bet they look like your mom."

Belanger dropped his head and looked at her professorially over his glasses. "Are you seriously telling me that 'yo mama' jokes made it into English 2.0?"

"No," she giggled, "just your mom."

As they finally reached the top of the ramp where Ping and Vroom waited, one of them raised his hands to his head and pushed up to remove his helmet. Destiny burst out laughing.

"Hey now," Belanger chided, "that isn't very nice!"

The ramp retracted back into the hull of the saucer, which then rose into the air and sped away faster than possible for any man-made craft.

Meanwhile back at the control center, Saraswati Banerjee, Kan Ji Hee, and Beata Puškarić released their colleagues from the conference room in which they had been locked. And in the nick of time, too, as they had just run out of donuts and coffee. The two senior scientists on the team walked carefully across the debris field to the gaping hole in their building to assess the damage.

One of them was a boyishly handsome British man, clean-shaven with brown eyes, bangs, and collar-length hair. His plain black t-shirt, black blazer, and blue jeans seemed far too casual for his obviously senior position. Yet there he stood, his full lips downturned as he sighed at the wreckage left behind by the rescue team. "Looks like we need to invoke Protocol ID 10-T. *Again.*"

His African-American colleague nodded in assent. He was the more distinguished of the two: about a decade older, with closely trimmed hair and moustache, and a tailored suit. The only detail that detracted from his formal appearance was a brightly colored necktie that depicted the planets of the solar system. "Right," he said with the distinct round tones of an east coast American. "I'll send out a fake press release saying that we're shutting down the LHC again to do more 'upgrades.'"

34

T HE SAUCER FLIGHT back from Geneva was more leisurely than the breakneck airdash there. Much to Destiny's disappointment, she did not require one of the gray suits that protected passengers from the excessive g-forces produced by high rates of acceleration. Nevertheless, the pilots humored her and allowed her to try one on. They also took a photograph of her and Belanger (with his helmet) to post online. Having arrived here before 1980, they were, after all, the friendly type of alien.

The photo reminded Destiny how glad she was that, in space, no one can hear you break FAA regulations about in-flight smoking.

With Tweezer, she asked the aliens to restore her account to its original base of followers. She wanted to build that list honestly. Besides, access to a billion monkeys was just too much power. In the short time since her recent high-profile posts, she picked up a large cadre of new followers, along with three marriage proposals, several hundred pieces of Internet porn, and a thousand lolcats.

As for Nicholas Young, the aliens explained that he was a trans-dimensional entity impervious to destruction. His quantum state impinged simultaneously on all of the Many Worlds possible. Thus, when the black hole back at CERN absorbed him, it dispersed his energy into alternate timelines. "In a universe of Many Worlds," Belanger asked as an armchair cosmologist, "wouldn't that mean that in some of them Nicholas actually successfully destroys the world? In fact, if there's an infinite number of other worlds, wouldn't it mean mathematically that Nicholas succeeds an infinite number of times?" Wisely, the aliens resisted the Kobayashi Maru of explaining to a liberal arts professor who was never very good at maths the fine points of Georg Cantor's proofs about cardinality and infinities of different sizes. Instead, they simply assured him that no matter how many worlds there were, the probability of Nicholas successfully destroying *any* of them was less than that of a catfish becoming sentient and reciting poetry.

To illustrate their point, they magnetically transformed a stream of neutrons into an antineutron beam and penetrated a parallel bubble universe to intercept a local-access cable TV network. In that reality, Nicholas was of all things a televangelist, albeit not a very good one. He addressed the camera from behind his pulpit—a lectern on which he had crudely drawn a cross in thick black marker. His priestly vestments consisted of a black dress shirt worn backwards to give himself a collar, to which he paper-clipped just below his chin a folded-over piece of white paper. "Most God-fearing folks don't know this," he preached, "but the Devil often appeared before the Apostles disguised as JEE-suss in order to confuse and deceive them. Fact is, a dozen guys who do whatever they're told are really easy to fool. That means the true teachings of Jesus—like at the wedding of Conan when he fed some fishes with a loaf of bread; or when he cursed the goats because he didn't like chèvre as much as feta; or when Mary Amygdala washed Jesus' feet and all the Apostles sang 'What's the Buzz?'—all those true teachings have gotten mixed up with the bogus sayings of Spurious Jesus, like 'rich folks should give their money to the poor.' So how can you tell the *real* teachings of Jesus from the false and inconvenient ones? Why, you'd need some kind of a Prophet. Ladies and gentlemen, *I* am that Prophet!"

The Nicholas Young of that universe sought to bring about the End Times by filling the role of the False Prophet from Revelation. Unfortunately, he really didn't know his Bible very well and made a very unconvincing preacher. His biggest obstacle, however—judging from *The 666 Club*'s homely production values—was that only about a dozen people seemed to watch his program. In a world where actual preachers proclaim in all sincerity that God hates fags, that fornication causes hurricanes and earthquakes, or that love of money is *not* the root of all evil, it's pretty much impossible to stand out as a false prophet. It was frustrating enough to make a false prophet want to blow up the world. If only he could amass more than a dozen followers.

With that settled, the aliens obliged Niels and Destiny and returned to a few spots along their past week's fateful journey, allowing them to tie up loose ends.

They began with a visit to Saint Louis No. 1, where Belanger had a fateful and prescient Tarot card reading that also happened to be utter pseudoscientific bollocks. Here he introduced Destiny to a nervous and clearly overcrowded resident tech-support guy. The hermit loosened up considerably when called upon to help Ping and Vroom fix their tractor beam by cycling the power off and then on again. The grateful aliens gave him a space-aged pair of Goggle Glasses, which allowed him to provide technical support from a fully functional virtual office. "Holy Glycon!" he exclaimed as he tried it out for the first time, "it's like I'm some kind of a magician." Indeed, adorned in those goggles, the tall shaggy hermit looked like Hagrid about to ride Sirius Black's motorbike. He was going to be the envy of all the other hermits…if they ever talked to one another.

Next they stopped at the hotel in Hulett where Destiny met Belanger. The latter gave a fiver to the bartender, whom he had neglected to tip on account of being shot at. In return, the barman offered them a complimentary taste of their popular new signature cocktail. "Hold on to your butts," he proclaimed as he poured passion fruit liqueur, limoncello, and bourbon into a martini glass mounded with crushed ice. He presented it with a curly strip of lemon rind on the rim and declared, "One of our customers named it the 'snow cone.'" Belanger and Jones looked at each other with wrinkled noses. Ping, however, stuck hir long index finger into the glass and, to everyone's surprise, absorbed the entire beverage into hir digit.

"*That,*" s/he proclaimed, holding up the finger, "beeee gooood." This meant Vroom was now driving while Ping drunk-dialed home.

Visiting the remains of the only gas station in Sidewinder, they thanked Lloyd again for his help. They were heartened to see that the convenience-store portion of his business remained unaffected, and they felt confident that it would continue to look the same as it did in 1970 until the end of time. Destiny became intrigued with the ancient vending machine in the corner. She drew a quarter from her purse, placed it in the machine, and pulled one of its knobs to purchase a pack of cigarettes that was older than her parents. "No, I'm not going to smoke them," she responded to Belanger's disapproval face. Instead, she popped into the Overlook Hotel and asked the concierge to deliver them, along with a note from her, "To the smoking-hot tattooed guy in room service."

Moving on to Roswell, the four of them donned flight uniforms and helmets then ventured out into the evening darkness. They proceeded to Wesley and Simon's Dungeons and Dragons gaming night. Pressing their noses against the dining room window, they witnessed a tangential debate sidetrack the adventurers from pillaging the Tomb of Horrors of all its treasures.

"The Star Wars prequels do *so* have Ewoks on the Galactic Senate!" insisted Wesley the Half-Orc paladin.

"No way, son," Simon disputed, bogarting the dice and refusing to roll his saving throw until this important matter of canon was settled. The game master simply rolled his eyes impatiently. "Ewoks lack basic technology, let alone spacecraft. How would they even *get* to Coruscant?"

"Maybe they catch a ride with someone else."

"Yeah, just like you need a ride to work every day."

One of the other players—a Drow druid—guffawed. "Ewoks don't even have outhouses!"

"What if *Return of the Jedi* took place in the hillbilly part of Endor," Wesley countered, "and we only got to see the Amish Ewoks?"

"Huh-huh, Ewok luddites," the Drow guffawed.

"They aren't very bright, either," Simon added another point, still rattling the dice in his cupped hands in a roll that seemed like it would never come.

"Gungans are in the Senate, and they're freaking idiots!" the paladin parried.

"Pffft, Ewoks are just adorable teddy bear people."

"—who will beat your head in with *a rock!*"

"More like Gizmo meets Chucky," the druid agreed.

The space-age onlookers, unable to contain themselves any longer, finally knocked on the dining room window. The sight of the waving grays caused the mighty band of warriors to let out a collective girly scream. Wesley spilled his Mountain Dew down the front of his pants—or that's what he claimed it was. Worst of all, Simon dropped the percentile dice in his hands and unintentionally rolled a natural 1, which the game master declared meant that Simongast the Brown's fireball completely missed the gelatinous cube blocking the hallway and instead incinerated himself and his entire party. As Destiny, Niels, Ping, and Vroom ran off into the night laughing hysterically, Simon turned on his outdoor flood lights and leaned out the door, hollering indignantly, "And stay away from my chickens, you...you...*p'tak!*" Despite his bluster, Simon prayed that the hostile visitors did not speak Klingon.

Finally the group returned to Rachel, where they used the saucer's newly repaired tractor beam to raise Phil into his tree to retrieve his man purse. Afterwards, Tammy caught Ping and Vroom up on the latest gossip from Alpha Centauri. Throughout these proceedings, a mysterious ranger watched protectively from the woods…which, being in the middle of the desert, consisted of some tall grass and a telephone pole. As the visitors prepared to resume their journey, the watcher reached into his cloak, drew his museum-quality collectible replica of the sword Andúril, and gave them a warrior's salute.

Only one unfinished piece of business remained. Destiny asked the aliens to do her a tangible and drop her off at home in New York City. As she put it in her own inimitable way, she had other potatoes to boil. She didn't want to do the walk of shame all the way home from Devils Tower. And besides, her cat sitter would be wondering what happened to her.

As they approached New York, Ping and Vroom activated the spacecraft's transformation optics and metamaterials invisibility cloak, rendering the craft and its passengers imperceptible. The saucer descended silently and deposited them in Washington Square Park near Fifth Avenue and Waverly Place.

Although Belanger and Destiny spontaneously appeared amidst a large crowd at Washington Square Fountain, thanks to alien mind-cloaking technology—or New Yorkers' focus on their cell phones— no one noticed. The fountain sat in the center of a depression formed by a ring of concrete steps that descended from the Washington Square promenade. During the summer, the fountain sent streams of water high into the air and filled the depression with a shallow pool. This being winter—with temperatures just slightly above freezing— the depression served simply as a dry extension of the promenade.

Destiny led Belanger through the sea of scarves and coats, away from the fountain and through Washington Square Arch, a seventy-seven-foot-tall marble commemoration of George Washington's presidential inauguration. As they passed through its thirty-foot-wide arch, Belanger—who, despite his recent visit to Manhattan's Javits Center, had never been to Greenwich Village—paused to admire its architecture and detailed sculptures of Washington. He was actually stalling, trying to postpone the inevitable.

On the other side of the monument, he found himself at the southern terminus of Fifth Avenue. He followed Destiny another two short blocks, where they came to a halt in front of her apartment building. It was much too soon for his liking.

Thus began the awkward goodbye. Belanger shuffled his feet, avoided eye contact, and searched for something worth saying. *I had a corking good time with you this week being shot at and chased by homicidal maniacs.* That wouldn't work. *I'll call you in a couple days.* Too cliché. *That was the best acid I've ever dropped.* If only he were in a lecture hall, this would be so much easier; he would simply say *Read the next chapter, and we'll see you next week.* But that wouldn't do here either. He ultimately decided on, "I will never forget this adventure we had." He regretted it as soon as he spoke the words. *That's too final sounding!* he second-guessed himself. *It's practically "Have a nice life." Why didn't I just say "I'll call you in a couple days"?!?*

Sensing his obvious anxiety, Destiny remained stoic and relaxed. "When I went to Devils Tower to chase after some obnoxious guy," she said, "I never imagined that I would meet a completely different obnoxious guy." She winked and smiled at him. "It's funny how even a bad decision can open the door to something wonderful." She held her outstretched hands about six inches apart. "Who knew there was room for so much behind an open door? I'm glad I met you."

He nodded. "Yeah, me too. I mean, I'm glad *I* met *you*, too."

"It was an amazing experience. Thanks for bringing me into your crazy world."

Belanger mused that she handled being shot at very well—much better than Bree. He didn't want this farewell to end, not so soon. Yet he was at a loss for words, no meaningfully reply.

Undeterred by the awkward silence, Destiny reached out and straightened his lapel and tie. Then she leaned in and kissed him on the cheek. "I might really have gone for you if you were just a little younger." She raised her eyebrows, flashed a devilish smile. "And a lot cooler."

Belanger laughed and looked down self-deprecatingly. He felt like a shy twelve-year-old.

When he raised his head again a moment later, Destiny Jones was gone. There was no trace of her. She couldn't possibly have gone anywhere in that instant; he would have seen her running away. Yet there he was, alone. It was as if she had vanished into thin air. He looked around quizzically.

Finally, on the telephone pole directly in front of him—where she had just been standing a moment before—he spotted her photograph. It graced a homemade poster that read "MISSING SINCE NEW YEAR'S EVE." Produced at home on standard letter-sized copy paper with someone's bare-bones inkjet printer, it announced to the neighborhood—and any of the countless tourists who may have happened upon it—these basic facts: She was twenty-four years old, her height was five-foot-nine, and she weighed one hundred ten pounds. She was last seen leaving a New Year's Eve party on the Upper East Side at approximately 10:30 p.m. She did not return home that night, nor did she show up for her next work day. The reproduction quality of her photograph was not very good, but it had obviously been taken on Christmas Day. She was unmistakable and characteristically dour.

In that moment of realization, his heart broke. Belanger lamented that he would never get to spend time with Destiny under less stressful circumstances. Yet he was equally amused that she got the last laugh by fooling him with one last urban legend. The hitchhiker who asks for a ride home, only to disappear into thin air on arrival as a phantom who had formerly lived there, was in fact the most famous contemporary myth of them all. Its scholarly literature dwarfed all others in modern folklore. Jan Harold Brunvand's *The Vanishing Hitchhiker* in 1981 traced the story to as early as 1940, while Gillian Bennett, whose name was synonymous with the phantom hitchhiker, established in the following year that elements of the story traced back to much older sources which were anything but modern or urban. Thereafter hundreds of subsequent publications referenced the story. While folklorist Alan Dundes offered a Freudian take on the myth—which essentially concluded that once one has lost one's innocence, virginity, or virtue, there is no "going home"—Bennett accepted the story as a simpler metaphor for the tragedy of an unfulfilled life.

Belanger stopped his mental recitation of the facts, realizing that he was again being a 8===D. He still heard the echo of Destiny's voice in his ears. If she was indeed a phantom, then the world was poorer for her loss.

Knowing that Destiny would never return home from that fateful New Year's Eve party, he reached out and pulled the sign off the telephone pole. It was the only tangible reminder available to him of this remarkable and unusual woman, and he desperately wanted a keepsake. He folded the paper in half one, twice, three times, then slipped it into his vest pocket next to his heart. Placing his hand over it, he held it there for a moment and mustered a bittersweet smile. Then he turned and walked away, crossing the street and entering Washington Square Park where his ride home awaited.

EPILOGUE

I N THE FORESTS OF CHINA sprawled a hundred recently unemployed apes, aspiring playwrights all. Whether recumbent on the ground, perched on a hill, or suspended on a tree branch, they morosely poked and prodded at their ill-gotten tablet computers, despondent in the knowledge that even if collectively they were the next Roth, Tartt, Danielewski, or Pynchon—or even the next King, Rowling, or Martin—their output would never be taken seriously. It would forever be dismissed as dumb luck, the exhaust of an infinite improbability drive, soulless fingers that produced something without conscious intent.

One of them tapped away half-heartedly in their word-processing app, "It was a darkened stormy night," then after consideration deleted the misguided words altogether. Another typed "Call me Isherwood," but also found it uninspiring. Propped up against a rock, one even managed to tap out "riverrun, past Eve and Adam's, from swerve of shore to bend of bay, brings us by a commodius vicus of recirculation back to Howth Castle and Environs," but his word processor complained of a host of typographical and grammatical errors: The first word of the sentence was not capitalized and should probably be two words. The sentence lacked a clear subject and verb. "Environs" should be lowercase. And the helpful autocorrect changed phrases to "commodious virus" and "Hot Castle." Weary of fighting the software, the ape simply pinch-closed the app without saving his work.

Others had long since abandoned trying. Some played *Angry Birds* instead of typing, or tried their hands at *Minecraft*. Still others played *Words with Friends*, even though the random combinations of letters that they attempted were more often than not rejected by the game's dictionary. Some simply surfed the web, endlessly tapping from link to link to link, idly curious to see what random images would appear next.

One of the troop suddenly sat upright in response to an onscreen image. After staring at it for a while, he knuckle-walked to a nearby companion and touch-swiped the webpage over to the other's tablet. The second ape gazed curiously at the screen, then stared quizzically at the first, who nodded sagaciously.

Thus the second ape made a full closed grin and scrambled over to a third, while the first one sought yet another troop-mate to share the curious webpage. As the third monkey looked at the new image on her screen, the second chattered excitedly. And so it went. The third passed the link to another, stood upright, raised her arms overhead, and screamed. Another thumped his chest and let out a throaty series of hoots. Another responded by throwing grass and sticks overhead into the air.

As the webpage made its rounds, the commotion grew increasingly frantic. More distant apes drew near, instinctively curious to determine what had excited the troop so. And thus the page passed around progressively faster and faster until all one hundred of the apes had the same image on their screens. Finally they all simultaneously dropped their tablets and began to pound their chests, throw objects into the air, slap the ground, or drum on trees. The forest reverberated with a hundred varied but united outcries of fear and danger.

The cause of this scene was a webpage that featured two photographs: One was of the latest addition to the British Royal Family. The other was of an iguana. Above these photographs ran the headline: DESCENDANTS OF THE QUEEN MUM ARE SECRET REPTILIAN ALIENS: MEET YOUR NEW ILLUMINATUS OVERLORD.

ACKNOWLEDGEMENTS

I write not because it is easy or lucrative (turns out it's neither) but because I must. Pen and paper have been my constant companions since second grade, when I wrote the best time-travel novel *ever* starring All The Dinosaurs. (It mercifully remains unpublished.) I have been writing ever since. While acknowledgements may be the hardest of the not-easy things to write, recognizing all the good and talented people who make it possible is the most rewarding. I therefore express my deepest gratitude and love to everyone who helped bring *The Billionth Monkey* from concept to book.

Thanks first of all to my wife, Kerry Kurowski, for merging her nerd life with mine, for patient encouragement while I prattled on for two years about urban legends and bad puns, for offering manuscript suggestions, and for going on adventures with me to do research and take photos.

Gratitude also goes to my other readers—Kate McPherson, Chris Weiss, and Page Brunner—for their valuable feedback. To my editor, Kathy Glass, for polishing my manuscript and sparing me embarrassing errors, and to Erin Weigand for hooking me up with such a fantastic editor. To Christian Hartman for meticulous proofreading. And to Steve Englehart, Lon Milo DuQuette, and Don Webb for honoring me with their blurbs.

Aaron Tatum designed the front cover and laid out the back cover. Special thanks to Ordo Templi Orientis for permission to reproduce "The Fool" from the *Thoth Tarot* by Aleister Crowley and Frieda Harris. My mini graphic novel would have been impossible without Greg LaRocque, who drew the pages, and Rus Wooton, who lettered them; Paul Baker and Jenny Randle, who shared their expertise in graphic novel and book design;

Martin Hayes, who reviewed my script for *Hamlet: Special Edition*; and especially Robert Randle, who painted the back cover artwork, added gray tones to Greg's artwork, and otherwise generously gave me the benefit of his friendship and artistic experience.

For this book's contents, thanks to the immensely kind and cool Stoya for permission to use her likeness, and to steve prue for permission to use his photography of her. To Conzpiracy Digital Arts for putting Stoya/Destiny on a spaceship of which even J.J. Abrams would be envious. To Steve "Stewie" Pattee at HorrorTalk.com for permission to use his photos of the Roswell welcome sign and Walmart, and to Anthony Hernandez, manager of the Roswell Walmart, for the property clearance to use a photo of his store. To Troy Schreck of Alfred Music and Aimee-Leigh Lerret of Hal Leonard for permission to quote my favorite band, Yes. To Terry Draper and Magentalane Music for permission to quote another of my favorites, Klaatu. And to Kittle Palakovich for answering all my intellectual property and legal questions, and for doing her level best to keep me out of trouble.

Gratitude to everyone who played along by being part of *The Billionth Monkey*'s virtual presence, including Tom Cole, Mark Evans, Christopher Feldman, Jimmie Gilmer, Sophia Horodysky, Kerry Kurowski, Devin McPherson, Gordon Olmsted-Dean, Daryl Serrano, Jon Sewell, and Justin Towson; to Lynne MacAfee and Chuck Rozanski at Mile High Comics for allowing me to use an interior photo of their store; and to Robert Maiolo for technical help and advice about websites.

Finally, thanks to Philip Smith, who offered suggestions on my query letters; John Tulles, public affairs director at the Timberline Lodge, for taking the time to talk to me during my visit; to Sophia Horodysky for being a real trooper, driving me around Tulane, and making a mad dash with me in the pouring rain to look at Newcomb Hall; and to Josh Secrest and Stephanie Olmstead-Dean for answering my noob questions about guns.

If it takes a village to raise a child, then it takes a metropolis of friends, supporters, artists, and other professionals to raise a writer. Thanks to everyone for helping this fiction become a reality.

HAMLET
SPECIAL EDITION

93 kr 1 FEB
02685

THE AUTHORIZED GRAPHIC NOVEL

HAMLET
SPECIAL EDITION

HEY KIDS!
LOOK AT ALL THIS GREAT STUFF!

X-RAY SPECS!
Be a creeper while *simultaneously* giving people cancer!

Why pass notes in class when you can have your own **ENIGMA MACHINE**

GMO CORN
Toss it at your science-illiterate friends and watch them run!

Whether it's 95, 94, or 93, you too can **NAIL UP YOUR THESES!**

COCKTAIL RECIPES guaranteed to make mom stop yelling.

BRAIN BACKUP!
Save the contents of your cranium for the upcoming singularity!

MAD SCIENTIST KIT
Everything you need to dress up and act crazy.

EXPLODING AA BATTERIES!
Slip these into mom's nightstand and wait 'til she uses them!

Learn the long-lost **SECRETS OF MASONRY**

HILARIOUS PRANKS you can pull with other people's cars!

TIN FOIL HAT
You can keep the government out of your head ... or let the aliens inside!

After a hard morning at the construction site, dad will laugh & laugh when he bites into our **RUBBER SANDWICH!**

SCARE THE SHIT OUT OF PEOPLE
with our creepy clown makeup and costume.

With our extensive reading list, you too can be an **ARMCHAIR MAGICIAN!**

HOW TO TALK TO GIRLS WITHOUT BORING THEM

Nobody expects **THE SPANISH INQUISITION!**
Start extracting confessions now.

Imagine the look on dad's face when you hand him a stack of **COUNTERFEIT CASH!**

FAKE PEANUTS
Slip a few of these into the allergic kid's lunch and watch all the fun!

Be the first kid on your block to have our exclusive **LASER SWORD** (imagination not included).

BUILD YOUR OWN MODULAR SYNTHESIZER with our DIY kit.

IT'S *Easy*

WRITE TODAY FOR YOUR
FREE CATALOG!

FREE

A long time ago in a kingdom far, far away…[1]

[1] Unless you're already in Scandinavia.[2]

[2] My cousin Bljúgr in Sweden says that on a clear summer day he can see Elsinore across the Øresund Strait during Helsingborg's *kräftskiva*.[3]

[3] One year during a *kräftskiva*, Bljúgr was pinched by a *kräftor* right on the *pekfingret*. Crayfish pinches can be nasty.[4,6]

[4] This sentence is ironically typeset to contain the phrase "**something is rotten**" in the font Denmark.[5]

[5] Not to be confused with this sentence, which has "the play" set in Scottish Modern…kind of like Sam Worthington's movie.

[6] I would still rather be pinched on the *pekfingret* by a *kräftor* any day than hit in the head with a frozen haggis.[7]

[7] At this point the damned don who was writing these notes was mercifully struck by lightning.

STANLEY KERBIE PRESENTS: HAMLET: SPECIAL EDITION

WILLIAM SHAKESPEARE
WRITER

GREG LAROCQUE
ARTIST

RUS WOOTON
LETTERER

ROB RANDLE
COLORIST

RICHARD KACZYNSKI
EDITOR-IN-CHIEF

ACT 1, SCENE 1

ELSINORE.

MIDNIGHT.

A PLATFORM BEFORE THE CASTLE.

WHO'S THERE?

NAY, ANSWER *ME!* STAND, AND *UNFOLD* YOURSELF!

FZZZEEW!

REVENGE *OF THE* KITH!

HAMLET: SPECIAL EDITION® is published by STANLEY'S MARVELOUS COMICS, Stanley Kerbie, President. Cover art by Rob Randle, cover layout by Aaron Tatum. Copyright ©2015 by Richard Kaczynski. For more information on Stanley's Marvelous Comics superstore, visit www.stanleysmarvelouscomics.com. Stanley's Marvelous Comics is a fictitious subsidiary of Richard's novel, The Billionth Monkey, www.thebillionthmonkey.com. Any resemblance between this homage and any living or dead person or franchise is…well, just look up "parody" in the dictionary.

CPSIA information can be obtained
at www.ICGtesting.com
Printed in the USA
LVHW022016240120
644726LV00013B/1485